# ARTHUR O. FRIEL

writes a great and timeless classic of fantastic adventure fiction.... TIGER RIVER is possibly the finest novel of its type ever written.

Here are white Indians, uncanny green men, and ruthless savages who haunt every foot of a strange and unknown land. Deep in a hidden treasure valley of the Andes lurks a Circe whose strange attractions have lured many a missing man of the Tiger River into her evil clutches. How draughts of her forbidden wine transformed them into mindless beasts, and how her spell was finally broken, are a part of this fantastic and unforgetable book.

# TIGER RIVER

## ARTHUR O. FRIEL

WILDSIDE PRESS

Cover by Jeff Jones

CONTENTS

TIGER RIVER

## I. WHERE WATERS MEET

At the edge of the jungle a rifle roared. High up among the branches of a tall buttress-rooted tree — more than a hundred feet above the soggy ground — a big, red, bearded monkey lurched out into space. Headlong he fell. A swift rip of breaking underbrush, a dull thump, and he lay lifeless on the earth.

At the base of another tree a man quietly levered a fresh cartridge into his gun barrel. For a few seconds he stood motionless, weapon up, eyes sweeping the surrounding tree butts and bush clumps. Then he let the rifle sink and, velvet-footed, stepped forward.

"So, Senor Cotomono," he said softly, "you will make your hideous howling, eh, to tell all the world that I am here? You will yell to the tigres of this Tiger Water to come and tear Jose Martinez, yes? Too late you learn that it does not pay to make too much noise with the mouth."

A sardonic smile played under his fierce black mustache. Even as the words slipped from his tongue his gaze lifted from the motionless animal and once more plumbed the vistas about him. Tall, sinewy, hawk-nosed, bold-eyed, red-kerchiefed, belted with a long machete, alert and wary as the great hunting-cat he had just mentioned — he looked a buccaneer chieftain marooned in a tropic wilderness, poised to fight man, beast, or demon.

A minute passed. No sound came, except the ceaseless rustle of unseen small life creeping about in the shadows during the hot hours of midday. With a lightning shift of manner he relaxed.

9

"Hah!" he growled. "Jose, you are overcareful. You have hardly left the Amazon — you have only just landed on the Tigre Yacu — and yet you stand as if you were far upstream and had shot a head-hunter instead of a poor cotomono. You disgust me, Jose mio. Come, little howler of the heights, and toast your toes at my fire."

In one motion he swooped up the dead monkey and whirled on his heel. A few strides to the rear, and he halted at water: clear water, about seventy yards broad, flowing southeast, at whose margin floated a small canoe. Some rods downstream the limpid little river ended, merging into a turbid yellow flood rolling eastward — the mighty Amazon, here known as the Maranon.

Two swift glances he shot to right and left — one upstream, one out at the tawny monarch of rivers. Only empty water, glaring under the sun, met his gaze. Leaning his rifle against a handy tree butt, he drew his machete and sliced some tindery bamboo into kindling. A few deft slashes with the same blade dressed the monkey for roasting. Then, adding more fuel, he squatted and concentrated his attention on the cooking of his meal.

A stiff breeze came rocketing down the clear-water stream, snatching the smoke of his fire and flinging it playfully down to the great river. And almost at once, as if the tang of smoke and the savory odor of broiling meat had evoked life from the depths of that river, something came crawling into the yellow vacancy at the end of the jungle shores. Foot by foot, yard by yard, it nosed its clumsy way out of the west until its whole length floated there, only a little way from the land. There, for a moment, it hung motionless.

A grotesque, misshapen monster of the jungle, it seemed: a low-bodied thing some thirty feet long, with half a dozen short, rigid legs on each side; a humpy creature with a small square bump in the middle, a big round one near its tail, and more than a dozen smaller protuberances along its back. Presently its little legs moved backward, lifted, came forward — flashing glints of sunlight from its wet feet — and slid backward again. Its blunt nose turned up the clear water. It grew larger, crawling toward the spot whence the smoke rolled. And the rough little breeze, as if it had done its duty in summoning the riverbeast, passed and was gone, leaving the smoke to rise straight above the squatting man like a telltale finger.

The man did not see the thing approach. Around him stood waist-high grass, which now, in his doubled-up position, rose just above his head and shut off from his view all but the fire and his meat. The river-creature advanced quietly, as if a bit wary. Fifty feet off shore it paused. From it burst a roaring voice.

"Hey there!"

The man in the grass started, spun about, lengthened himself toward his rifle, and in one second was behind the tree with gun cocked. His narrowed eyes stabbed through the sun-glare at the clumsy thing which had slipped up so smoothly within pistol-shot of him. In one tight squint he saw what it was.

A Peruvian garretea, or river-canoe, with a pile of supplies corded in the middle, a curve-roofed cabin at the stern, twelve copper-skinned paddlers and a steersman, and four khaki-shirted white men: that was the monster. The second glance of the lurking Jose told him that all the white men were deeply tanned and well bearded; that two of the beards were black, one yellow, and one unmistakably red. Then the voice spoke again.

"Come on out. We're not hunting anybody. I see you've got a bandanna, so you're no Indian. You understand English?"

The eyes of Jose widened.

"Por Dios!" he muttered. "Is it — it is not — yet the voice is the same! And a red beard — "

He stepped forth, rifle still ready but not aimed.

"Si, I savvy, senor," he answered. "Who comes?"

"Friends," clipped another voice. "Any objections to our tying up here? Want to sell that meat?"

"It is my dinner, senor, and not for sale," Jose replied coolly, still squinting at the boat. "Tying up here is as you wish. I do not own this river."

"All right. We'll shoot our own meat. Paddle!"

At the command the paddlers swayed in unison. The garretea floated nearer. Then out broke the first voice.

"Cap, look at that fellow! Isn't he a dead ringer for old Hozy, the lad that was with us last year on that Javaree river down below? By gosh, I wonder — Say, maybe this is a sassy question, but what's your name?"

The speaker was the red-bearded, red-headed man: a broad-chested, muscular fellow whose blue eyes peered keenly from under a cupped hand and whose wide face glowed with eagerness. Into the hawk face of Jose flashed the light of certainty. His teeth gleamed and his rifle sank. In three strides he was at the water's edge.

"It is the Senor Tim!" he cried. "I thought — but I was not

**11**

sure. And El Capitan McKay – Senor Knowlton – si, yo soy, amigos! It is I, Jose Martinez, at your service!"

"Well, by thunder!" laughed the blond man. "Welcome to our company, Jose, old top! I'll pump your arm off as soon as I can get out of this blooming boat. Give you a drink too – the occasion calls for one."

"Right you are looey. Hozy, you sure are a sight for sore eyes! Look out there, you gobs, Timmy Ryan is landing."

And land he did – crowding himself between the Indian paddlers and launching himself over the bow as it touched shore. As his boots plunked into the mud his right hand seized that of Jose and wrung it in a mighty grasp.

"You old son-of-a-gun!" he chuckled. "You old slashing, tearing, hip-shooting death's head! Just as homely and full of cussedness as ever. Mind the time we blowed the Red Bone cannibals all to glory? Damn, that was a scrap, I'll tell the world!"

"I remember it well," laughed Jose. "But you need not break my hand, amigo. The Senor Knowlton seems to wish to use it."

The blond man too had landed, and now he shouldered the exuberant Tim aside and proceeded to make good his promise to pump the Spaniard's arm, meanwhile giving him a running fire of banter. After him, cool and unhurried, came a tall, black-bearded, wide-shouldered man whose set face and bleak gray eyes now were softened by a welcoming smile. Last of all debarked a stocky man of medium height, with hat pulled well down over his brow.

In contrast to the red Tim and the blond Knowlton, the blackbeard spoke no word as his hand grasped that of Jose. but his brief, hearty grip and direct gaze spoke what his tongue did not. And to him Jose gave a look and a tone of deeper respect than that accorded to his predecessors.

"Capitan!" he bowed. Then, as their hands parted, he turned suddenly away. When he swung back his bold eyes were a trifle misty and his smile strained.

"Pardon the weakness, senores," he said. "It is sudden, this meeting. And there are few men who care to take the hand of Jose Martinez, outlaw – though there are many who would take his head."

"Grrumph! Let them come and get it – they'll have a fat time while this gang's here, Hozy!" erupted Tim. "We don't give a damn if you're a dozen outlaws. You're square and there's no yellow streak in you, and we know it. Besides, there's no law in this neck of the woods, unless they lugged

**12**

some in since the last time we were here, which I sure hope they haven't. There's too much law in the world now, most of it made by crooks. But say, haven't you got a word for Dave Rand here? You ought to remember him."

He motioned toward the last man ashore, who stood impassively waiting.

"Rand?" echoed Jose. "Senor Rand I do not — Ho! Por Dios! Is this the man who was the Raposa — the Wild Dog of the Javary?"

"The same," answered Rand himself. As he spoke he lifted his broad hat, revealing green- gray eyes and dark hair in which an odd white mark stood out above one ear.

"The man who was a crazy captive of the Red Bone Indians," he went on, "and whom you last saw as a naked, painted wreck being dragged home to the States by McKay and Knowlton and Tim here. No wonder you didn't recognize me. Shake?"

"Indeed, yes, senor, with pride." And the final handshake was completed. "But how come you here in South America again — and, of all places, on the banks of this dangerous water? You had best move on quickly, comrades, all of you."

Tim interrupted.

"Aw, who's afraid of a little brook like this? And say, your meat is burning. Get out of the way and I'll save it. We've got to eat."

Jose wheeled, pounced, retrieved the blackened meat, and gazed at it ruefully.

"A third of my dinner gone," he grumbled. "But this cotomono was a big one, and we can each get a few mouthfuls of fresh meat from him. Your Indians can find meat of their own if they will hunt back from the water."

But the Indians seemed to want no meat. They did not even show any intention of landing. Every man of them had remained in the boat, and, though they sniffed wistfully at the odor of the cooking, their eyes were continually watching the thick tropical tangle near at hand. Uneasy mutterings went among them, and repeatedly they grunted two words:

"Tigre Yacu."

The northerners stared at them. Jose,the jungle rover, alone seemed to understand. He gave the paddlers a brief glance, nodded, and let his own gaze go roving upstream.

"What ails them?" wondered Tim. "Is this place haunted or something?"

"This, Senor Tim, is the Tiger Water," Jose explained, "and it is bad country. Above here — "

**13**

He stopped. Across his words smote a dread sound.

From the jungle behind them broke a coughing roar: a hoarse, harsh, malignant note of menace which struck both brown and white men like a blow. It was the voice of the South American tiger, savage king of the jungle, eater of men; the voice of the Tigre Yacu, on whose banks lurked unknown things; the voice of Death.

## II. THE RIVER OF MISSING MEN

For a moment the jungle and the river were still. No man moved; and the rustle of small things in bush and branches was hushed as if all life held its breath. Then, calmly, tall Captain McKay spoke.

"Sounds hungry. A hungry jaguar is bad medicine. Get aboard, men, and we'll shove out a little. Come along, Jose. Want to talk to you."

Jose glowered into the tangle as if half minded to go seeking the tigre. But when Knowlton seconded the invitation he shrugged and nodded.

"Climb in," said the blond man. "Nothing to stay here for. The Indians won't come ashore, your meat is cooked, and we can talk better where that brute won't drop on somebody's back. Besides," with a laugh, "we have to dig up that bottle I spoke of."

"Your last reason is much the best one, senor," Jose grinned. "Now that I think of it, my throat is most dry."

Back into the garretea the white men clambered, and at once the paddlers shoved off. But for McKay's sharp commands, they would have driven the boat back to the Amazon. As it was, they reluctantly stopped work after a few strokes, and a moment later a sixty-pound weight plunged over the bow. Fifteen yards out, the boat swung at anchor.

Four of the whites went aft to the shelter of the shady hoop-roofed cabin, which rose importantly from a ten-foot palm-bark deck. Tim, the fifth, halted amidships and sought something among the supplies, straightening up presently with a quart bottle on which the Indians fixed a longing gaze. Not until the red-bearded man entered the cabin did they take their eyes from his liquid treasure. Then they silently moved forward and made a fire in a big clay pot in the bow – the "galley" of their crude ship.

"Well, Hozy, old-timer, here's how!" proclaimed Tim, flourishing the bottle. "Good stuff, this is. Take a husky gargle of it before you eat. You get more of a jolt on an empty stomach. Shoot!"

14

Jose shot. The anisado gurgled down his throat like water. When he handed back the bottle his eyes glistened and a fourth of the liquor had disappeared from mortal view.

"Gosh!" muttered Tim. "Half a pint to one swallow! You got me beat. But I'll do my best."

Measuring off another half pint with a thumbnail, he opened his capacious mouth, nipped his nose between his free thumb and forefinger, and let the bottle gurgle. Presently he gasped, shot the bottle to McKay, seized a gourd, and seemed to dive overboard; but his legs and body remained on the deck, and the gourd came up full of river water. Several gulps, and he arose, breathing hard.

"That's what we came up here for, anyway – clean water," he alibied. "So I'm getting mine now. That Amazon water is alright if you let it settle, but it sure needs some settling. Don't you want a chaser, too, Hozy? No? Then eat something quick, before you get violent. We don't want to have to fight you."

But Jose only grinned and licked his mustache, bowing to Knowlton as the latter saluted him with the bottle and took a short pull. McKay drank without a quiver. Rand barely touched the glass to his lips, then replaced the cork.

"Hard case, this fellow Rand," winked Tim. "Last time he got hold of a bottle he swallowed the whole thing and then chewed up the cork for a chaser. Right after that he sat down hard and the bottle busted inside him, so he has to go easy for a few days. If you don't believe me, kick him, and you'll hear the glass jingle."

"You'll be more likely to hear the angels singing," countered the green-eyed man, with a tight smile. "Fact is, Jose, I'm not drinking any more. Drink got me into hell once. Maybe you remember."

The Peruvian nodded.

"Si. It was drinking which got you into a fight at Manaos some years ago when you were traveling up the Amazon. You struck down a man – a German – so hard that you believed him killed, and you hid on a steamer and fled up the river. Then you went into the wild cannibal country on the Rio Javary, fought another German – Schwandorf – who tried to make you steal Indian women for his slave trade, and were shot in the head by that man. The bullet crazed you, and for years you wandered among the cannibals, who let you live only because they feared you. The Raposa – the Wild Dog of the jungle! I heard of you long before I ever saw you."

"And if it hadn't been for Mac and Merry Knowlton and Tim, who came hunting me and knocked sense back into my

**15**

head with a gun butt, I'd be there yet," Rand acquiesced grimly.

Jose nodded again.

"Es verdad. But that time is past, and you are a strong man once more. Yet I am much astonished to see you again in the jungle. If I have it right, these senores came seeking you because you were heir to a great estate and they were commissioned to find you. A North American millionaire is the last kind of man I should expect to see here, even if he had not suffered here as you have."

Rand smiled wryly.

"But I don't happen to be a millionaire. I haven't even a million cents, not to mention dollars."

"Por Dios! There were two million dollars — did you not say so capitan? And that was hardly a year ago! How have you spent so much money in so short a time?"

"Didn't spend a cent of it. Never had it to spend. It's this way:

"My uncle, Philip Dawson, died. His son, Paul, who fought in the great war, was supposed to have been killed in action in the Argonne Forest. So the Dawson estate was legally mine — for a while.

"But Paul wasn't killed. He was badly wounded, captured, and treated none too well; and he got aphasia — forgot who he was. The War Department mixed up things, recorded him as dead, and shipped home the body of some other soldier as his. A lot of those blunders happened in the war.

"Just about the time these chaps were finding me down here, a friend of Paul's found him over there. He was working as a field hand, and even thought he was a German — he had traveled a lot as a boy and could talk German as easily as English; so when he found himself among German people and didn't know who he was or how he came there, he thought he belonged there. Of course his friend got him back to the States at once, and by the time I showed up he was there in the hands of specialists who were bringing his memory back to him. So that let me out."

Jose carved a section of monkey haunch. Slicing it with careful exactness, he passed portions to his companions. All fell to chewing.

"But I thtill do not thee, thenor," lisped Jose, his mouth nearly full, "why you return to thith plathe."

"We're partners, chasing the rainbow," Knowlton vouchsafed after swallowing his morsel. "We three were well rewarded for getting Dave back, even though he wasn't the

**16**

heir; the estate had to make good its contract with us. Dave wasn't broke, either – he had some money of his own in a couple of banks. So we got restless, pooled our money, and came down to the Andes to make ourselves billionaires by finding the treasures of the Incas or anything else lying around loose.

"But we were out of luck. We poked around the upper Maranon awhile and tried a couple of other prospects, but got nothing but hard knocks. So we got this boat and came along down. Thought we'd take a whirl at the Napo country, just below here. Loads of gold in the Napo, we hear; Indians pick it out of the river bed, and so on. Want to join us and try your luck?"

Jose did not answer at once. His black eyes searched the face of each man as if seeking some sign of derision or amusement. He found none.

"You jest, senor," he said presently.

"Not a bit of it. What do you say, Rod – Tim – Dave? Is Jose a welcome member of this gang?"

"I'll say he is! rumbled Tim. The other two nodded decisively.

The Peruvian's face glowed. But he shook his head.

"I thank you, senores, but I cannot. I have no such outfit as you, I have no money, I am not one of you but Jose Martinez – outlaw. I could not be on an equal footing – "

"That's rot, Jose," McKay cut in. "If we didn't want you we wouldn't ask you. Money and outfit are immaterial. You have something we lack – intimate knowledge of this region. Put your knowledge in the pot with our outfit, and you owe nothing. Coming in?"

Again Jose held his tongue before answering. Pride gleamed in his eyes, but those eyes went up the Tiger River as if visioning something the others could not see. Absently he rolled and smoked a cigarette. Not until he snapped the charred butt overboard did he speak.

"Senores," he said abruptly, "the tale of gold in the Napo is old. Too old. Everybody knows it. True, gold is there: gold dust washed from the Llanganati mountains of Ecuador. But men have known of it for hundreds of years. Many expeditions have gone in after it. Some have come out, some have not. Savages – accidents – fever – there are many men's bones in the Napo jungle. There will be many more.

"Gold is there, yes. But why journey to the Napo, and hundreds of miles up the Napo – it is eight hundred miles long, amigos – to seek a thing which is nearer at hand? Why

**17**

poke about a river where the workings are known and covered by fighting men, when before you opens a stream where you can take anything you find?"

The Americans stared. Their glances darted up the Tigre Yacu.

"You mean — " Knowlton began.

"Sssst!" Jose hissed warningly.

Two of the crew were approaching, bearing salt fish and hot coffee to their patrones. The Peruvian eyed them narrowly, but none gave sign of having heard or understood the talk. Stolidly they placed the food on the raised deck, turned, and went back to the bow.

"Speak on," said McKay. "They know no English except a few words like 'paddle,' and so on."

"Bueno. You guess it — I mean this Tigre Yacu.

"Behold, companeros. It is but a little brook, yes, if one thinks of the great Maranon or the Napo. Yet it runs a long way up — one hundred fifty miles or more — and it is deep; canoes can travel far on it. And it heads between two long mountain spurs, which form the split end of the Cordillera del Pastassa. And that cordillera, amigos, is itself a spur from those same Llanganati mountains whence comes the gold of the Napo and its tributary river, the Curraray!

"See. It is thus."

Dipping a finger into his coffee, he drew on the bark deck a figure somewhat like a crude, elongated "h." Between the legs of this symbol he traced another line running southeast.

"The long line is the Cordillera del Pastassa, the curved one its spur," he explained. "And the third line is this Tigre Yacu. North of this cordillera runs the Curaray, which, as I say, bears gold. Some of its tributaries flow from this cordillera. Who shall say that the cordillera, an offshoot of the Llanganati, is not bursting with gold? Who shall say that much — or all — of the gold of the Curaray does not come from this cordillera instead of the Llanganati? Madre de Dios! Quien sabe?"

His face was flaming now. And, looking into his hot black eyes, the blue and the gray and the green eyes of the northerners suddenly flared with the reckless light of the gold lure. Rainbow-chasers all, hardy, venturesome, fearless, they were of that breed which plunges straight into the jaws of death if within those jaws lies a prize worth the daring. In one flashing instant the projected journey to the Napo vanished from their minds like wind-blown mist. The Napo was old. The Tigre Yacu, unknown, mysterious, had caught them in a spell.

It was McKay, canny and controlled, who spoke first.

"If there's gold here, why has it been passed by?"

One laconic word answered him.

"Jiveros."

"Hm. The head-hunters! Thought we were past their country."

"Oof! The Jiveros?" blurted Tim. "They the ones that shrink your head to the size of an orange?"

Jose nodded and smiled slightly.

"Their country is farther west, as el capitan says: the rivers Pastassa, Morona, Santiago; but they know no boundaries and they roam far. It is more than possible that even now some of them lurk yonder in the bush watching us. Wise men do not go up these rivers west of the Napo — only fools like Jose.

"That was why I hesitated so long before telling you of the treasure that may be up this stream. To risk my own life is nothing? to lure my friends into a death trap with me is much. But — we were together among the southern cannibals not long ago. So I tell you."

He gulped some coffee. At once he went on: "Nor is that all. Somewhere up this stream is something — I know not what — which makes men mad. I am not the first fool who has thought of gold up here and gone after it. How many men have gone in here I know not. But until recently no man has come out.

"Two weeks ago came one Rafael Pardo down to Iquitos. A hard, reckless man he was; a killer and other things. I say he was. He no longer is.

"Months ago he went up this Tigre Yacu, boasting that he feared no man, beast, God or devil. Days ago he came back, naked, bearded, filthy, raving. But with him he brought gold. A hide bag he had, and it was heavy with nuggets. Yes, nuggets, no dust. His skin was seamed with scars like those of a whip. His toes were gone — every one cut off. How he walked through the jungle, how he lived without weapons, I do not know. But he came — and he brought gold."

"Did anyone learn what he had been through?" asked Rand.

"No. He was utterly mad. He screamed frightful things, but such as made no sense. Then some one stole his gold. When he found it gone he ran about yelling, fell down frothing and died."

For a long minute there was silence. All peered up the stream. The flush of excitement had died from their faces, but no indecision or fear showed in them. Their jaws were set and their eyes narrowed as if they were sizing up an enemy. And they were. In each man's mind flamed a challenge to the river of missing men.

Then, all at once, their heads jerked to the right. The Indians in the bow had risen from their squat and were facing toward the spot where the Peruvian's little fire had smoked, and where his canoe still lay. The blaze now had died. And through the waist-high grass something large, something stealthy, was creeping from the jungle.

### III. THE CONQUISTADOR

Ready rifles slid out from the cabin. From four of them sounded the quiet snicks of safeties being thrown off. The hammer of Jose's big-bulleted repeater clicked dully and poised at full cock.

"The shot is mine, amigos," he reminded them. So, of the five guns, his was the only one to take aim.

The telltale grass stood still. For a breathless minute no sign of movement was visible. Slowly then it swayed again above the creeping thing, marking another few inches of advance.

Crash!

Jose's muzzle jumped. Blue smoke drifted along the water. The grass shook. From it burst a screech of appalling fury.

The dense growth of green split. At the water's edge a great black cat creature poised, eyes glaring, fangs gleaming, tail thrashing the grass like a maddened snake. On one ebony shoulder a streak of red flowed and widened.

"Hah-yah!" mocked Jose, his own teeth bared in a tigerish snarl. "Here am I, you devil! Come to me!"

The devil came. In one leap it shot ten feet from the bank. Its big paws, with long claws unsheathed, commenced swimming almost before its powerful body splashed. Eyes fixed in malevolent hate on the man who had wounded and mocked it, teeth still bared in a soundless snarl, the brute lunged straight for the boat.

From the Indians broke guttural gasps of fear. From the white men sounded short growls. From four high-power rifles cracked whip-like reports. From the Peruvian's black-powder gun another blunt roar thumped out.

The black tiger, suddenly motionless, sank in a red welter.

"Guess it was just as well that we did our talking out here," Knowlton observed. "Sorry to horn into your party, Jose, but I just had to slam a bullet into that fellow."

"It is nothing, senor. I had first blood — and last." Then, grinning, he added: "I have made a good beginning on the Tigre Yacu. I have shot a black tiger and a curaca."

**20**

"Curaca? A chief? How come?"

"Ha, ha, ha! That is my little joke. 'Curaca' means an Indian chief. But the male cotomono monkey, with his long beard, also is called 'curaca.' You have just eaten some of my chief-monkey."

"So I been chewing a chief's leg, hey?" muttered Tim. "It was tough stuff, anyway."

"If you go up this stream with me, Senor Tim, you may have to eat worse things before you come out," was the ominous reply. "But our coffee cools. Let us finish it."

Back in the shade of the cabin the five chewed and sipped in the silence of thought. When nothing but bare bones and empty gourds remained and tobacco was burning, Knowlton reached to a peg at one side, took down a roll of rubberized fabric, extracted a number of maps, and spread one on the bark floor. After a moment of study he nodded.

"Your cordillera starts from the Llanganati, all right," he said. "And it splits into spurs, with the Tigre starting between them. Guess this country has been explored."

"I think not, senor," Jose differed.

"Then how would the map makers know what was in there?"

"How do I know what is in there?" the jungle rover countered. "Because I have talked with Indians who know. Canoemen of the Napo, they were, whom I met on the Amazon. Is it not quite likely that the maps were made by men who never have been here, but who have taken the word of others who in turn had asked Indians?"

The blond Northerner was momentarily silenced. But presently he added: "Well, see here. The map agrees with you as to the mountains, but it gives this country east of the Cordillera del Pastassa to the Zaparos, not the Jiveros. The Jiveros are west of the Rio Pastassa."

A faint smile twitched the Spanish mouth.

"Si? That is a great relief, senor. Now we can go on without caution. If we meet Jiveros and they seek to cut off our heads, behold! we shall show them that map and tell them they have no right here, and they will go speeding back to the Pastassa."

Tim snickered. McKay and Rand smiled broadly. Knowlton flushed, laughed in a vexed way, and shoved the map back among the others.

"Faith, being an army officer gets you into lots of bad habits," remarked Tim. "These two were officers in the big war. Cap was a real captain and little old Knowlton was a looey — lieutenant. Course, they had to use maps a lot, and those maps of Europe are right: everything's just like the map says, except maybe the enemy. So looey got so used to believing the map he hasn't gotten out of the habit yet. But what kind of men are those – uh – what do you call them, looey?"

"Zaparos."

Jose waved a contemptuous hand.

"Animals. Wandering beasts of the forest, nothing more. They are short, flat of nose, with little eyes set slanting in their heads. They cannot count above ten, and for any number above three they must use their fingers. They have no towns, make only flimsy huts, live apart from each other in any place they like, then move on elsewhere. The only thing they make is the hammock: they are the hammock makers of the Provincia del Oriente. Oh, I was forgetting – they make also a drink called ayahuasca; but it is the stupid drink of a stupid people, which only makes one sleep. They are not even interesting. There is no danger from them."

"Uh-huh. Well, what about the head-shrinkers? They ought to be interesting."

The outlaw smiled grimly.

"You have said it, Senor Tim. There, amigos, is a race of men! Never have they been conquered. Neither my people of Spain nor the old Incas before us could make them bend their necks. They are fighters – fighters like my own ancestors, who, por Dios, were no such sleek potbellied politicians as they now have become! And though I do not intend to lose my head to any man, and will fight like ten devils to keep it, if it must be lost I would rather give it to the warriors of the Jiveros than to the sneaking,foot-lapping police of my own race. Si!"

His swarthy face, tanned deep by years of jungle sun, twisted in sudden savage bitterness. Abruptly he shot up to his full height, took a pantherish step, whirled, gazed slit-eyed at the four who had made him their partner.

"Listen to me! he rasped. "I, Jose Martinez, am of the Conquistadores! In me runs the blood of a man who dared the seas – dared the Andes – dared the jungle – and made this a land of Spain! But for him and his comrades, what would this Peru – that Ecuador – Colombia, Venezuela, the accursed Chile, Argentina – what would they be today? Indian lands. The strong hand, the cold steel, the fire and blood of my fathers, won all this great country.

"And what are their sons today?" Perros amarillos! Yellow dogs! Dogs who yelp out from among them like a wild beast a

**22**

man who still has the strength of his ancestors — dogs who hide behind their police — dogs who fight only with cunning and treachery and law, law, law!

"The Conquistadores were heroes, because they fought and killed. Yet never have I killed a man who woould not kill me. Not that I have always waited to be attacked — else I should be dead, long since. I have seen the death in a man's eye and I have acted. So I live. But I live with a price on my head. Why? Because I first killed a greasy politician, beyond the mountains, who had sent hired tools to murder me because he wanted my woman — "

He broke off short and struggled for control. But the flood of his fury burst forth again.

"The slime! The crawling scum! I killed him — si! — and his paid assassins too I killed. Hah! But he was a politican — a maker of laws. His brother makers of laws lashed the police — the army — all of Peru — on my trail. So am I an outlaw.

"Bueno! So be it. I am a man. I am among men. If I lose my heads to those Jiveros I lose it to men. And my bones will rest quiet, and my shrunken head hanging in a Jivero hut will grin at men — fighting men!"

His chin lifted sharply, and his eyes blazed at the farther shore. As if he saw Jiveros there, he did grin — a hard, deadly grin. And the four North Americans silently watched him level-eyed and knew he spoke truth. Piratical, flamboyant, fiery and fearless, he needed only a coat of mail and a sword to become the reincarnation of the long-dead conquerors whose iron will and bloody deeds had crushed a continent. He was a man born to late to live in the Peru beyond the mountains; but here in El Oriente, where the quick hand and the ready steel still ruled, he was at home. In him blazed the same flame that had burned in the veins of Pizarro, Orellana, Aguirre, and their bold and violent followers; and it would drive him up this Tigre Yacu, to gold or to death, as it had driven them into the dread jungles of the Napo and the Huallaga.

Slowly the fire in his face died out. At length, with a shrug, he turned back to them.

"But you would hear of those Jiveros, not of Jose," he deprecated. "Something of them and their habits you must have learned before now, but I will speak what comes to my mind.

"They too are wanderers, like the Zaparos; but in no other way are they like those sluggish ones, and even in their wanderings they differ. Instead of miserable palm-leaf shelters separated one from another, they build at chosen places two or three strong houses of logs standing on end, each house holding fifty or more people, and a tower for use in fighting enemies who attack them. When they move to another place all go together; and they move every few months, no matter how good the place where they are. It is in their blood, senores: they can no more live years in one spot than a tigre can make himself a house cat.

"Often they move back to some other place where they have been before and where their old houses wait, but it is not always so. Many times they go on and build new fortresses and plant new crops. And when the drive to go becomes too strong to be satisfied by this moving about, they strike out in fierce raids far from their old homes, killing all men who block their way.

"They fight with the poisoned arrow, the spear, the club, and sometimes with ax and knife and gun. In time of peace they trade rubber and gold for steel weapons — at Macas and Canelos and Loja — but they are so often at war that they cannot keep themselves in ammunition; so they do not depend much on their guns. And one of the big tribes of the Jiveros — the Huambisas of the Santiago — will seldom trade with the whites, so they have no guns, except those taken from white men killed while hunting gold in their region. But they need none. Their own weapons are more than enough."

"Yeah," nodded Tim. "Especially that poison that kills you if the arrow only scratches, but leaves you fit to be eaten. I suppose they barbecue the rest of you after they get your head off, hey?"

"No," Jose smiled. "They are not cannibals. All they do to you after you are dead is to shrink your head, and perhaps braid your hair into a belt made from the hair of other slain men. The Jivero who kills you, amigo, will surely put your red hair into his girdle. It will shine brightly among the black strands."

"Yeah? Well, unless he gets me from behind he'll have a two-handed job giving me that hair cut. What kind of men are they?"

"They are most clean, and take much care of themselves. They bathe often, and whatever thing they get from a white man they wash at once. The one thing of which they have fear is disease, for many of their people have died of smallpox and measles and other ills caught while trading at towns; so they are suspicious of all things belonging to strangers until washed.

"Many of them are light of skin and have beards, with faces

like those of Spaniards burned by the sun. It may even be that some Spanish blood is in the veins of such men. I have heard that long ago – three hundred years or more – the Jiveros and the Spaniards fought a bitter war in which the white men were swept out of this land, and the wives of those Spaniards had to become the women of the Indian conquerors. If that be true, the Spanish children born to those women after capture would grow up as Jiveros. It may be so – I know not. But I do know this: that up this very Tigre Yacu are white Indians!

"The Yameos, they are. White Indians who are restless rovers; they even cross the great Maranon and journey hundreds of miles southward up the Ucayali. Little is known of them. But it is known that they are white."

"Maybe more will be known about them when we come out," commented Rand.

"Si – when we come out. Many things may be known about this river – when we come out. But before coming out we must go in. Yes? No?"

There was a short pause. Captain McKay's keen gray gaze plumbed each face. Then he perfunctorily suggested: "Contrary-minded, vote no."

Instead, his three mates nodded. Jose smiled.

"It seems that I am to have company," he observed.

"Seems like this game has swapped ends," Tim grinned. "Little while ago we thought we were electing you: now you're adopting us. Well, let's go."

"Not so fast," Jose demurred. "There must be a new boat. And fewer men."

"Correct," approved McKay. "Boat's too big. Indians won't go up here. Got to shake them and paddle our own canoe. But can we get a smaller craft?"

"I think so, capitan. Just below here is a small settlement, San Regis. It is not much – a few huts on the bank, that is all – but canoes are there. No doubt you can make a trade. But – no word of where we go, comrades."

"Sure," agreed Knowlton. "This little cruise is strictly private. All aboard for San Regis, then. Popero!"

In answer to the summons, the steersman arose from the group of Indians still clustered around the cooking pot. His mates, facing aft, watched and listened. Sullen dread lest they be commanded to go farther up the Tigre Yacu was stamped plain on their faces.

"Abajo. Downstream," McKay ordered.

The face of the popero lit up. The sulky expressions of the paddlers vanished. With monkeylike agility the steersman

**25**

swung himself atop the cabin roof. Eagerly the others turned to haul up the crude anchor. When its wet bulk glistened again in the bow they scrambled to their places in haste to be gone.

"I think, amigos, I will await you here," said Jose, as the big craft began to surge around. "If you will land me — "

"Hitch your canoe astern," Knowlton interposed. "We'll all get plenty of paddling soon. Take it easy while you can."

"Ah, yes. But it may be as well for you if I am not seen with you. I am not well known up here, more than three hundred miles above the Javary, but a bad name travels far."

"Rot!" snapped McKay. "You're our partner. That's enough. Unless, of course, you'd rather not run the risk — "

"Ho! Risk? Jose Martinez skulks from no town, capitan! Who would imprison me must first take me."

His fierce mustache bristled, and his right hand tapped the hilt of a knife under his waistband. McKay nodded shortly.

"Then you ride here," was his curt answer.

A word to the steersman, and the garretea swung shoreward. Tim, grabbing a length of fiber cord, clambered to the extreme stern. While every Indian eye anxiously searched the grass and the trees, the big boat halted at the bank long enough to allow the taking in tow of the Peruvian's canoe. Then it sheered off and slid away toward the yellow water below.

## IV. THE POWER OF GOLD

Out into the turbid flood of the continental stream plowed the long boat. There the paddlers settled themselves for their regular long-distance stroke. Hardly had they begun to sweat, however, when their tall captain ordered them to swerve toward a cleared space on the high left bank, where the peaked roofs of a few dingy clay houses showed against the encompassing wall of the jungle.

Bewilderment showed in their faces as they glanced back toward the cabin, but they obeyed without hesitation. Once more on the broad Maranon, with the demon water of the Tigre left behind, whatever the white men said was right.

Into a sizable cove below the village they floated. Up ahead, sheltered by the land from the power of the giant of waters, a number of canoes lay at the shore? and from them a crude footpath — hardly more than a gully in the clay — rose to the village. Down that path were coming a couple of wooden-faced Indians, shirtless but wearing tattered breeches; and as the garretea slowed to a stop they also stopped, staring.

"Umph. We don't get a four-man boat here," declared Tim,

after a glance along the meagher stock of canoes.

"A couple of three-man dugouts will do," said Knowlton. "Put two men in each and split the outfit. There's one three-man boat over yonder. Looks good, too. Find another and we're fixed."

But finding the other was not so easily done. The others all were too small — all, that is, except one hulking craft at the end of the line, which bore a striking resemblance in size and shape to the garretea of the adventurers. At this Jose scowled.

"We come at a bad time," he muttered. "Traders are here. Ho, Indios! Whose boat is that?"

The staring pair on the footpath did not answer. One mumbled growlingly to the other, and they resumed their downward way, turning, at the bottom, toward the long boat.

"Sangre de Cristo!" snarled the Peruvian, his eyes snapping. "Put me ashore! I will put tongues in the heads of those surly men!"

McKay, unspeaking, motioned shoreward. The popero grunted, and the paddlers sank their blades.

"Go easy, Jose," Knowlton cautioned. "We came here to trade, not to fight."

"Es verdad. But let them escape with their insolence, and what trade should we make?"

Without awaiting a reply, he made a flying leap to the stern of a dugout near at hand; landed cat-footed, and in three more bounds was ashore. Fierce face shoved forward, red kerchief flaring sinister in the sun, he strode at the two Indians.

One of them, cowed by the truculence of the outlaw's eye, gave back. The other stood his ground and dropped a hand to the hilt of a machete. The menace of his attitude was plain. But Jose did not honor him by drawing his own steel.

His open hand shot out, the heel of it smacking sharply on the Indian's jaw. The man went down as if slugged by a clenched fist.

"Whose boat is that?" rasped the son of the Conquistadores.

The second, cringing, answered promptly this time.

"Maldonado, from Moyobamba, senor."

"Moyobamba!" Jose spat the name as if it were a curse. "You are his man? Why in ten devils did you not answer when I called? Where is that accursed Moyobambino master of yours?"

The man retreated another step, blinking with fear, and pointed a hand up the bank.

"So. He shall soon see me," announced Jose. "Their master

is a sneaking Moyobambino trader, one Maldonado. If you know not the Moyobambinos, learn now that they are cheating, lying, thieving dogs, known from Lima to Para for their rascally tricks. Their one thought is money. If one of them heard that a dead man with three pesetas in his pocket lay on the shore, he would not rest until he had smelled out the corpse and torn the money from it. Such is the Moyobambino."

"Seems to me I've heard of those fellows," said Knowlton.

"A Moyobambino can never be trusted," Jose said grimly.

"One of the worst massacres on this Maranon was caused by one of those curs. It was at Santa Teresa, between the rivers Santiago and Morona — a town which exists no more.

"A party of bold young men from the Rio Mayo determined to seek gold on the Santiago, though that is the country of the fierce Huambisas. They started up the Maranon to carry out their plan. But there was a Moyobambino trader, one Canuto Acosta, to whom some of the Santa Teresans owed a little gold dust; and he was worried lest the coming of the gold hunters might spoil his chance of collecting his debt. So he scurried up the river ahead of them and reached the little town just as a big party of Huambisas came in from the Santiago to trade.

"To these bloody savages he said that a great army of white men was coming up the river to crush their tribe and make them slaves. The Huambisas at once killed every man in the town — forty and seven of them — and carried away sixty women as their slaves. They left alive only two boys, whom they put on a raft and sent down the river to tell the gold-hunters they would kill them also if they came on. So, senores, one hundred and seven people went to death or misery because of one Moyobambino."

"Huh! And I suppose he got away with a whole hide," growled Tim.

"No. He was the first man killed."

"Yeah? Good!"

"Good indeed, comrade. If only the Huambisas had stopped with killing him — but that is not their way. Nor is it the way of Moyobambinos to let other men get money if they also can smell it. What that Acosta did, this Maldonado would do if he suspected where we go and why. He would try to betray us in some way, if only to keep us from finding treasure he could not have. Capitan, if this cur seeks to know our business, let me handle him."

McKay's set lips twitched slightly.

28

"He's your meat," he agreed. "I'll handle the trade, though. Tim, stick here on guard."

"Right, cap." The red-haired man swung his left hand carelessly to his gun barrel in rifle salute.

Up the slope clambered the four, each carrying his rifle. Tim got back on board and leaned against the cabin, where he could watch everything without effort. The crew lounged at ease, incurious, unaware that their voyage down the river was likely to end here. The two men of the Moyobambino effaced themselves by entering their own craft and squatting in the bow.

At the top of the bank the northerners threw one glance around the weedy, slovenly little village, wrinkled their noses at the odor of decaying offal, and headed for a damp-looking mud-walled house around which clustered a knot of sluggish men and frowsy women — Indians and mestizos. A boy, spying the approach of the newcomers, let out a shrill yell. The adults turned with a suddenness that sent a small cloud of flies buzzing up off their unclean skins.

"Estranjeros!" shrieked a number of the women. Then, they began simpering with affected shyness and furtively attempted to pat their hair into something approaching tidiness.

With an aggressive stride, as the men stood and gaped, the four tramped straight up to the pack before speaking. The townspeople, scanning the bleak face of McKay, and meeting the hard eye of Jose, involuntarily shrank together, presenting a compact front.

"Buenas tardes, amigos," spoke McKay. "Where is your head man?"

"Within, senor," answered a fat, pompous-looking man. "The Jefe Pablo Arredondo. But he is engaged in affairs of business."

"So. We bring him further affairs. Have the goodness to step aside."

"But the Senor Torribio Maldonado — " began the important one.

"Can step aside also," McKay broke in. "We have haste."

"And we dislike your town too much to wait," Jose added with a hard grin.

The fat man swelled as if mortally insulted. Then, catching the glimmer under the black brows of the outlaw, he suddenly began laughing in a scared way and backed a step.

"Enter, amigos!" he squeaked. "Ha, ha, ha! A rich joke! He, he, he!"

**29**

With a contemptuous glance Jose forthwith began shouldering his arrogant way through to the door. The three northerners, with less violence but no less firmness, pressed forward and forced a path which otherwise might not have opened to them for an hour. A moment later they were inside the musty house.

The "affairs of business" were in plain sight on a rickety table. They comprised the contents of a large bottle, which the Senor Torribio Maldonado and the civic authority evidently had already discussed to some extent; for the bottle was far from full, while the head man showed slight signs of being on the way to becoming so. His face was heavy with liquor and displeasure at being disturbed. One direct look at him told the newcomers that trading might be a protracted affair involving much patience and diplomacy — unless a shrewd stroke could be delivered at the outset. McKay instantly decided on the nature of that stroke.

But first he and his companions studied the other man, whose predatory face hung over the table like that of a vulture. Hook-beaked, slit-mouthed, beady-eyed, scrawny of neck and humpy of shoulder, with one skinny hand lying like a curved talon on the table — here was the Moyobambino. Already his cunning eyes were agleam with speculation as to whether he could make anything out of these travelers.

McKay turned his gaze back to the frowning visage of the big man of the village. Without speaking, he casually drew from a pocket a gold coin and flipped it whirling into the air. In a shaft of sunlight shining in at a small side window the spinning gold flashed yellow darts at the two men beyond the table. Into the sodden face of Arredondo leaped an answering flash of life.

Gold! Gold money! Here where money was so scarce that canoemen were paid with stingy yards of cloth and business was done by primitive barter, where a paltry peseta was something to be proudly exhibited and a silver sol was to be hoarded — gold money, tossed carelessly into the air! The glittering rise and fall of that coin accomplished more than half an hour of patient talk would have done. Hardly had it thudded softly back into McKay's palm when the headman was leaning forward, his loose lips writhing in an ingratiating grimace. The Moyobambino — his hand had clenched like the claws of a swooping hawk.

"Senores!" gurgled Jefe Pablo. "What is your pleasure?"

"Canoes," laconically answered the captain, closing his hand but allowing the rim of the yellow disk to peep between

**30**

his fingers. "Two three-man canoes. For them we will trade a fine large garretea."

"A garretea!" The other's face fell. "What should we of San Regis do with so big a boat? And two canoes of that sort — no hay."

"There is one in the port," disputed McKay. "Think hard, my friend. There must be another."

"No hay," was the doleful answer.

Then the Senor Torribio Maldonado intruded himself.

"Amigo mio," he began.

"Liar!" spat Jose. "No man is your 'friend.' No man wishes to be. Hold your tongue!"

The man of Moyobamba, after one look, obeyed. Meanwhile McKay took another tack.

"Then we must keep our garretea. Also we keep our gold. If there were canoes — but there are none. Good day."

Dropping the coin back into a pocket, he turned doorward.

"Wait!" blurted the pride of San Regis. "If there were canoes, you would buy them — with gold?"

"Yes. But — no hay." McKay took a step outward.

"Senor! Have the goodness to wait — one little moment. One canoe there is, si. And — "

"That canoe is mine, Pablo!" yelled Maldonado. "Before these strangers came you agreed to let me have it, and also to give me a new crew for my big boat — "

"And now it comes to my mind that there is another," pursued the headman, ignoring the trader. "I had forgotten — it is just finished — it will be put into the water immediately, caballero mio! Mariano — Juan — Mauricio — you others! Put beside the garretea of these gentlemen the new canoe! At once!"

"But it is mine — they are mine!" screeched the Moyobambino. "I will sell them to you, senores — "

"You have not paid for them," Arredondo harshly retorted. "So they are not yours. Senor — Capitan — that is real gold in your hand? You will give it me now? How much?"

"Twenty gold dollars of the United States of America," McKay solemnly answered, opening his hand halfway. "Gold. Gold of the finest. You shall have it when we have the canoes."

"Santo Domingo! San Pedro! Madre de Dios! The canoes are mine!" roared Maldonado. "He has no right to sell them. Give the gold to me!"

Jose burst into a roar of mirth.

"Oho-ho-ho!" yelped the outlaw. "A Moyobambino beaten

in a trade! Twenty golden dollars, Torribio, which go not into your claws! Yah-hah-ha! It is too good!"

The trader, beside himself, sprang up, knocking over the flimsy table. Like a flash Jose's face froze.

"Sit, senor!" he said softly, a sinister sibilance in his tone. For one instant the other glared — for one instant only. Then, his face that of a man who had just looked Death in the eye, he slowly, very carefully, sank back. He still sat there when the adventurers and the greedy-mouthed Arredondo had passed outside.

But a little later, when the two new canoes were hitched to the garretea and all San Regis stood clustered on the bank, the man of Moyobamba appeared and bent a long look on the gold-piece now reposing in the dirty palm of the double-dealing Pablo, who gloated down at its yellow luster as if hypnotized. Then his sly glance lifted to Pablo's fascinated face, and he grinned a cunning grin.

To the men out on the water, already outwardly bound, he yelled boldly: "Where do you go with all those boats?"

Rand, lounging against the cabin, spoke his first words since leaving the Tigre Yacu.

"To the devil!" he snapped.

"A quick voyage to you!" came the jeering retort.

"Faith," muttered Tim Ryan, "maybe you spoke a true word at that."

## V. EYES IN THE BUSH

Gripped again by the current of the Maranon, the long river boat and its trio of canoes floated downstream. It traveled slowly, however, for McKay had ordered the paddlers to rest. Meanwhile a council of war proceeded in the cabin.

"We have to get rid of this garretea and its crew," stated McKay. "May as well drift until we figure out how. It won't take us long to go back upstream, and it's as well to get away from San Regis and that snooping trader. Now what'll we do with this cumbersome craft?"

Frowns of thought ensued. The big boat had become a veritable elephant on their hands. It was Jose who suggested a solution of the problem.

"Perhaps this may do, capitan. Send boat and crew to Iquitos, and with them a note to a man I know, telling him to pay off the crew and hold the boat for us. I have a friend there — oh yes, even an outlaw has friends — who will do this if I write the letter. The boat is worth as much as the wages of the paddlers, is it not so? Then he will lose nothing if we never come to get it.

"Promise the Indians more pay if they reach there by a certain time, and they will travel fast enough to keep ahead of that spying Maldonado, who surely would question them if he overtook them. Still, perhaps he travels up, not down. I wish I knew what is in his garreta."

"I can tell you that," volunteered Tim. "I got tired standing on board, so I rambled over and peeked at his cargo. It's heavy stuff — copper kettles and hardware and crockery — "

"Ah! Esta bien! He goes upstream. If he were down bound he would be carrying straw hats, sarsaparilla, sugar, and such things, for the down-river trade. Then we need not care how much time these paddlers take. Only give them the letter, explain to the popero, and let them go. Is the plan good, capitan?"

"Why not pay 'em off ourselves?" Rand demurred. "We've got lots of trade-cloth — "

"If you pay them they will go straight back home as soon as we are out of sight," Jose interrupted. "Let us make a good start up the Tigre Yacu before anyone learns of our journey. Not that many will dare to follow, but — "

"Jose has the right idea," clipped McKay. "That looks like a good cove over yonder. May as well transfer our stuff there. Popero! Adentro! Inland, over yonder!"

The puzzled steersman obediently swung his rudder and growled at the paddlers. The flotilla veered, plowed into a gap in the bank, bumped to a stop against the shore. At once began the work of transshipment.

The paddlers, much mystified, found themselves stowing in the two newly acquired canoes the sealed kerosene tins — which held not oil but reserve rations, cartridges, and such necessities, soldered tight to keep out moisture and thievish hands — and other paraphernalia of their patrones. Meanwhile the Peruvian, equipped with paper and pencil by Knowlton, laboriously composed a brief note which he signed, not with name or initials, but with an undecipherable symbol. When it was done he laughed in derision.

"Look at the miserable scrawl!" he jeered. "When I was a little boy in — a certain town beyond the mountains — I wrote such a hand that the padre used to pat my head. And now — caramba! one would think this note was written with a machete instead of a pencil. Years of the paddle and the gun have destroyed the writing trick. I move the whole arm to make one tiny letter."

Jose set a bewildered Indian right with three sharp words

and a gesture, and thereafter aided in speeding up the shifting of the equipment. The crew, who knew they would be kicked or struck by the North Americans, were taking their time in all they did; but when they heard the Spaniard's crackling oaths and found him looming over them in apparent eagerness to decapitate any who dawdled, they jumped. Under the lash of his tongue they finished the job in half time.

Then after a final inspection of the garretea to make sure nothing was forgotten, McKay told the men that their ways parted here. Carefully, patiently, he explained just what they were to do, until it was evident that it was understood. The letter he gave to the popero, who took it gingerly and turned it over and over. Then he glanced along the huddle of Indian faces, which stared glumly back at him as if their owners wondered if they were not the victims of some white-man treachery.

"Jose, you're sure these chaps will be paid in full at Iquitos?" he demanded.

"I am positive, capitan," the Peruvian answered earnestly. "I know that man as I know my right hand, and he will do as I have written. He will pay them their just wage and get them places on some upbound boat. They will have no trouble in receiving what is due or in returning home."

The captain nodded. In direct, curt, but kindly phrases he pledged them his word that no trick was being put upon them, and that the paper in the hands of the popero would bring them the full reward for their toil. The sooner they reached Iquitos, he pointed out, the sooner they would be paid; they had best not dally on the way, and above all they must not lose the paper or allow anyone to turn them aside from their journey. For a moment they stared back at him, searching his face. Then they stirred and muttered their belief in his words.

"We leave with you," McKay added, smiling a little, "to help you on your way, a little aquardiente. It is here in the cabin. Adios."

The glum faces lit up. Teeth gleamed in joyous grins, and as the captain went over the side they scrambled into the cabin to drink his parting gift.

"Nothing like it to send them away happy," laughed Knowlton, who had suggested the idea of leaving the raw liquor. "Poor fellows, they get little enough pleasure."

And as the three canoes slid out into the river they all looked back and tossed their paddles in response to the shouts of the sons of the western mountains: "Hasta luego, senores!

34

Goodbye for a while!"

They were the last cheery words the five were to hear, except from one another, for many a long day.

Into the glare of the westering sun surged the canoes, driven by the powerful strokes of fresh muscles and the impetus of a new quest. The twin dugouts, built for three men each, held two pairs: McKay and Knowlton in the one, Rand and Tim in the other. Jose, alone in his smaller craft, slipped along with the careless ease of a tireless machine. Before long, he knew, his four mates would become conscious of hot palms and fatigued shoulders; for weeks of traveling in the confinement of a garretea give men scant chance to keep fit. But he said no word.

San Regis drew near, crept past, and fell away behind without sign that the passage of the little fleet had been observed. Evidently the population of the town was again clustered at the door of the great man Arredondo, listening to every word uttered and watching the progress of their Moyobamba visitor's campaign to get possession of the American double-eagle. The adventurers, remembering the cunning gaze of the trader at the gold-dazed Pablo, had not the slightest doubt that before morning the up-river man would have that coin in his pouch. But that was a matter for Pablo to worry about. They had their canoes — stout boats worth double the price paid — and were on their way.

Soon the one-man canoe drew a little ahead and swung inward. It curved athwart the eddying shore current and glided into the bank, out of sight. The others, following close, slowed beside it and came to a pause. Once more clear water flowed around them. Behind rolled the Maranon. Ahead opened the Tigre.

For a moment, holding their boats steady with slow strokes, the five men gazed around. One last look they took at the tremendous river marching onward in savage power through the wilderness — a grim monster which, even though it now rested between the periods of its engulfing floods, gnawed ceaselessly at its jungle walls and from time to time brought miles of tree-laden shore tumbling down into its insatiable maw; which, already a thousand miles away from its birthplace in little Lake Lauricocha, would sweep on eastward for three thousand miles farther, growing more and more vast, until it hurled its yellow tide two hundred miles out into the Atlantic Ocean; a sullen serpent of waters, malignant, merciless, untamable as the colossal mountains whence it sprang.

Yet the level-eyed voyagers in the hollowed-out log boats

**35**

gave the monster only the casual look of men who cared no whit for its power. It was the smaller stream that held their searching gaze — the frank, clear water which seemed to hold no evil thing in its limpid depths, yet which lured bold hearts into a dim land of sorcery and there swallowed them utterly or flung them back scarred, mutilated, and mad; the flowing road to mountains of golden treasure, but a road beleaguered by ferocious beasts and by man-demons who belted themselves with human hair and shrunk human heads into leering dolls.

"Once upon a time," said blue-eyed Knowlton, "when I was a little kid, I used to read fairy tales and Arabian Nights yarns about caves where dragons would come out and shoot fire from their noses and broil wayfarers to death; and about ogres who trapped travelers into their castles and stewed them for supper, and one-eyed giants who picked men up by the feet and bit their heads off, and so on. And when I went to bed and the room was dark I could see those things standing in the black corners and glowering at me. I used to sweat blood!

"Then when I grew older I sneered at myself for ever believing such things. But lately I'm not so sure that I sneered rightly. There isn't much choice, after all, between a fiery dragon and a tiger that tears out your throat, or between a fellow who bites off your head and one who cuts it off and keeps it so that he can spit in your face whenever he feels grouchy."

"Getting cold feet?" smiled McKay, who more than once had seen the former lieutenant plunge recklessly into an inferno of blood and flame among the shell-torn trenches of the Hindenburg line.

"Uh-huh. Numb from the knees down. But, on the level, I'm beginning to wonder if we're not a lot of jackasses to go in here. Seems as if those San Regis bums would have some gold if this river of theirs was gold-bearing."

Jose spat. "Bah! Those sons of sloths? If the ground beneath their miserable hovels were full of gold, teniente, they would not have enough ambition to dig it up. And to go up this stream seeking it — not they! They lock themselves into their houses at night for fear of the tigres."

Rand nodded. "Same way over in the Andes," he said. "Indians, poor as dirt, shivering and lousy, living on top of millions in gold and silver and never digging down to it. Takes a man to hunt treasure. What's biting you, Tim?"

Tim, who had been twitching his shoulders as if to dislodge something, now lifted a hand and scratched.

"Nothing — yet. Maybe it's only imagination, but I've been

feeling crawly since we left that town. Those people aren't human. I bet the only time they get a bath is when they get caught in the rain. And — talking about dirt, did you see the naked kid eating it?"

All shook their heads. But Jose smiled understandingly.

"It is so. He was clawing up hunks of clay and chewing them — I saw him swallow the stuff!"

"That is nothing new," Jose said calmly. "Children who are eaters of dirt are common enough in this country west of the Napo, and east of it, too. But unless we are to go back to San Regis, let us move now and find a place to make camp tonight. The sun swings low."

"Right you are. Let's go. I'll fight all the headhunters this side of Heligoland before I'll go back there."

The water swirled behind the paddles and creamed away from the prows. Three abreast, the canoes surged away up the River of Tigers. They passed the spot where the dead ashes of the Peruvian's noonday fire lay hidden in the grass, and where the mud still held the broad tracks of a cat creature which long before now had been torn assunder by down-river crocodiles. On they swept, gradually growing smaller, until at length they slid out of sight around a turn.

Then, at the edge of the thick growth above the point where they had paused, a man moved. Across his flat, coppery face, expressionless as that of a crude idol, passed a flicker of hatred. One hand, resting on the hilt of a machete, tightened as if around the throat of a Spaniard. Beady eyes glancing warily around him, he began silently working his way eastward, down the bank of the Maranon.

He was the Indian whom Jose had knocked flat on the shore of the port of San Regis. And he was on his way back to the town where waited his master, the Senor Torribio Maldonado.

## VI. IN THE PATH OF THE STORM

Between two hundred-foot walls of vivid verdure, starred softly by delicately tinted orchids and tipped by yellowish bud-flowers of palms, the Tigre Yacu shone like polished silver, unruffled by the faintest breath of air. On its placid bosom were mirrored great flowering ferns, fifty feet tall, curving stems and drooping fronds of the giant of grasses, the bamboo; the high reaching branches of the jagua, the enormous plumes of the jupati, the feather-bunch crown of the ubussu, the white trunk and flat top of the lordly silk-cotton, and the looping, twining, dangling network of aerial vines.

Even the emerald gleam of the huge green tree-beetles, shining like jewels in the glare of the westering sun, was reflected from the flawless surface of the river of the evil name. Over it wheeled and floated clouds of gorgeous blue and yellow butterflies. Across it winged flocks of green parrots, and along it hopped and yelped huge-beaked toucans gaudy in feather dresses of flaring yellow, orange, and red.

A captivating, alluring river it seemed, beckoning the wanderer on into an Elysium where no evil could wait and where stingless bees would pour their honey into his bowl. But to those wanderers who even now were stroking up into its luxuriance and furrowing its smooth surface into uneasy ripples it was not the Eden it looked. Every man of the five was tormented by scores of red-hot needles.

Though their distance from shore might protect them from savage man or beast, it only made them easier prey to the tiny torturers whose ferocity has for centuries aided the head-hunting barbarians to keep the tributaries of the Maranon almost uninhabited by civilized man: the bloodthirsty zancudos, the almost invisible piums, the big black montuca flies whose lancets bore so big a hole in the flesh that blood drips long after the bite. Out on the broad Maranon itself, where the east winds swept strong and steady across all floating craft, the North Americans had suffered little from such pests. But now, well up the Tiger River, they had long since lost that wind; and the exposed skin of every man was blackened with the minute scars of the piums and scabbed with the wounds of the montucas. And, with merciless persistence, fresh hordes kept swarming to the attack.

Yet, in days of dogged journeying, they had suffered nothing except this constant bloodletting. Not once had human foes appeared. Not once had any animal or snake assailed them – though each night the roar of more than one tigre had sounded too close to camp for comfortable rest, and from time to time during the day as well there came from the maze of shore growth the menacing note of some jungle king voicing his resentment at the invasion of his domain. They received no response to their challenge, those fierce animals: for Captain McKay had issued strict orders to ignore them.

"Let them alone unless they attack," he commanded. "We're here for something more important than cat shooting, and the less noise we make the better. No firing unless necessary."

So, except for the volley which had blown the head off the

38

big black cat at the Maranon, neither the high-powered bolt-action rifles of the Americans nor the big-bored repeater of Jose had spoken since the five-cornered partnership had been formed. Hunting was done at the end of each day's traverse, but only with a light .22-caliber table gun, which made little more noise than a breaking stick, and with bow and arrow, which killed in silence.

The archer of the company was the taciturn, green-eyed Rand. For five years, before being found and rehabilitated by the three former soldiers who now were his comrades, he had been a wild creature of the jungle; and grim necessity had made him as expert in the construction and use of bows and arrows as any of the savages among whom he lived. Moreover, it had given him the keen hunting instinct and the instantaneous perception of the presence of animal life to which no civilized man can attain without living long amid primeval surroundings. And now, though no longer a "wild dog," he had not lost either his hunting-animal sensitiveness or his deadly skill with the weapon of primitive man.

In fact, his markmanship with the bow was much better than with the rifle. Though he had equipped himself in the States with the same rifle and pistol favored by his companions, and familiarized himself with their use, he still was only a fair shot. In comparison with the shooting of his companions, his was not even fair. McKay, Knowlton, and Ryan were all crack shots, and Jose, veteran jungle ranger, was deadly with either rifle or machete. In such company Rand was low gun.

Whether because of a natural dislike to feeling himself inferior to his comrades, or because of an atavistic urge to return to the barbaric implement of death after returning to the primordial land east of the Andes, on his way down the big river he had quietly built for himself a new bow, with a quiver and a goodly supply of arrows — five-foot shafts made from straight cane and tipped with barbed tail-bones of the swamp sting-ray. Equipped with these and minus his boots — which, despite the ever-present danger of snake bite, he refused to wear while hunting — he now would slip away into the bush late each day, silent and deadly as any prowling beast of the forest. With him, carrying the little .22 rifle, went — not Jose, the other bush-trained hunter of the party, but Knowlton. While they were out Jose and the other two would make camp for the night. And before the sun slid down behind the distant Andes and night whelmed the forest the absent pair always returned with ample meat.

Jose, who under normal conditions, should have been one of the hunters, remained at the river bank from choice; the choice being due to the fact that he was not allowed to shoot his own heavy gun. On trying to snap the light, short, low-power rifle to his shoulder and catch the sights quickly he found himself, as he said, "all thumbs." After a few vain efforts to accustom himself to it he handed it back with a rueful grin.

"With a man's gun, amigos, with that old iron bar of mine, I can shoot," he said. "But with this toy rifle – this little boy's plaything – no. And these tiny bullets – por Dios, they feel like fleas in my hands! If I shot a monkey with one of them I should feel that I had insulted him."

So it was Knowlton, who had amused himself many a time by popping the little gun at crocodiles' eyes during the long days of drifting, who followed Rand on the stealthy pot-hunting trips. Despite his comparative inexperience at jungle travel afoot, he could step quietly and spy game quickly, and he could shoot like a flash. With Rand as his guide he had no difficulty in getting about, and now and then he knocked over some bird or small animal in places where his partner's long bow was at a disadvantage. Thus the pair formed a very efficient team.

Now another day was nearing its end. A sweltering day, it had been; a breathless, cloudless day on which the vindictive assaults of the insect hordes seemed to have been redoubled. Ceaselessly they hunted skin spots not already hardened and scabbed by the bites of their predecessors; they burrowed into beards and shaggy hair, they crawled into noses and ears, they sneaked inside shirts and strove to dig under the sweatbands of the hats. The paddlers, smeared with clay which they had applied in the vain hope of defending their tortured skins, grinned and bore it; grinned not with mirth or contempt, but with the fixed facial contraction of acute discomfort which must be endured. Tight-mouthed, slit-eyed, their faces were masks of unbreakable determination. Their shoulders swung with regular unbroken sway, and the paddles rose and fell as if moved by machines driven by inexorable will. Bugs might come and bugs might go, but it seemed that the three boats would surge on with never a halt to the journey's end.

But the eyes under those slits were scanning the shores, which now were closer together than back at the Maranon, and from time to time the heads turned in a brief look at some possible campsite. It was nearing the hour when the voyagers must land, hunt, throw up pole-and-palm shelters, sling

**40**

hammocks, eat, and seek badly needed refuge from their tormentors inside the drab insect bars. And in his stubborn heart every man was glad of it.

With a wordless grunt Jose veered out of line toward the left shore. The twin dugouts followed. Into a shadowy creek between small bluffs they went. Within the entrance thick brush flanked them like impenetrable walls. But a few rods farther upstream Jose drew up to shore and paused. There the tangle was thinner, and the Peruvian pointed to an arm-thick sindicaspi tree.

"Will do," grunted McKay, speaking through lips swollen by bites. The pair of San Regis dugouts drew up, and their paddlers rose stiffly and stepped ashore.

A moment of wary looking around — then Jose slashed his machete with whirling deftness through the nearest bush stalks, clearing a small space. The travelers pulled from their canoes dry clothing and large gourds, and, with such speed as their tired muscles allowed, they stripped. Insects swooped exultantly at the bared skins. But the pests had hardly alighted when they were swept away by the gourdfuls of water with which their victims deluged themselves from hair to heels. A copious drenching, a swift rubdown, a hurried donning of dry garments, and the five stood reinvigorated. With one accord they produced tobacco and papers and rolled cigarettes.

"Got firewood, anyway," remarked Tim, eyeing the sindicaspi tree and luxuriously blowing smoke into the cloud of bugs around him. "Better get busy and make camp. Bet you we have another thunderstorm soon. We didn't get a shower today. Same way our first day up — no rain that noon, but we caught it at night."

The others nodded. The regular noon rain, usually arriving from the east as punctually as if turned on by prearranged schedule, had failed to arrive that day. The air now was oppressively heavy, though nowhere near so hot as out on the river; in fact, the change in temperature was so marked in the damp forest shadows that if the travelers had not shed their sweat-soaked clothing promptly on landing they would have speedily become chilled.

"The rain must come," Jose agreed. "The path of the sun is the path of the storm, as the Indians say. The sun has nearly passed, and the storm is not far behind."

With which he drew his machete again and renewed his destruction of the small growth. Tim pulled a half-ax from his canoe and advances on the sindicaspi tree — one of the few dependable fuel woods in the humid forests of the upper

**41**

Amazon. McKay, with a smiliar ax, looked about for material for the cornerposts and ridge-pole of the night refuge. Rand, who had remained unshod after his bath, got out his big bow, and Knowlton picked up the scorned but useful little rifle. Every man was at his job.

With no word of parting, the pair of hunters slipped away into the woods, working upstream. Oddly mated they seemed, and incongruously armed: the one stolid-faced as an Indian, black-bearded, hatless, barefoot, carrying the most archaic missile-throwing weapon known; the other light of eye and hair, sensitive-mouthed, appearing more like a dreamer than a man of action, bearing a puny weapon which indeed looked the boy's toy Jose had called it. Yet they were brothers at heart – brothers of the long trails and the lawless lands – and each was equipped to fight the most ferocious beast or man; for strapped to each right thigh swung a heavy automatic, and down each left leg hung a keen machete.

For a short distance they stole along in file, eyes searching the branches, feet subconsciously picking clear going. All at once Rand stiffened and paused, but only for a moment. Then he moved on. Up from the creek-side rose a brown bird resembling a pheasant, which whirred away aloft and vanished among the dense foliage. Knowlton's rifle, instinctively lifted, sank again. Both men had recognized the gamy-looking flier as a chansu, whose flesh is so musky that the Indians refuse to eat it.

Onward they crept, threading the pathless tangle like somber shadows for perhaps another hundred yards. Then the light increased. Just ahead the tree tops thinned, and after a few more stealthy steps the hunters halted behind trees at the edge of a small lagoon. At once each threw up his weapon. A few feet beyond, at the edge of the water, were feeding a splenddid pair of huananas – big ducks, armed with small horns on the wings.

Rand, extending his bow horizontally, loosed point-blank. At the low twang of the cord both birds jumped and shot out broad wings in the first beat of flight. But neither rose. With the thrum of the bow blended the snap of the little rifle. The extended wings fell asprawl, the reaching necks collapsed, and both birds floated dead on the water.

Exultantly the men started forward to retrieve their game. In that same moment two things happened. A couple of rods farther on, a bush swayed. As Rand's quick eye caught the movement, the light suddenly dimmed and behind them sounded a rising roar like the onrush of a mighty tidal wave.

42

For an instant Rand watched the bush. Then, deciding that the movement was caused by some animal, he glanced up. Overhead loomed black clouds, hurtling westward at terrific speed. Behind, the roar of the onsweeping wind culminated in a crash of thunder. Storm was upon them.

Dropping his rifle, Knowlton plunged thigh-deep into the muddy pool and seized the birds. Rand swept a searching gaze along the shore, seeking shelter — and found it. Just beyond the spot where the bush had wagged stood a patriarchal old tree in whose base opened a black hole. Shouting, the green-eyed man pointed to it, grabbed up the rifle, and ran. Knowlton, floundering ashore with a duck dangling by the neck from each fist, raced in his wake.

Another crash — a searing flash of lightning — a smashing deluge of rain — then Rand reached the hollow tree and plunged into it. In the same instant Knowlton heard a startled yell and glimpsed something darting out of the hole: a thing that seemed only a thin, vanishing streak elbow high from the ground. In mid-stride he dropped both ducks and snatched his pistol from the holster. Then he hurled himself into the dim tree-trunk.

Struggling bodies plunged against him and spun him outside again. A sheet of rain lashed into his face, blinding and choking him. Lightning flared anew, casting a ghastly greenish glare through the sudden darkness. By its weird flicker he saw two fighting men reel about in the blur of falling water, then pitch headlong back into the hole.

Into that hole he leaped again. The light of storm winked out. Dimly he made out a man tangle at his feet. As he strove to see which was his partner they heaved over violently, knocking his legs from under him. His pistol flew from his hand. Falling, he grabbed fiercely at the man on top.

Then, before he knew whom he had seized, above them sounded a straining, creaking groan of wood. The ground rose under them. A rending crack — a rushing sound — a tremendous blow. Then darkness and silence.

## VII. THE CLAWS OF THE TIGRE

Night engulfed the jungle in such blackness as only the jungle knows.

The vast sea of tree and bush and vine, by day almost impenetrable but nevertheless composed of myriads of separate parts, now was a solid bulk. Far above it the tropic stars shone in a clear sky of deep dark blue, dropping a faint light which, to such creatures as moved above the matted roof of branch and leaf, gave form and substance to those things near at hand. But down below, where shadows lay thick even at noonday, the gloom now was that of an abyss. Through it could pass only such life as could dilate its eyes to the rims, the noisome things which have no eyes and need none, or that unbeatable creature — man — who can carry light with him.

Yet, among those Stygian shades, life moved. Misshapen ant-bears stalked slowly about, their gluey tongues drooling out, in search of ant-hills. Giant cats, hungry and savage, hunted in ugly impatience. And down beside a little pool on a creek of the Tigre Yacu, a man struggled dizzily to sit up.

His first conscious impression was that a tigre had snarled. He could not see that beast, but some primitive instinct, inherited perhaps from apelike ancestors on whom the terrible sabertoothed tiger had preyed ages ago, told him it was only a few feet away, at his right. Moved by the primordial impulse associated with that ancient instinct, he reached above him for a branch to seize as his first move toward safety in the upper air. His hand hit solid wood. At the same instant the invisible brute snarled again.

His head whirled, and he slumped down. For a moment he lay supine, trying to think. He had been fighting — storm had flashed and crashed — something had struck him —

Abruptly the menace of the present knocked all thought of the past from his struggling brain. Hot, fetid breath poured against his bare right leg. A sniffing sound came to his ears. He yanked the leg back, and just in time; for great claws hooked into his breeches, scraping the skin.

Heaving himself over, he felt the cloth yield and heard it rip. Then he caught the malevolent gleam of a big eye.

Tardily, something told him he was armed. His right hand slid to his thigh, yanked a flat pistol from a holster — and at the same instant the huge paw reached for him again.

The claws sank with a cruel grip into his flesh. Again glimmered the eye. He shoved his weapon forward and fired.

Crash-crash-crash-crash! Four shots shattered the night.

The claws bit deeper in a convulsive spasm. Squirming with pain, he struck at them with his pistol. The barrel hit something hard, unyielding, and the weapon was nearly knocked from his grip. With an inarticulate growl he dropped it and attacked the clutching paw with both hands.

Though it clung to its hold, that paw now was motionless. He tore its hooks loose and threw it aside. Then he scratched around him in a mad effort to recover his gun. One hand hit it and closed around it. At once he lurched up,

A cruel blow on the head downed him. He struck on something softer than earth, slid down it a little, dropped a hand on it. His dazed brain told him it was warm human flesh.

Another snarl beyond him! Then a hoarse, harsh roar of rage. Would that tigre never die? It sounded more malignant, more powerful than ever. Pistol shoved forward, hair bristling, he settled himself forward on his knees and awaited attack. He could not see the thing; he must hold his fire until —

"It was here, amigos. I cannot have it wrong — Hah! What is that? Sangre de Cristo! The tigre himself!"

The voice struck across the black void with startling suddenness. With it came light. With both voice and light came a louder snarl from the unseen beast.

"Yeah! That's him. Let him have it!"

Rifle reports split the air before the second voice ceased: sharp cracks merging with a blunter shock of exploding gunpowder; two high-velocity guns and an old-fashioned .44 pouring out a ragged volley. Silence followed.

After a tense pause the first voice spoke.

"Dead, I think. But it is best to be sure."

The black powder smashed out for a second time. Another pause ensued.

"Si. Dead, comrades. And now if we can find the one whose gun we heard — Senores! Knowlton! Rand!"

"Hey, Dave! Looey! For the love of Mike make a noise!"

The crouching man, who still could not see his rescuers, shouted hoarsely.

"Here! Come closer! This is Dave!"

Sounds of movement began. The light increased. Rand, peering about, found himself walled in. The light shone beyond a jagged hole near him, a scant foot wide.

"I don't know where he is," came Tim's puzzled tones. "Sounded right over here — Huh! Look, a tree down! He must be under that. Hey, Dave, are you all right? Where's looey? That bloody tiger didn't get him, did he? Look at this — another tiger! Under the tree, dead as a herring!"

The torchlight shone brightly now beyond the hole. Rand spoke again.

"In here, fellows. Penned up in a little coop. Can't stand up or get out. Merry must be here, too — I'm sort of woozy yet. Got knocked cold a while ago. Pass in a light."

"We'll get you loose in no time. Just a minute, till we yank this cat out."

Another hole opened, lower down, as the dead paw was pulled out from the opening through which it had reached the imprisoned man. Then into the upper hole came a torch and a fist.

"Here you are, Davey. You aren't busted up, are you? Good! Then look at looey, if he's there with you. How's he?"

Rand snatched the torch, turned on his knees, and looked down. Just beyond him lay the former lieutenant. His blond hair was blond no more, but a dull red. From under him protruded the naked legs and lower torso of another man whose head and shoulders seemed to be hidden beyond Knowlton's body. Both were motionless.

Starting up to lift his comrade, Rand struck his head once more against the solid obstacle above. The blow dropped him back to his knees, and he shook his head to clear it. Pressing one hand to his sore scalp, he took his first look about his prison, seeking a way out.

He had spoken more truly than he knew when he said he was penned in a coop. Around him rose the encompassing shell of the big old tree, now uprooted and thrown back prone. Over him was the broken butt, and beyond him were great fang splinters drive into the torn earth. The tree, strained too far by the storm wind, had broken across its hollow base, collapsed on itself, ripped its own stump loose and shoved it back, then folded and closed like the broken halves of an enormous oyster shell. Within the cavity the three men were imprisoned.

All this he saw in one slow sweep of the eyes. Then he hunched forward and pulled at Knowlton, who seemed wedged among gigantic slivers. He could not move him. But he could, and did, determine that he was alive and, though senseless and bleeding from a split scalp, not fatally hurt.

The smoke of the torch choked him. Hastily he pivoted about and pushed it out through the hole.

"Merry's pinned down," he told the anxious men outside. "Got a cut head, and knocked out, but seems all right otherwise. Got an ax or something? Maybe I can cut him loose."

"Got both axes," Tim informed him, shoving one through. "We been looking all over for you, and we came prepared for anything. Here's the flashlight, too. We'll cut this hole bigger while you get looey clear. How'd you ever get into this trap, anyway?"

Rand wasted no time in explanation just then. He wedged the flashlight in a crack and commenced the difficult task of cutting Knowlton free. So scant was his headroom that he had to hold the short-handled ax by the back of the blade and make mere pecks at the long wood fangs. But the edge was keen, and after steady, careful work he managed to liberate his companion.

By that time the hole behind him had been enlarged enough to give easy ingress or exit. As he passed back the ax, McKay ordered him to come out. But he turned back to Knowlton. Forthwith iron hands gripped his feet, and he was hauled backward out into the air.

"Come out," clipped McKay. "You're done up. I'll get Merry."

And, shoving aside both Tim and Jose, the captain crawled into the cavity. Rand, feeling suddenly weak, sprawled where he had been left.

"Humph! Who's this fellow?" came McKay's muffled voice from the hole.

Rand made no answer, and the captain did not spend time in examining the man he had found under Knowlton. He emerged feet first, dragging the limp form of the lieutenant.

"He's all here," blurted Tim after a close look and a hurried examination. "Scratched up and bleeding, but only asleep. That's the way, Hozy! Dump it on his head."

Jose, who had brought a hatful of water, dumped it as requested. McKay, after a searching glance, nodded and turned back to the hole. Rand rolled over, crept on hands and knees to Knowlton's side, and saw the blue eyes flicker open and stare upward. Tim reached to his hip, produced a flask, uncorked it and held it to the blond-bearded mouth. The lieutenant promptly swallowed a mouthful of anisado, coughed, grinned, and struggled up.

"Not so fast," chuckled Tim. "You're too fast for your own good – I was going to give you another shot of this. If you want it, take it now or you won't get it."

"Not now," mumbled the blond man. "My head aches! Hello, Dave. What's all the row?"

"Row's all over, Merry. Cap is bringing out the chap we found in the tree. Tree busted and fell on us while we were waltzing around in there. Guess the other fellow got busted, too."

"He did," McKay's voice corroborated. "Who was he?"

Tim and Jose, who until now had know nothing of any other prisoner of the tree, voiced their amazement as they saw what the captain had hauled forth. Rand and Knowlton, too, got to their feet and stared downward. In the wavering torchlight the five men stood in silent contemplation of the sixth.

He was a muscular man of medium stature, black-haired,

strong-faced, light-skinned, naked except for a loin-clout of dark red cloth and a necklace of tiger claws: a man whose solid frame indicated a strength that would make him an ugly antagonist in hand-to-hand combat. But he never would fight again. His head lay slanting to one side, and his throat was torn open.

"Big splinter killed him," McKay explained. "It's in the tree there. I had to pull him off it."

"Find his bow there, too?" queried Rand.

"Didn't notice it. Found a couple of arrows, though, and the little twenty-two gun. Found a side-arm, too. Yours, Merry?"

He extended a service pistol. Knowlton, after touching his fingers to his empty holster, took it with a nod of thanks.

"Well, the bow must be there, unless it knocked outside," Rand asserted. "He was there when I dived out of the storm. Knew we were coming, too, and didn't care for our company. Had his arrow drawn, and let go as soon as I popped in. Guess he shot a shade too soon — arrow zipped past my chest and missed. I jumped him. Merry pranced in and fell all over us. Then the world came to an end."

The others nodded. Jose sank on one knee and studied the dead man.

"An Indian, amigos, though light of skin," was his judgment. "A Jivero, perhaps; but I think he is a Yameo — one of the white Indians. This is Yameo country. A lone hunter. But his people cannot be far off."

Heads lifted and eyes searched the gloom. To all except Knowlton, who had been unconscious at the time, came realization that the rule against loud gunfire had been broken, and that those reports might have reached hostile ears. But there was little chance that any searching party would seek the gunmen before dawn, and dawn was fully eight hours away.

"We can stow him away out of sight," said McKay, jerking his head toward the tree. "But first, what about that leg of yours, Dave? Looks bad. Jam it?"

"No. Cat tried to haul me out where he could get me." And Rand briefly related his experience in the tree.

"You sure had a time of it," rumbled Tim. "Luck's with you, I'd say. You had about once chance in a million of living through that tree smash, and if you hadn' woke up when you did and had your gun handy — oof! Better wash your leg right now, before you get blood poison."

"Right," McKay seconded. "Both of you fellows clean up before we start back to camp. Jose, help Dave. Tim, give

48

Merry a head-wash. I'll attend to this chap."

Stooping, he gripped the dead man and dragged him back to the tree. There he shoved him into the cavity where he had died. Glancing around he saw the dead tigre which had attacked Rand. With a grim smile he lifted it and laid it against the opening.

"Hm. Female," he mused. "Leave it to the female to claw a man when he's out of luck."

Turning, he stepped aside a few feet and found the other brute, a powerful male. This also he carried to the hole and dropped beside its mate. Picking up Knowlton's little rifle and Rand's quiver of arrows – the bow was broken and useless – he returned to the water, finding the two hunters bathed and being temporarily bandaged with handkerchiefs.

"Did you babes in the woods get any game to pay us for our work?" he demanded.

"Couple of huananas. Beauties, too," Knowlton replied. "Ought to be right over back of you somewhere. I dropped them."

"And the cats ate them," Jose added. "I saw feathers scattered around in the bush there."

"A great pair of hunters you are," chaffed Tim. "Kill a couple of huananas and let the cats get them. Next time you stay home and let somebody hunt that can bring in the bacon. Come on, let's get back to camp and open a can. We've been thrashing around looking when we ought to have been eating."

The torches moved. In squad column the little band filed slowly away into the gloom. The lights faded out, and the jungle night again brooded over the little spot where the gun-bearing intruders had violated its solitude.

On the black bosom of the placid little lagoon the big stars shone, mirrored upward in a frame of reflected tree tops. On the trampled shore, where the sunlight would reveal them to the first Indian eyes to scan the mud, were the imprints of white men's boots. Those leather-heeled tracks converged at the cavity in the shattered butt of the prone tree. And there, in a crude tomb bearing the fresh marks of white men's axes, a savage son of the jungle who had died fighting white men lay waiting, guarded by two bullet-torn tigres of the Tigre Yacu.

## VIII. THE WHITE INDIANS

Dawn broke. Up in the tree-tops birds and mammals started from sleep and hurled a discordant chorus of squawks, squeaks, hoots and howls out into the gray blanket of night-formed fog. Down beside a little creek men stirred, peered at their insect bars, yawned, stretched, and sat up in their hammocks. From one of them sounded a muffled grunt of pain, instantly subdued.

"How's the leg, Dave?" asked Knowlton, protruding a white-swathed head.

"Little sore," admitted Rand, inwardly cursing himself for the groan. "Nothing to speak of. How's the head?"

"Head?" with elaborate carelessness. "Forgot I had one."

"You're a couple of cheerful liars," rumbled Tim. "Dave, you ought to be on crutches and looey, your neck's three inches shorter than it was yesterday morning, not saying anything about a bump as big as my fist and scalp. Lay down again, like good dogs."

Knowlton scowled with official severity, forgetful of the fact that the frown was hidden under his bandages.

"Sssst! Hush, teniente!" Jose cut in .

His hawk face was shoved forward. His thunderous gun had slid into his hands. All froze into postures of listening. Except for the animal noises, no sound came to them save the monotonous drip of moisture in the dank jungle round about.

"Something moved yonder," the Peruvian muttered, twitching his head. "An animal sneaking past, perhaps. It is too early for Indians to be moving. But not too early for us to move."

With which he arose, rolled his hammock, and pitched it into his canoe. The others, with wary glances at the murky shadows, followed his example. In less than a minute the little palm hut was bare.

But none embarked. Men must eat, and Tim voiced the general sentiment when he growled: "I'm going to have coffee before I hit the river, and have it hot. Anyone who wants to mix it with me before I'm ready to go can come running, poison arrow and all."

So, with ears alert but with no haste, the five made their morning meal by the aid of the faithful sindicaspi wood, which burned smokily in the heavy air but did its duty. When the frugal meal was finished all hands rolled the usual cigarettes and squatted beside the coals until the butts scorched their hardened fingers. But there was no more banter, and each man's gun stood within elbow length of him.

Then, when remaining longer would have been mere bravado, they moved into the canoes and pushed away. Rand limped while getting aboard, and in his dugout he sat on some supplies, his torn leg eased out in front of him. Knowlton gave no sign of feeling less energetic than usual. In silence the small flotilla slipped away toward the misty river.

Once more on the wider water, they found the fog still too thick for any but slow travel. It was thinning, and patches of it wavered and almost dissolved, giving short views of one or the other of the banks; but the great body of it clung stubbornly to the ground. Stroking lazily, they progressed gradually upstream, awaiting the dissolution of the murk. Tim found time and inclination for a little grumbling.

"Pretty slow so far," he declared. "Nothings happened but shooting three cats and getting looey and Dave out of the hole. Where's the head-hunters and the thing that bites off toes and drives men batty? Where's the bags of gold? All we get from the Tiger River is bug bites, seems like."

'Well, you're getting plenty of them, aren't you?" countered Knowlton. "One thing at a time. Trouble with you is that you're sore because you missed getting into that tree racket of ours."

"Oh, yeah. You're so sore you can't see straight because you did get into it. All the same, I'd like to get a little action out of this trip. I wasn't brought up to push a paddle for nothing. When do we get to the gold?"

"Wouldn't be a bad idea to pan a little dirt before long and see what we get," suggested Rand. "Water's pretty shallow now, and we're well up."

McKay nodded.

"Been thinking of that," he conceded. "Might give us some idea of what's ahead."

Jose, the real source of the expedition, said nothing, though he heard all. His eyes kept plumbing the slowly clearing shores. Gradually his strokes lengthened as the mist rolled upward, and the others automatically adapted their pace to his. At length the fog burned away completely, and the canoes swung into their regular speed.

For several hours they forged on, silent as usual, hot as usual, bitten as usual by the insect swarms. Along the banks little life showed: macaws, quarrelsome toucans, surly male cotomonos which howled monkey execrations at the intruders while the females scurried away through the branches, carrying their young clinging on the backs. Then on the quiet surface appeared bubbles, floating down from ahead; and to the ears of the canoemen came a soft, elusive sound like wind among high leaves.

"Ah! We approach a mal-paso — a rapid," Jose announced. "Do you not hear the water, amigos? It now is low and quiet; but soon we shall reach rocks."

The mechanical swing of the paddles quickened a bit. Rocks! For many long days the voyagers from the Andes had seen not the tiniest stone: nothing but clay banks and the everlasting walls of tree and bush. Now the arrival at rock country meant harder work and slower progress, but it also meant that the mysterious Cordillera del Pastassa, offshoot of the precious Llanganati, was creeping nearer to them. And up there to the northwest might be — what? The dream city of El Dorado? The fabulous mother lode of all gold? Who knew? Save for one man whose brain was twisted, none had ever come back to tell.

Peering over-side for the first time in hours, McKay saw gravel on the bottom. His iron face lightened a little, and he put another pound of power on his paddle.

But when the rocks appeared the eager faces of the North Americans fell. Accustomed to the fierce mal-pasos and the gorged pongos of the upper Maranon, they had unconsciously looked for a chasm, even though small. The obstacles now before them could hardly be dignified by the name of "bad pass." They were only a few boulders at a bend, protruding above the surface like dingy, worn-down molars, visible only because of the low stage of the water. Yet they were rocks, real rocks, the farthest outposts of the host of mountain fragments waiting beyond. And, despite their insignificance, the treasure hunters smiled at them and at the sleepily murmuring water flowing down between them.

"Here's where you can exercise your manly right arm, Tim, and pan some gold," Knowlton chaffed. "Just hop over with a shovel and dig down to bed rock. We'll get lunch."

"Huh! I could dig halfway to China before I'd hit bed rock in this mud country. But I'll pan her once anyway just to see the color."

And, when the canoes had been forced beyond the barrier, he did. With a dexterity betokening much practice somewhere farther west, he swirled the water and the mingled mud and gravel in his pan until he was down to the dregs.

"It's here!" he exploded. "Nothing much — just a few flakes — but it's color! Free gold, men! Look here!"

Eager heads clustered over his pan. For a moment there was silence. "Uh-huh," commented McKay. "Pretty poor showing, though."

"That's true, but maybe farther up we'll hit the real stuff. This bed is all gummed up with mud. I'll give her another whirl, just for luck."

His luck seemed not to improve, however, though he

scooped up several more pans from below and worked them with extreme care. His first enthusiasm oozed away. After giving the last pan a couple of tilts and a sour survey he desisted without trying to wash it.

"She's got to come across better than this or I won't tell anybody she's a friend of mine," he asserted, clawing out some muddy gravel. "If only these stones were something beside dirt — "

He stopped, his mouth open. His red lashes lifted, and his eyes seemed to bulge. Very carefully he set the pan down on the nearest rock. With the fingers of his free hand he rubbed the stones in his cupped palm against one another. Then he picked one out and grated it along the boulder beside him.

Mute, he held up the stone. From its scraped side flashed a yellow gleam.

"Nugget!" barked Knowlton.

With sudden energy Tim scraped his find again, then scrubbed it under water with a hard thumb. When he again held it aloft it shone like a gilt ball.

"Sure as God made the kaiser crazy, it's a nugget!" he exulted. "Mud stuck to it and camouflaged it. Weighs a couple of ounces, easy. Forty dollars, gents — eight apiece for you that haven't panned a thing. Now let's see you work for yourself. Come on in, the water's fine. Beat old Timmy Ryan if you can! Oh you little yellow baby!"

His exuberant challenge met with instant response. Into the river splashed his companions, heedless of hunger and of recent injuries from tiger claw and falling tree. They brought up fistfuls of gravel which had lodged around the boulders, and with minute care inspected each one. Tim, carefully buttoning his nugget in a pocket after assuring himself that the pocket had no hole in it, fell to scraping and rubbing each of the little stones which had suddenly become potential treasures.

One by one, however, he cast them away. The whole pan received a rigid inspection, but no glimmer of yellow showed. He brought up another panful from the same spot where he had caught the nugget. This, too, yielded no results.

At length the dripping company ceased work, empty-handed.

"Guess you're the only lucky one in the crowd, Tim," admitted Knowlton. "Let's see that nugget again."

Tenderly Tim drew it out. "Don't drop it," he adjured. "If it gets back in the muck it's gone. Water's all riled up."

With a nod, the lieutenant studied the chunk of metal.

Then he passed it to McKay.

"No wonder we didn't find any more," he said. "That nugget never rolled down this stream."

"Huh? Oh, I suppose it rained down last night, then, or maybe it fell from one of these trees," jeered Tim.

"It never came down in the water," insisted the other. "It's too rough. Water would wear it smooth. Look at the stones around here — even these big ones are smoothed off. Not a sharp edge on any of them."

"Right," agreed McKay. "It's well rounded, but not smooth. You can feel the edges, and see them, too."

"Um. You're right, cap. But how did it get here — one lonesome nugget like that? It isn't right."

All stared at it, groping for a solution. Presently Knowlton laughed: "Old Dame Fortune left it here for us, maybe, to encourage us. Sort of a come-on stunt, eh? Like a girl dropping her handkerchief on the sidewalk when you look good to her. She's a flirty old dame, is Lady Fortune."

"Si," grinned Jose. "But you are forgetting Rafael Pardo, comrades. It may have been he, not the old lady, who dropped this here. It is less than a month since he returned to Iquitos, as I have told you, with his bag of gold. Is it not quite likely that he lost this, and other nuggets as well, on his outward trail?"

"Guess you've hit the only sensible answer," agreed Rand. "Come on, let's eat."

The close-drawn knot of men drew apart and turned toward shore. With a sudden gulp Tim halted short. His mates froze.

Armed Indians confronted them. There on the bank, arrows drawn back and aimed with deadly accuracy at each man's breast, stood a dozen hard-faced savages. Their skins were light, their hair black and cut straight across the brow, their bodies naked save for tooth-and-claw necklaces and red loin cloths. In stature, in build, and in expression they might have been brothers of the dead man left last night in the tree-butt tomb beside the black lagoon.

Motionless from surprise for an instant, the men in the water then began reaching stealthily toward their wet pistols.

"Alto!" snapped a sharp voice behind them. "Lift those hands or you die!"

The five heads jerked around. On the other bank they beheld eight more of the white Indians. These held no bows. Instead, seven of them squinted down the barrels of big-bored rifles. The eighth, standing a little to the rear, had a similar rifle but was not aiming it. His face had a markedly Spanish cast.

The hands of the North Americans poised exactly where they were. The situation was utterly hopeless. But Captain McKay's voice, when he replied, was as cold and calm as if he held the power.

"If we do not die here we die hereafter. When and how?"

Across the mouth of the Spanish Indian twitched a fleeting smile. "You are cool. Die now if you will. All men die. If you do not die here you may live long. Strong men live."

"Live through what? Torture?"

"No torture. We kill swiftly. Among us a man is all alive or all dead."

McKay glanced once at the bowmen, running his keen gaze along their hard eyes. He looked back at the seven riflemen and the Spanish-speaking leader.

"No good, boys," he said quietly. "We haven't a chance. Better surrender."

His hands rose. Reluctantly his companions followed his example. Turning about, the captain waded across to the shore where the leader stood. In his wake swashed the others, still covered from both banks. Up on the land they went, and there they halted.

"We live on," said McKay, smiling bleakly. "Now what?"

The leader grunted something. The riflemen closed in. Five put their gun muzzles against the abdomens of their captives. The other two passed behind the explorers.

"Now you will put the hands down. Behind your backs."

As the order was obeyed the two spare riflemen lashed the wrists of each prisoner tightly with fiber cord. In less than two minutes all were securely bound. Their weapons were left in their sheaths.

"Now what?" demanded McKay again.

The evanescent smile fled once more across the Spanish face. "Now we walk. One of you shall die. The others — quien sabe?"

## IX. A LIFE FOR A LIFE

Gloomily the pinioned men stood on the bank and watched their captors gather around the canoes. Despite the firmness of their bonds — every one of which had been sharply inspected by the leader of the gang — they still were guarded by two riflemen, one of whom stood at each end of the line, ready to shoot any prisoner making a sudden move. The other gun-bearers had waded across the river.

Now, under direction of the leader, half a dozen of the wild men busied themselves in thoroughly washing every piece of

**55**

equipment. The rifles, the axes, the clothing, the bags and heavy tins, the cooking and mining utensils − everything was plunged into the river, swashed about and scrubbed by rough fingers, then thrown upward on the shore. Watching the immersion of the guns and the puzzled examination given the bolt actions afterward, the captives silently raged over their carelessness in leaving their rifles while they clawed in the mud for gold. The wrath of Jose was not quite silent.

"Sangre de Cristo!" he hissed in an undertone. "Caught like the fools we are! Snared while we snatched at stones! I, Jose Martinez, trapped like a child! Si, wash those guns, you measles-fearing man-killers! I hope you catch a hundred sicknesses!"

Forgotten was his recent statement that he would rather fall prey to savages than to his own countrymen; forgotten the fact that these wild men had spared his life, at least for the time. His pride in his ability to protect himself was cut to the quick, and in the same hissing monotone he heaped vitriolic maledictions on his captors.

The two guards stirred, scowling at him and moving their gun muzzles into line with his stomach.

"Let up, Jose," muttered Knowlton. "We all feel the same way, but mum's the word. Less talk and more thinking may pull us out of the hole yet."

The outlaw's teeth clicked, and he said no more, though his eyes still smouldered. Then came a call from the Spanish-speaking leader.

"What is here?" He pointed downward at one of the sealed tins. Baffled by the heavy solder, none of his men had been able to open them.

"Open it if you dare," snarled Jose. "Those boxes are full of diseases which kill quicker than the bite of a snake."

The effect of the retort was remarkable. Every man of the Indians jumped back from those harmless tins as if they truly were filled with sudden death. Several, who had handled the containers, leaped into the river and frantically scrubbed their hands.

The outlaw broke into a jeering laugh. Maddened, the leader of the tribesmen plunged in and came straight for him, the rest following close. Their glittering eyes and hard mouths spoke death to the captives.

"Halt!" snapped McKay. "Do you kill a man for warning you? He has done you great service. The diseases cannot harm you unless you let them out. Now that he has told you, you will not let them out."

**56**

His quick wit saved his party. The Indians, though set to kill, glanced at their leader. That leader stared into McKay's inscrutable face.

"You have promised that only one shall die," added McKay. "Is your tongue forked?"

The other's gaze swerved to his own men and came back.

"My tongue is straight," he declared. "What I have said shall be."

He gave a sign to his men. Their weapons sank. He spoke, with a backward jerk of the head. They turned slowly, went back into the water, and began bringing across the equipment — all except the tins, which they avoided.

"You are a good leader," McKay complimented. "Your men obey."

A touch of cruel pride flitted over the other's face.

"They know it is best to obey," was the significant retort. With which he turned his back to the prisoners and watched the transportation of the loot.

The Scot's compliment had been no idle flattery. The sinewy white Indian was a good commander. He handled his followers almost as if he were an American or a European, instead of a savage son of the jungle; and, despite their position, the ex-soldiers watched with appreciative eyes.

"Spanish blood here," thought McKay. "It sticks out. Wonder if Jose's tale was right, and this chap's descended from Spanish stock. Wonder who they all are, anyhow. Wonder why we're not killed at once. Oh well, we may learn."

Aloud he asked: "Who are you? Yameos?"

"Men of the forest," came the curt answer. "Now walk."

He tilted his head to the left, indicating the direction. The captives turned downstream. A couple of Indians glided in front of them and led the way. Behind the adventurers the main body closed in, walking in file, carrying the plunder from the canoes.

Almost at once the five found themselves in a path. A narrowing, twisting trail through the forest, it was, and scarcely visible even to a man following it. But it was a path, perhaps a rod back from the edge of the bank, where the voyagers had supposed the bush to be utterly trackless; and along it the guiding pair slipped ahead as fast as if it were a broad highway. The bound men following found themselves hard put to it to maintain the speed set by the pacemakers, for their walking wind had been shortened by many days of river travel. Rand, limping along on torn leg muscles, found the going doubly hard. But he set his teeth and strove to keep up.

**57**

It was the commander of the party who gave the word to slow down. He trod close at Rand's heels, and he saw the lameness of the green-eyed man; but he made no effort to ease the prisoner's difficulty until he himself felt the consequences of it. The injured leg, stiff and sore, failed to clear a projecting root, and Rand stumbled and fell. The Indian behind tripped over him and bumped his head sharply against a tree. He was up instantly, glaring at the prostrate man and at the tree he had hit; but he realized that the blame rested not on the prisoner but on the pace at which they were moving. He snapped something at the guiding pair, who had continued on. They stopped.

The leader glowered suspiciously at Rand's leg, as if he thought the prisoner to be malingering; for Rand now wore his boots, concealing the bandages around the limb.

"What ails the leg?" he demanded. "The forest is no place for the lame."

"The claws of a tigre," panted Rand, still prone and snatching a moment's rest.

A quick light flickered in the hard eyes.

"When did the claws of the tigre strike?"

"Last night."

A short nod and a tightening of the mouth followed. Roughly he hauled Rand to his feet. To the pair ahead he grunted briefly. They resumed their advance, but at a slower pace. Wondering what was in the leader's mind, but thankful for the slower progress, Rand went on.

For perhaps two hours the march continued without a halt. Glancing from time to time at the sun-slanted shadows, the captives observed that they were working steadily southward. Now and then they caught gleams of water at their left, where the river wound close to the path and then veered off again. At length, at a cool little brook, the whole band stopped to drink.

Here McKay asked a question which had been puzzling him.

"Where do you get your guns?"

"From men who came here before you," was the straightforward answer. "We use them only for war. The yellow things that kill are few. From those men I learned the tongue you speak. From you we shall learn how to use these new guns — before you go."

As he spoke he frowned down at McKay's own rifle, which he held in one hand. McKay had seen him trying to pull back the bolt, without first lifting it. So far as the Indian was concerned, the gun was locked tight. The captain did not enlighten him regarding the method of working a bolt action.

58

"Before we go where?" he demanded.

"Where the other men went." His eyes strayed to Tim, red-bearded, red-headed. His shadowy smile flitted across his mouth and was gone. Abruptly he arose and gave the sign to move on.

As they resumed their march, a chill crept up the backs of the five. All had seen that brief stare at red Tim and the slight smile that went with it. All knew this man had said that one of them should die. And all recalled the grim jest of Jose, made days before: that Tim's hair would be braided into the hair belt of the Jivero who killed him. That careless joke now loomed as a prophecy.

Yet on the heels of this thought came another — not one of their captors wore a girdle of human hair. They might not be Jiveros. Their commander had promised life to four of them. And — they could only march on, hoping for some miraculous change of luck.

For another hour or more no word was spoken. The occasional sidelong glances of the captives showed them that they had left the river, for no water-gleam now came to their eyes. At length they did meet water again, but it was a creek, not the river. Up along this they filed for a couple of hundred yards. Then they debouched into a clearing.

An oval-shaped house of up-and-down logs, thickly thatched with palm; a knot of armed men standing before the door; several small mud huts around it; a plantation at the rear, with women at work — these were the first impressions of the white men. McKay, striding at the head of his unfortunate company and bulking tall over the heads of the two guides, noted three more things as they neared the big house: that it was big enough to hold a hundred people, that it looked much more new than the mud huts beyond, and that the warriors before it showed signs of travel. Their faces lit up as they saw the captives, and they grunted as if they now saw something for which they had been hunting. The captain, used to watching faces, guessed that this party also had been out beating the bush in a search for strangers.

Almost up to the door the captors and captives went. Then the guides stopped. The prisoners halted. The Indians behind spread out and surrounded them in a half-horseshoe, open end toward the door. Through that door, without awaiting a summons, now came a man whom the newcomers knew to be the chief.

Slightly taller than his men, past middle age, harsh of face, with brown eyes burning like tawny coals in deep sockets, he

**59**

was a grim figure. In his thick black hair, unblanched by any sign of gray, parrot plumes rose as his crown of rank. Like his men, he wore a necklace of tiger claws; but, unlike them, he had also arm bands of big fang teeth, and – a hair girdle.

Wide and thick and black was that sinister cincture, reaching from the waist to the loins. In it gleamed no lighter shade: no brown, no gold, no red. But every man of the five saw that the hollow eyes of the ruler, after passing along their faces, returned to the blond beard of Knowlton and the glinting red of Tim's hair.

He said no word until the report of the capture was made. When the white Indian holding McKay's gun finished his tale he pointed at Rand. The chief followed the gesture, looked down at the lame man's boots, lifted his gaze and somberly studied the impassive face of the former Raposa. Then he spoke.

In a tone low but harsh as his face he ground out a curt sentence. Two men went to one of the little mud huts. Immediately they came out again, bearing between them a pole litter on which lay a rigid figure covered with big leaves.

Straight up to the prisoners they came. On the ground before them they put the litter down. With a few swift motions they stripped the leaves from the still form.

The five looked down at the dead face and the torn throat of the wild man who had fallen fighting in the hollow tree.

For a moment there was utter stillness. Then the captives, looking up, found the chief's eyes boring into their faces. Abruptly he spoke again. The Spanish-speaking leader translated his words.

"You have killed this man of mine. You have torn the throat of a hunter of my tribe and let out his spirit. For that you all should die. But there is other use for you. You shall live to pull the wheel. All but the man who killed my warrior. That man dies. Who is he?"

McKay answered. "The great chief has it wrong. This man was killed by a tree splintered by storm. We took him off the splinter. We laid him back in the tree where no tigre could destroy him. We left two dead tigres to guard him. Let the chief blame the storm."

The hard mouth of the chief only grew tighter.

"The storm harms us not. You men have killed my hunter. One of you must go down his trail and pay him for his life. One goes or all go."

His eyes dwelt on Rand, whose tiger-clawed leg had been reported to him. Then they shifted to Tim. Plainly he believed

**60**

Rand to be the man most implicated in the death of his subject. Yet he obviously coveted the red man's hair, and hoped he might be the guilty one.

"You know the man who killed," he rasped. "Who is the man?"

For a moment there was silence. The three soldiers, who had fronted death many times on another continent; the outlaw, who lived by his own deadliness; the former Wild Dog of the Javary jungle, who had roved for years among violent endings of life — all searched the relentless visage of the chief. Through each man's mind went the same thought: that through the death of one the rest should live.

Moved by the same impulse, all stepped forward. Like one man all answered:

"I!"

## X. RED SPOTS

For an instant every man of the five stood defiantly fronting the chief. Then each became aware of the fact that his comrades also had volunteered for death.

"Get back!" Tim muttered. "I'll take this on! — "

"It is mine!" hoarsely disputed Jose. "I am but an outlaw — let me — "

"You both shut up!" growled Knowlton. "I was there and you guys weren't — "

Rand cut short the tragic argument. He strode across the body, limped up to the chief, and nodded. The chief nodded in response. The Indian directness of the move went straight to his mind, and the steady green eyes convinced him that here was the right man.

Once more he spoke in the same harsh monotone. As before, the interpreter translated.

"The sun of today sinks. Those who live shall see more suns rise. This man shall see one sun. While the stars shine you shall stay there."

The chief pointed to one of the mud hovels. Without another word he went back into the big house.

Forthwith the five were herded to the designated hut. At its entrance the leader halted them. At a word from him each man's belt was unbuckled and, with its weapons dangling from it, taken away. Then, still bound, they were shoved into the dank interior.

Leaving four warriors on guard outside the house, the rest went back to the tribe-house and busied themselves carrying in the loot. Until it was all transported, the dead man lay stark

**61**

and still on the ground. Then two men grasped the litter and carried it away toward the rear of the place.

"Thought so," nodded McKay, who had been coolly watching. "They found that fellow early and saved him for a third-degree stunt. Sent one gang up-river and the other down. They traveled fast, and the upstream bunch caught us cold. The down-river detachment got back just before we came."

After eyeing the guards who stood suggestively ready, he turned and looked about the bare prison from which Rand was to go forth to death at the next sunrise. As a place of confinement it was almost ideal, at least from the standpoint of the jailers; for it had no windows, its roof was a solid sheet of sun-baked clay supported by close-laid poles, and there was no possible means of exit except through the doorway, which could easily be blocked up and guarded. To men confined in it, however, it was a miserable hole – damp, clammy, unprovided with either conveniences or necessities. No hammocks, no water – nothing at all was in it except a small cracked clay jar in one corner.

"I don't think much of this town's guest house," remarked Knowlton, sourly surveying the place.

The others nodded.

"They may cut us loose later," McKay encouraged. "If not, I'll do it."

"Huh? How?" asked Tim.

"Jack-knife. Got one here in my right pocket."

"I got one, too, but I can't get to it with my hands tied like this."

"Simple enough. One of you fellows get a couple of fingers into my pocket and fish it out. We can open it somehow and cut one man's cords. Then he'll free the rest of us."

McKay's glance strayed to Rand, who had sunk down against a wall and eased his aching leg out before him. Catching the look, Rand smiled somberly.

"This leg won't hurt me tomorrow at this time, Rod," he said.

Black scowls met his stoic jest. Think as they might, none could see any possibility of evading the execution at dawn. But none would admit it.

"Por Dios, I would not be too sure of that, Senor Dave," protested Jose. "We have all night to work ourselves out of this place, even though they will bar the door. And if once I can get at the guards with cold steel – "

He moved his jaw eloquently toward his throat.

But Rand only shook his head slightly and contemplated

62

the opposite wall. One by one the others sank down beside him and silently stared at the same wall, thinking, thinking, but seeing no hope.

"If you'd stayed where you were, Dave, instead of walking right up to the chief, you'd be safe," Tim asserted morosely. "He wants this red hair of mine in his corset. Why didn't you keep quiet?"

"Why didn't you keep quiet?" countered Rand. "I'm the logical candidate anyway. I jumped that Indian in the tree. Merry only fell on top of us, and you three weren't there at all. Besides, I haven't any folks up home, and I'm crippled for awhile with this leg. Now shut up. There's no more to say."

Tim growlingly subsided. For some time all sat wordless, moving only to ease their positions. Outside, the guards stood watching steadily through the open doorway, and other tribesmen came, stood, stared, grunted among themselves, and went away. The sun-shadows, already long, slid faster and faster to the eastward as the earth rolled toward darkness. Within the house, the dimness shaded into dusk.

At length Knowlton hitched forward, got to his knees, and heaved himself up.

"Guess I can get that knife when you're ready, Rod," he said. "My hands aren't quite so numb now. I've been holding my wrists close together to ease the cords."

"Wait for dark. We're too closely watched now."

The blond man began pacing up and down. After a few turns he approached the cracked pot, kicked it out where the light was a little better, and peered at it.

"Ugh!" he grunted. "Dried blood!"

He gave it one more kick, knocking it back to the wall. It struck sharply and broke into chunks. One of them spun against Jose. The bushman glanced at it, then bent and looked closely.

"Not blood," he corrected. "It is too red. This is an old pot of anatto dye, which they use to color their red loin cloths."

Yawning, he got up and strode to the doorway. The guards drew together and fronted him with weapons ready.

"Oh, do not fear, poor little ones," sneered the outlaw. "I will not attack you – not yet. I want water. Water, you fools! My throat is parched."

The Indians made no response. They only watched, uncomprehending.

"Agua!" roared Jose. "Water - agua!"

From a group near the door of the big house came the leader of the gang which had caught them.

"Agua!" Jose yelled again. "Water, and food, too! Will you starve us and choke us with thirst? Agua! Carne!"

The advancing Indian scowled at the imperious tone. But, after a gesture with one finger, he grunted something to another man near by. The man went along the curving wall of the tribe-house and barked something at women near a rear door. Presently several women approached, bearing clay jars and platters.

Reaching the guards, they stopped and stared fearfully at the gaunt red-capped outlaw, who still stood scowling in the doorway. They were young and good-looking, as light-skinned as their men, clothed only in short hip-bands of the red fiber cloth worn by the warriors: but Jose showed them scant courtesy.

"Make haste!" he snarled. "We do not want to look at you, but to eat and drink. Come here!"

Instead, they retreated. The Indian leader spoke curtly. They hastily put down their burdens and fled back to the rear door. Men came forward and carried the victuals into the prison pen.

"How are we to eat without hands?" demanded Jose. "Are you afraid to untie us even when we are penned up and without weapons? You are brave!"

The commander scowled again. Then his eyes fastened on something peeping over the Peruvian's waistband. In two steps and a slutch he had it – a hidden knife, whose hilt had worked up into view unnoticed by its owner.

Without a word he turned the chagrined outlaw around and cut his bonds. Then, with a sneering smile, he threw down the knife and stalked out.

With a muttered oath, Jose worked his stiffened fingers a minute or two, then picked up the keen weapon in mingled relief and rage – the rage due to the contemptuous manner in which the Indian had answered his taunt. Outside, the savage watched, then spoke.

"Eat well. When you are on the wheel you will not feast. Use your knife to kill yourself tonight if you will. It may be better for you."

While Jose stared at him he strode away. In less than half a minute the floor was littered with several cords, the Americans were rubbing their numbed hands together, and Jose's knife had vanished into its secret sheath. In another minute all were squatting in jungle style around the food and water. The bill of fare was fish, fruit, and meat – the first two sweet and fresh, the meat offensive to both nose and palate. However, the meat

64

went the way of the rest: and when Jose, with an ironical bow to the guards, put the dishes outside the door they were bare.

"I notice they keep speaking of a wheel," remarked Knowlton, when his cigarette was going. "Seems to be something unpleasant."

"I believe the old Spanish Inquisition had a wheel," suggested McKay.

"Umph! Hope it's nothing like that. Besides, that fellow promised no torture. What do you make of it, Jose, and of these people?"

"Of the wheel I make nothing, senor. I cannot guess what it may be. Of the people I make only this: they are not shrinkers of heads, unless the heads are kept in the big house, which may be possible. We have seen none. At the same time, they have the Jivero custom of keeping the women apart from the men; there is a separate door at the rear for them. They are like Jiveros in some ways, unlike them in others — keeping us alive, for one. They have not been here many months; their big house is too new. If I could have my way they would not be here one hour longer, but in hell."

"Yeah," contributed Tim. "But wishing doesn't get us anything. If it did I'd wish for one of those diseases they're so scared of. I'll bet if we broke out with smallpox or measles over night they'd knock down the whole jungle running away. Hello, here comes more trouble."

A dozen men were coming across the stumpy clearing, bearing spears and short but heavy logs. The prisoners arose and stood alert — Tim with fists shut, Jose with a hand on his knife, McKay and Rand feeling for clasp-knives in their pockets, Knowlton holding a jagged section of the shattered dye-pot. But none of the Indians entered the hut. They dropped their logs at the doorway. Two more came up with stout poles.

While the prisoners watched, the poles were set into deep holes at each side of the doorway. The log sections were piled on one another, between poles and wall, across the entrance. In a few minutes the doorway was blocked by a solid wall of logs reaching from the ground to within a hand's breadth of the top, where a small opening was left to admit air. Then came sounds of men walking on the low roof, and the barrier, which had hung outward a little against the poles, was forced back tight against the door edges as if drawn by ropes around the uprights.

"Crude jail door, but mighty effective," commented Rand. "They've roped it back against a big tree just behind here. It

**65**

would take us a week to break out."

As if in answer, through the air-hole came the warning voice of the Spanish-speaking Indian. "Men watch through the night. If this wall moves they kill."

No answer came from the prisoners, who now stood in dense gloom. Voices grunted outside, and a whiff of smoke drifted in. Almost at once the last sunlight vanished from the farther jungle. The night noise of animals and frogs broke out. Through the air-hole a yellowish light glimmered and the hiss of flames sounded. The guards had started a protective fire and were settling themselves for their vigil until dawn.

"Well," came Rand's unemotional voice, "guess I'll curl up for a good sleep."

"Wait a minute," shot Knowlton, a quiver in his tone. "Thanks to Tim, I have an idea. Thanks to a chafed knee, I have a little can of talcum powder in my pocket. Thanks to luck, we have water and some dried anatto dye. Rod, is your flashlight in your shirt pocket as usual?"

"Yes. Why?"

"Here's why. Those fellows outside are dead afraid of disease. Now listen hard."

His voice mumbled rapidly for a minute. Then sounded a subdued chorus of approval.

"Por Dios, it will do!"

"It's good, looey!"

"Good head, Merry. We'll try it out."

Jose stole to the door and, through the airslit, watched the guards at their fire. The others huddled in a corner, where, in the white sheen of the little electric ray, they worked with powder and moistened dye. They worked slowly and with extreme care. At length McKay strode to Jose and muttered: "All right. Your turn next."

The outlaw stepped to the corner, and the tall captain stood guard at the slit. For a while longer the white light in the corner burned. Then it winked out.

"All set, Rod," said Knowlton. "We can turn in now."

The five stretched themselves on the floor.

The night wore on. To the ears of the squatting guards came the roars of prowling tigres, the howls of cotomonos, the other night noises of the tropic forest. But from the prison came no sound.

At length two of them arose, advanced with a torch, narrowly inspected the log wall, listened, passed around the house, looked at the roof, listened again at the door. At that moment came a dread sound from within: groans of a man in deadly pain and sickness. Followed other voices and a sound of water being poured. Then, except for more groans, all was still.

The pair stared soberly at each other. Then they slipped back to the fire and told their mates. None went near the door again. All watched it and listened.

Came a babbling voice, broken by louder groans and piteous appeals for water. Presently it rose to a shrill, terrible note like that of a death-scream. This was followed by an outbreak of exclamations, questions, calls to one who did not reply, scaling down into mumbling tones. Then came silence again.

The stars rolled westward. The dank chill of the hours before dawn made the guards shiver and draw close to the fire. At last a wan light came into the sky, brightening fast. The animal world roused itself to its daybreak clamor. The door of the tribe-house opened. Men emerged, and the guards rose to meet them.

They grunted rapidly, pointing to the clay prison. A worried scowl came on the faces of their auditors, among whom was the leader who spoke Spanish. After a moment of hesitation he walked to the mud house and ordered the others to release the door. As quickly as possible they obeyed, pulling out half of the logs. Then they retreated.

Within the hut the leader saw only dimness. He stepped closer and leaned inside. For a moment he stood petrified. Then he sprang back.

Rigid on the floor before him lay the man who was to have been executed that morning. His jaw hung slack. His upturned face was ghastly with the pallor of death. And against that awful pallor stood out a thick sprinkling of malevolent reddish spots.

## XI. THE LOOTER

A hollow groan echoed out from the dank pen. Before the starting eyes of the Indians, one of the captives came reeling from a dark corner at the rear — the tall black-bearded one. His groan was echoed by another, and a second figure staggered into sight: the blond man with the bandaged head. Both were blanched and haggard of face. And on each of those faces, on their necks, and on their arms as well, flamed virulent spots far more red and appalling than those of the corpse.

They lurched to the doorway and hung there, staring glassily. Hoarsely they begged:

"Agua! Water — for the dying!"

**67**

Frozen, dry-mouthed, the savages stood staring speechless at the frightfully diseased creatures who yesterday had been strong men.

"Agua!" croaked the pair again. Then, with the desperation of beings already doomed, they came crawling over the logs and lunged straight at their captors, reaching for them with the malignantly spotted hands. Behind them appeared two more men — the red-headed one and the hawk-faced Spaniard — and on them, too, glared the blotches of deadly contagion.

In that instant the wild men of the jungle ceased to be men. They became screaming creatures bereft of sense and reason by frenzied fear. From bullets, from cold steel, from poisoned arrows or spears they would not have retreated an inch; but from those lunging, reaching corpses whose touch meant hideous death to all their tribe — they recoiled, collided, struck and clawed one another, fought madly to get away, and, shrieking, bolted for their tribal house.

But that house, a fortress against jungle enemies, was no defense against the dread thing pursuing them now. Somehow the dying men found the strength to run after them, treading close on their flying heels and reaching, reaching, reaching for them, grinning horribly as they sped. There was no time to throw the stout door of their home into place and bar out those awful creatures. Before they could even struggle through the opening the two foremost pursuers got their clammy clutches on three or four of them — clutches which did not hold, but which froze their hearts with insane terror.

Screeching like lost souls harried through Hades by malicious demons, they fought through the portal and ran madly on toward the door connecting the quarters of the warriors with those of the women. To their horror-struck fellows they gasped the frightful news as they fled. Paralyzed for an instant, those who heard the fatal tidings gaped at the doorway and saw the red-spotted apparitions coming relentlessly on. The wave of fear which had swept the first fugitives into flight engulfed them also. The big house became a chaos of frenzied men.

The chief himself, standing beside his hammock with a throwing-spear poised for attack, was caught in the mob terror sweeping the place. For a minute he stood his ground, fighting against the chill that enwrapped his heart. If the advancing dead-alive men had hesitated he would have held his position, hurling one javelin after another at them. But they did not hesitate, did not waver. With inexorable tread they came straight at him, grinning those grisly grins, stretching out hands empty but more menacing than if they held weapons.

His hollow eyes darted aside. His mouth writhed in repulsion. With a choking grunt he hurled his spear at the black-bearded specter in the lead. McKay, watching keenly, lurched aside. The missile flew wild. The chief spun about and leaped headlong away toward the thin partition beyond which were the women's quarters.

Under the weight of the men hurling themselves at the one small door, that partition caved in and collapsed. Among its fragments the howling mob struggled, fell, scrambled up and dashed on toward the exit, already jammed with women shrieking and clawing their way out. For a moment or two a panic-stricken maelstrom swirled about that door. Then at last, bruised and scratched and bleeding, the whole tribe was outside and rushing for the shelter of the forest.

Had any of them paused to look back toward the mud prison, he would have seen a thing which might either have restored his reason or knocked the last vestige of sense from his quivering brain. There among the stumps, halfway across the clearing and heading for the tribe house, was swiftly creeping a fifth red-spotted man: the dead man who had lain just within the doorway when the logs were taken down; the man who was to have borne the vengeance of the tribe for the death of the hunter. But none paused. Men, women, children, old and young, strong and weak, all tore for the protecting labyrinth of tree and bush. And the dead man reached the house and vanished.

Within the doorway, Rand found a scene of wreckage which suggested the devastation of an exploding shell. Hammocks were torn down, weapons lay scattered over the floor, clay cooking vessels were overturned and shattered, the debris of the partition jutted in jagged segments, and smoke from the newly lit breakfast fires drifted over all. In the midst of it he saw his comrades, grouped at the chief's hammock, swiftly buckling on their weapon-belts, gathering up their rifles and axes and hammocks, stuffing into pockets and shirts small parts of their plundered equipment which could be carried away without hampering their movements. As fast as he could he limped to them.

"Here's Dave!" rumbled Tim. "Hello, who said you could come alive? Don't you know you died with smallpox last night? Shake a leg. We've got to move, double time."

The green-eyed man was moving already. In a few fleeting second he was belted and armed like the rest.

"Hate to leave so much of our duffle," grumbled

69

Knowlton, "but we have to get away from here while the getting is good. If we can get back to the canoes we'll find our cans of grub and cartridges there, anyhow."

"Si," grinned Jose, "and if these Indios follow us there they will soon learn that I told no lie when I said those bullet-tins were filled with quick death. And when they return here they will find none of our plunder waiting for them. If we cannot have it, they shall not. Hold my rifle a moment."

With which he snatched blazing sticks from the chief's fire and bounded to the smashed partition. Swiftly he worked along the debris, firing it in a dozen places. It flamed up instantly, the blaze crawling rapidly up to the tindery palm-thatch roof.

"An affectionate adios to the gentleman who advised me to kill myself before morning," he chuckled, loping back. "Now outside, comrades! If we go quickly we may go unseen. They ran into the bush at the rear — we go out at the front — the house hides us. Come!"

Out to the entrance they strode. A quick glance around, and they struck for the path, which opened ahead. At every step they expected to hear a yell from the jungle behind, announcing that they had been sighted. But none came.

Into the bush they plunged. There, for the space of one brief glance, they paused to look back. Already the tribe-house was vomiting black clouds from roof and doors. Up from the smoke-hole at the peak darted a flare of flame. Even if the whole tribe should rush back to it now, it was doomed. So was any man who dared to enter it.

"Jose, take the lead," commanded McKay. "Dave, you march second. Tim and Merry, follow in file. March!"

Thus, in four crisp sentences, he arranged his little command in the most effective order: the veteran bushman as guide, the injured man where his bad leg would not compel him to fall behind the rest, and the bulk of his fighting force instantly available for rear-guard action. McKay, in the post of danger, strode behind, keeping a watchful eye and ear open toward the rear.

For a time all forged ahead in silence, Jose picking the dim trail with unerring eye, Rand stoically hobbling onward at good speed, Tim and Knowlton careful not to crowd their lame comrade. Presently Knowlton began to chuckle.

"Did it work?" he exulted. "We must be a handsome gang of corpses, from the reception we got. Dave, you missed the best show of your life."

"Didn't miss much," Rand denied. "I came to life in time

70

to watch you chase them into the house. Saw them come yelping out of the back door, too. Finest free fight I ever clapped an eye on."

"Yeah," assented Tim. "I almost laughed out loud when they went right through the wall."

"Quiet!" snapped the captain. But his mouth twitched as the ludicrous side of it struck him too. Again he saw the chief turn tail and fight madly with his own men in flight from four faces whitened with talcum and dotted with harmless dye-spots. And as he caught a subdued humming from Tim and recognized the air he laughed silently. The ex-sergeant was softly singing to himself an army tune beginning:

"One battalion jumped over the other battalion's back — "

But the smile vanished in a flash, and he wheeled. Muffled, almost deadened by the intervening jungle, a roar of raging yells sounded back at the clearing where the tribe-house now must be a belching furnace. The Indians had returned to their toppling stronghold.

"Sounds like the beginning of another party," muttered Knowlton, inching back his breech-bolt to make sure his gun still was loaded.

"Uh-huh. But they're crazy if they follow us," said Tim. "They haven't got anything to fight with but hands and teeth. They dropped everything when they ran, and all their weapons are burned. We could massacre the whole tribe."

For the first time the full extent of Jose's revenge on the Indians dawned on the rest. He had not merely burned their house: he had plunged the whole tribe into the most abject poverty, if not into actual tragedy. They were without shelter, save for the few small, wretched clay huts; without food except for the products of the plantation which they had trampled down in their flight; without weapons, in a savage jungle where weapons meant life. True, they could exist, and no doubt would exist, until they could rehabilitate themselves. But for a time they would be virtually at the mercy of any fate that came their way, and for a longer time they would be a weak, disorganized tribe.

"Guess their morale has suffered a severe jolt," McKay summarized it. "But they'll make it hot for us if they can."

And there was no relaxing of alertness as the little column went on. All knew that they left behind them a plain trail; that soon the absence of the dead man and the presence of the tell-tale broken dye-pot would be discovered; that somewhere an unbroken bow and a few arrows might yet remain; and that only five arrows, skillfully shot, were needed to wipe out their

**71**

whole party. Wherefore silence and vigilance again ruled.

But whatever the furious white Indians may have thirsted to do was not done. The adventurers, once more doggedly heading toward the mysterious cordillera to the north, wound steadily onward without attack. They passed from the creek into the streamless shadows, through them to the water-gleams of the river, up along the Tigre Yacu to the first rocks, where yesterday they had found gold and capture. Today, at the same spot, they found something equally unexpected.

Approaching it, they heard sounds which at first seemed to be the recurrent murmur of the water. A few rods farther on, they slowed and listened hard; for now the mutter seemed to be that of voices. Jose, scowling, slipped on ahead, motioning to the rest to wait. Hardly had he disappeared among the trees when an unmistakable noise broke through the curtain of brush – the thump of a heavily laden tin container.

"Somebody else at our stuff!" fiercely whispered Tim. "Let me get by, Dave."

Rand, however, declined to yield his place or to be hurried. Despite his injury, he was creeping forward with the old stealth that had been his when he was the Wild Dog of the Javary. Tim swallowed his impatience and trailed him in silence, Knowlton and McKay close behind.

The thumping sound came again, and with it a voice that seemed familiar, speaking Spanish. In it was a note of malicious joy, with an undertone of fear.

"So the illustrious gentlemen have gone to the devil as they said they would. Ha! Ha! 'A quick voyage to you,' I said, and so it was. My polite senores, I trust that you now roast comfortably in hell. Ha, ha! Quick, you clumsy ladroncillo! Take this one also. Los Indios blancos – the white Indians – may be close to us."

Another bump. Then the sarcastic voice of Jose.

"For your good wishes I thank you, Senor Bocaza ( Big Mouth ). But I think it is you who goes to the devil."

With a rush the Americans emerged from the bush beside Jose. The Peruvian, with a leering grin, was sighting down the barrel of his rifle. On the river lay a newly arrived canoe – a two-man craft. In it, bending over with his hands on one of the American cases, stood the Indian whom Jose had chastised at San Regis. On the farther bank, clutching another case, his face blanched yellow-white, crouched the Moyobambino trader, Torribio Maldonado.

Shocked speechless the rascally trader squatted rigidly for a moment, eyes and mouth gaping at the men whom he had just

72

consigned to eternal torment. Then his lips moved.

"Cien mil diablos!" he gasped.

"Do you say so?" mocked Jose. "A hundred thousand devils? I did not know there were so many. I know only one — the great horned devil of them all. The others must be mean little diablillos like yourself. If they are not too proud to associate with you they will soon have a new companion. How will you have your traveling ticket — in the head or the stomach?"

The yellow pallor of the other became ghastly. He tried to shrink behind the tin case, which was far too small to hide him.

"San Pablo! Santo Tomas! Sanata Ana!" he mouthed. Then, in desperation, he rose quivering to his feet.

"Amigo mio," he whined, "I was but taking your goods to a safe place where the accursed Indios would not get them, and where I could start a party to search for you. I thought you were captured - "

"And so we were," taunted the outlaw. "Perhaps you stirred up those Indios blancos to hunt us down, yes? That would be a true Moyobamba trick."

"But no — Santo Domingo, no! Never would I do such a thing. I am mad with joy to find you alive, amigos! Only put down that gun — it gives me a coldness in the middle, though I know you are only having your little joke — ha, ha! Only put down the gun, Don Jose."

Jose's eyes flickered over his gun-sight. His trigger finger tightened by a hair's weight. Then it loosened. "Don Jose?" he purred menacingly. "What is the rest of the name, you who know so much?"

"Martinez. Oh, yes, I know you, Don Jose. Who has not heard of the famous — "

"Pah! Your lies and your flattery both sicken me! Once I was a don, a caballero, but you know nothing of those days. All you know is that I am a killer of men. Of men, not of whining pups. I will not waste a precious bullet on you. I will save it for a beast or a snake — something worth killing."

The menacing muzzle sank. But, as the Moyobambino began sidling toward his canoe, it rose again.

"Not so fast! Pick up that case under your hands and carry it into the San Regis canoe nearest to you. Then carry all the others and pack them carefully, every one. If you miss one, you ladron, or forget to take one out of your own boat, you go floating down the Tigre with a hole in your liver. Now work!"

The Senor Torribio Maldonado worked. Perspiring profusely, he packed the cases with faultless precision and extreme dispatch. Meanwhile the Americans, though watching appreciatively, kept their ears open for any sound from behind. None came.

"Shall we let him go, capitan, or take him with us?" Jose queried in an undertone. "We can use the pair of them for work-slaves and punish them well for sneaking after us in this way, and we shall know they stir up no trouble behind us."

McKay studied him quizzically. The hard face of the descendant of the Conquistadores showed that he was not joking. Left to his own inclinations, he would make that pair sweat blood in the days to come.

"More trouble than they're worth," the captain refused.

"I will see that they give no trouble," was the significant promise.

"So will I — by not having them around. I told you, back on the Maranon, that this fellow was your meat, but I'll take charge now."

"As you wish, capitan."

McKay motioned, and his four mates went with him into the stream. Maldonado watched their approach with obvious misgiving, but he did not dare attempt to flee. On the farther shore McKay faced him.

"You! Do you want to live?" he snapped. "If you — what's the matter with you?"

Maldonado had shrunk back, staring from face to face, a new terror in his eyes.

"The spots!" he breathed. "Your faces — your hands — "

"It is la fiebre encarnada — the red fever," interrupted Jose, grinning wickedly. "You do not know the red fever? No? We caught it among your friends the white Indians, back there. They have it much worse than we. It drives men mad, Torribio. Those wild men were tearing their own house apart when we came away, they were so mad from the red spots. At any moment we, too, may become crazed. Hah!"

With a horrible grimace, he shot out one red-spotted hand and rubbed it over the Moyobambino's face. Squeaking with fear, the wretch tripped backward, sprawled over the edge, soused into the water. He came up gasping, and scrambled into his own canoe.

"Go!" rasped McKay, gritting his teeth to hold a stern face. "This is your last chance. Paddle hard to the great river and you may live. Otherwise — "

He paused. The trader, now all atremble between his fear of

Jose, of the white Indians, and of this new disease of the river of evil repute, did not wait to hear what might happen otherwise. He went.

His canoe bumped between the boulders and fled downstream, the Indian and his master heaving it away with strokes that bent their tough paddles. Rapidly it diminished to a blot at the apex of twin angular ripples, the paddle blades winking fast in the sunlight. Then it darted out of sight around a turn.

A chorus of chuckles sounded on the shore where the five watched the flight.

"And so the River of Missing Men sends back two more bold hearts," laughed Knowlton. "They'll have a brave tale to tell when they return to San Regis."

"The river has not yet returned them to that town," suggested Rand.

"Meaning they may get swallowed by something before they get clear?" guessed Tim.

"I have a feeling, comrades, that we have not yet seen the last of that pair," Jose somberly stated. "I wish I had them under my thumb — or that my old rifle had accidently exploded when it pointed at the Moyobambino. But they are gone, and we waste time here."

McKay nodded and gestured toward the canoes. With one more keen look at the surrounding bush and a swift survey to make sure nothing was overlooked on the ground, the voyagers returned to their respective boats. A little later the boulders around which had centered treasure-hunting, peril, capture, theft, mockery, and fear, were alone once more in a stretch of empty river.

A mile upstream the five spotted men slowed their strokes. Before them rose more rocks. Like the first obstructions, however, they were few, and not high enough or close enough to cause much difficulty to canoes. But before traveling much farther every man needed to get into the tins which had just been saved from the clutches of the Moyobambino. Their stomachs were empty and their cartridges few.

So, beyond the boulders, they halted. Jose, watching the flat boxes of cartridges emerge from one of the ammunition tins, smiled wryly.

"I should have brought with me a tin box like yours, amigos," he said. "Or else I should have remembered to find some bullets before leaving our Indian friends. Now all the cartridges they took from me are exploded in the fire I set, and I have only five left in all the world. Senor Dave, you must make for me a bow and some arrrows."

**75**

Rand smiled and shook his head. "Not unless we've lost a can," he said. "Tim, is the forty-four tin still there?"

"Uh-huh. Safe and solid. Wait a minute, Hozy, and I'll give you all the cannon balls you want."

To the Peruvian's amazement, he was speedily presented with a clean, dry carton of the heavy bullets that fitted his gun.

"Trade stuff," McKay explained. "It's so commonly used in the jungle that we brought a batch of it over the Andes. Lots of time a few forty-four slugs will buy more than you could purchase with five times their value in money."

"True, capitan. And to me they are worth more than all the gold that may be ahead. Now that I have them, I am curious to know whether that path of the white Indians still follows this stream upward. So I will take a little walk over yonder while you open some food."

Dumping his ammunition into his capacious right-hand pocket, he shoved his canoe across the stream, climbed the bank, and disappeared.

"Queer thing about that path," remarked Rand. "It's a good deal older than the clearing and the tribe-house of the Indians back yonder. Been here longer."

The others frowned thoughtfully. Their eyes were not trained to note the slight differentiations which were so obvious to the former wild man; but even they had noticed that the tribe-house seemed quite new. Now, while they labored with can-openers and gouged beef out of the cans, they pondered.

"Old trail, probably," hazarded Tim. "Been used a hundred years, maybe."

"Quite likely. Wish my leg was in good hiking condition. I'd like to leave the canoes and hit the trail. It probably goes to where we're heading for, and canoeing will be work from now on."

"Nope, me for the river as long as she holds out. And I'm going to use some of it right now."

He began scrubbing the sweat-streaked talcum powder and the dye-spots from his face. The others followed his example — but not all at once. Rand and Knowlton waited, with hands on rifles and eyes scanning water and tree line, until the other two were through. Then they took their turn, while their clean-faced companions watched.

"Funny we don't hear anything from Hozy," muttered Tim. "Thought he'd be right back."

McKay made no answer. But his eyes rested on the

76

Peruvian's canoe, noting that its owner, with habitual caution, had left it under some drooping ferns which would mask it from above. Then they roved up the creeping water, pausing at a spot some rods farther on, where other ferns formed a good covert. As Rand and Knowlton lifted their wet faces he pointed upstream.

"We'll move up there," he said. After a look at him and at the bank, the others dipped their paddles. The twin dugouts slid across and upward and floated under cover.

The lieutenant lifted inquiring brows, getting in return a noncommittal wave of the hand. For a little time all sat in silence. All at once Rand grew tense.

His fingers tightened over his rifle. He leaned a little forward, all his senses concentrated into listening. To the ears of the others came no new sound: no sound whatever, unless it was a barely audible rustle which held a moment, then died, like the soft sigh of a passing breeze. But Rand's head slowly turned, following that tiny murmur downstream. After it had died away he still held that alert poise.

Presently his gaze swung to the faces of his companions, who were watching him keenly. Soundlessly his lips formed one word: "Men!"

McKay pointed a thumb backward, mutely asking if the men had gone down the river. The ex-roamer of the jungle nodded.

All watched toward the rocks below. No sight or sound of human life came. From where they lurked they could not see the empty canoe of Jose. In every mind grew the same question: what had become of him?

At length the question was answered. Stealthy dips of a paddle floated to them, and a ripple curved along the water. The bow of the outlaw's canoe appeared, hugging the shore. Above it moved a black-haired head, minus the piratical red handkerchief. Stroking carefully, Jose slipped up to them.

"Por Dios, you are wise, capitan!" he whispered. "You shifted in good time. I could not get back to warn you, and I have been sweating blood, expecting to hear you attacked.

"The path is there, amigos. It is close to the water along here. And down it have just gone thirty Jiveros! The head shrinkers!"

## XII. FOLLOWED

McKay reached to the newly opened ammunition tin. Silently he extracted box after box of soft-point cartridges and passed them to his companions. With equal silence each of the

**77**

Americans received the flat packets, slit the thin paper seals with a thumb-nail, turned back the covers, and placed the boxes on the bottoms of the canoes, the grim brass heads ready within instant reach. Boxes of forty-fives followed, and the spare clips of the belt guns were given quick but thorough inspection. Finally Tim beckoned Jose closer, and, with a muffled grunt, lifted the entire case of forty-fours into the outlaw's craft.

"They're yours," he whispered.

The Peruvian made no reply in words, but his eyes spoke for him. So did the swift swoop of his hand into the tin and his affectionate gaze at the cartons of death-dealing cylinders he brought forth. But he wasted no time in gloating over his treasure. After exposing the shining discs and the dull gray leads to the sun he turned and watched downstream.

Minutes dragged away while the hidden five squatted under the ferns, holding the canoes motionless by gripping the bank, straining eyes and ears for sight of savage figures near the rocks or for any returning rustle. Then Jose let his gaze wander to the opened beef tins.

"I believe, senores, we halted here to eat," he suggested.

The broad hint met with immediate response. Hands relaxed from their grips on the guns, and the guns themselves were laid softly down. A minute later every one was wolfing food.

"No smoking," warned McKay, as Tim, after devouring his meat and gulping a gourd of river water, reached for his "makings." The big freckled hand hesitated, then reluctantly came away from the shirt pocket. "Grumph!" he growled, but his hand went to his paddle, not to his tobacco. "No use hanging around here. Let's go."

They went, slowly, stealthily, with open cartridge boxes beside them and rifles close at hand, but steadily forging on up the forbidden water toward whatever lay beyond.

Though they now were afloat once more, they tacitly held to the same formation in which they had traveled the trail that morning: Jose in the lead, with Rand following in the bow of Tim's canoe, and the pair of ex-officers trailing. The two jungle veterans thus were where their keen senses were of most use, while the rest of the expedition was in position for quick action toward front or rear. Yet, for all their readiness, there seemed to be nothing to do but the everlasting paddling. Since the passing of that sinister rustle in the western bush no sight or sound of anything but animal or bird life had come to them.

78

As they went, the sharp eyes of McKay dwelt thoughtfully on Rand. He was pushing his paddle as stoically as ever, and to all appearances his stroke was as strong as if he had had both legs curled under him. But the captain knew well that the lacerated limb was aching, and that the forced journeys through the tangled forest had pulled the torn muscles apart and undone whatever good had been accomplished by the first rough-and-ready surgical attention.

He knew, too, that unless the claw wounds were given a fair chance to heal there would be a cripple in his company for many days to come; and that the day might not be far off when, notwithstanding his dogged grit, that cripple's inability to handle himself with his normal ease might plunge the whole party into irretrievable disaster. Humanitarian reasons aside, it was imperative that the weak link in the chain be made strong again. Rand must lie up.

But he could not lie up in the moving canoe. Not only would this throw all the work of propelling that dugout on Tim, but if a real mal-paso should be encountered he would have to take to his legs with the rest while the boats were dragged and poled upward. Moreover, another band of savages using that hidden trail – or perhaps the same band returning – might at any time see and attack the expedition. Finally, the stubborn pride of the man himself would not let him rest unless the others also halted. Wherefore the only solution was to find a covert where a secret camp could be constructed and all hands could take a few days of ease.

So, saying nothing, the commander renewed his study of the slowly passing shores. Now and then he halted his paddle and scrutinized some indentation or dried-up brook mouth; but only for a minute. The canoes crawled on for some distance before he saw what he sought.

Then, on the eastern shore, a fair-sized creek opened. After a quick survey McKay spoke to Knowlton, and the canoe surged ahead at double speed, closing in on Jose.

"Think we'll look at that creek," said the captain. "First, take another look at the trail – see if it's still there. Then hunt for another on the other shore."

The Peruvian swung his bow inward, picked a landing spot, and slipped away among the leaves. Rand's eyes followed him. Knowlton's turned to McKay with a look of inquiry. The captain rolled a thumb toward Rand's back, then touched his own leg. The blond man's quick nod showed that his thoughts had been traveling in the same channel.

Jose returned, reporting that the path still ran beside the

water and that it showed no sign of use since the Jiveros had gone downstream. At once the canoes crossed and entered the creek. There Jose disappeared for a longer time, exploring the shores of the new stream. At length he stepped out of the tangle with news.

"There is no path here, at least near the water," he declared. "And this water is no real creek. It is only the outlet of a lago — how big I do not know, but only a little way up."

"All right. Let's inspect it."

The black eyes of the outlaw hung on the gray ones a moment, mutely puzzled. But he asked no question. Into his short craft he got, and up along the almost motionless arm of water he led the way. He knew the captain well enough to realize that this was no thoughtless waste of time and effort. Tim and Rand, too, wondered but held their tongues.

The waterway curved from northeast to north, cutting off all view of the Tigre Yacu. Only a few hundred yards from the river it opened into a lake, perhaps a mile long, rimmed with wide sandy shores from which rose stiff slopes of heavy timber. Nowhere on its placid bosom nor on its gleaming sands showed any sign of humanity.

"Will do," McKay asserted.

"For what?" demanded Rand.

"For a hangout," enlightened Knowlton.

"What's the big idea?" Tim wanted to know.

"Here you can smoke," said McKay, his face relaxing.

In three-fifths of a second the tobacco-hungry paddler's pouch was in service.

"We'll lie up here a few days," McKay went on. "A little rest will do us all good."

"Look here, Rod, am I holding the gang back?" Rand sharply asked. "If that's your idea I won't — "

"Yes, you will," McKay cooly contradicted. "You'll stick with the gang, and the gang halts here."

"But — "

"No argument, Dave. Your leg's bad. It's got to get well as fast as possible. We want no lame ducks. You've got to lie up."

"And eat up all our grub — "

"We'll get more grub here. Turn the little twenty-two gun loose on monkeys, jerk the meat, save our canned stuff. May lay in a stock of fish, too. There's plenty of salt."

"Si," Jose approved, scanning the sandy shores. "And this sand should be full of turtle eggs. The water must hold many fish. Those heavy woods beyond will mean easy hunting and good hiding. You could not have chosen a better place,

**80**

capitan."

Rand's mouth remained set, but he was silenced. Tim, with a sidelong wink at Knowlton, shoved on his paddle, and the Rand-Ryan boat moved onward. After a few more strokes from the stern, Rand began to ply his own blade.

A little way down, on the right shore, a sandy spit ran out into the water. Beyond it the five found a small cove. There they ran the canoes aground, and Jose and Tim were first to debark.

Jose, as scout, stepped off across the sand toward the steep bluff which, in the wet season, evidently formed the rim of the lake, but which now was some fifty yards distant. But he did not step far. All at once he bounded into the air, whirling like a cat, and ran for the lake. Knee-deep in the water he stopped, spluttering a hodgepodge of Spanish, Indian, and English profanity.

"What the — " Tim began. Then he sharply picked up one booted foot, hopped off the other as if stung, caught his balance, and rushed to join Jose.

"This is some place you picked out, cap!" he blurted. "Ouch! OO-ee! I bet my boots are gone!"

The three still in the boats stared up the sand. From it radiated intense heat, but nothing moved on it.

"What's the matter?" demanded Knowlton.

"Matter! Go ashore and you'll find out! That stuff isn't just sand. It's the top lid of hell!"

Jose, with lurid emphasis, assured him that he too was burned to the bones. But after the water had cooled his suffering feet he flashed a grin.

"I wish, amigos, I had my Moyobambino pet here now," he chuckled. "I would ride on his back. How he would prance! Hah!"

"Maybe he's dead already, and those hundred thousand friends of his have lit extra bonfires to welcome him," suggested Tim. "Anyway, this sure is the top crust of his winter home."

Jose tugged his bow off the sand and stepped in. "It is the sun," he explained. "On a cloudy day, or in the morning, one could walk here without trouble; but not now. All sand soaks up sun heat, but some sand is worse, and this is the worst I ever met. If we stay in this place we must find a shorter way to the trees. There is one, on the other side. See."

Following his pointing finger, the rest saw a spot where a deep indentation gave a water path to within a few yards of the tree growth. Pushing out, they passed over to it. The water shoaled to finger depth at a distance of ten feet or more from the edge of the beach, making a poor landing, but the space of hot sand intervening was so short that, with boots wet, it could be traversed without much discomfort.

McKay and Knowlton loped across the sand to the bush, arriving with feet hot but not painful. A short scout revealed nothing but animal sign. Returning, they brought strips of flexible but tough bark and some bush-cord, which they presented to Jose. The Peruvian, sitting in the water, fell to work binding the bark to his feet as protective coverings to his tender soles. Tim and Rand, after a thorough soaking of their boots, made a quick trip arm-in-arm across the hot space. Then Tim returned, picking up his feet with unusual spryness.

Half an hour later a camp had been made at a little distance from the entry cove and skillfully camouflaged with big leaves, and to it all the outfit except the canoes themselves was transported. Later on, when the sand could be crossed with impunity, the boats would be shifted to a better berth; but now they were left stranded in the shallows. Rand's leg was dressed anew by Knowlton, who was more deft at such work than the others, and he lay in his hammock, solacing himself with a cigarette.

Then, all at once, the hand holding the cigarette stopped in air. Into his face came that look of concentrated listening. Jose, too, turned from something he was doing and cocked an ear toward the river. The others glanced at one another and stood motionless.

The Peruvian shot a look at Rand. Then he picked up his gun and vanished among the trees. To the waiting four presently came a sound — a swishing, pelting sound which grew into a murmur, as if men were running and breathing in hoarse gasps.

A sudden nearer rustle, and Jose burst out of the forest. "Peace is not for us, amigos," he panted, with a hard grin. "That tribe of accursed white Indians is coming!"

## XIII. BURNING SANDS

Tim snorted and seized his rifle. "No rest for the wicked. Just when we get comfortable they horn in again. This isn't going to be any fun either — not unless they've dug up weapons somewhere."

The other Americans, too, though swift to arm themselves, scowled as if facing a disagreeable task. Not so Jose. His pride still rankled at the memory of having been trapped so easily and driven like a beast to a mud pen, and now, finger on trigger, he looked vengefully back as if awaiting the appearance of the leader who had flung his knife so contemptuously on the dirt and invited him to commit suicide.

When that leader did come loping into sight, however, the Peruvian stood stock still. Not only was the Indian weaponless and darting glances from side to side like a hunted thing, but he was followed by gasping women and children.

At sight of the five aligned beside their hidden hut and the five deadly muzzles menacing his breast he stopped as if shot. The running horde behind struck him and knocked him forward, reeling and clutching for support. One hand caught a tree and saved him from sprawling. He snarled something over his shoulder. The human herd slowed to a halt.

For a second the women and children stared at the hard, bearded faces fronting them — faces now without a vestige of the horrible pallor and virulent spots which had been there that morning. Then their heads turned back, and from them broke whimpers of terror. Behind them sounded the hoarse voices of their men, urging them on. But again the leader snarled, and instead of pressing forward they passed back his words.

"You fools!" McKay rasped. "Why do you follow us?"

"We do not follow," the Spanish-speaking Indian retorted. "We seek safety for our women and children. Death comes behind."

"What death?"

"The men who shrink the head. They found us helpless. They follow to take our heads and our women. Let us pass on. Or kill us quickly, before they come."

He glanced back, but his face held no fear. He seemed only coolly gauging the pursuit. When he turned again his eyes held a malevolent glow, and the thin smile glimmered across his mouth.

"We cannot live," he ground out. "But you who destroyed us go to death with us. Your heads hang with ours. Bueno!"

Though he spoke an alien tongue, the women behind moaned as if they understood; as if they were visioning the massacre of their men and their own slavery. At that sound the hard-set faces of the five turned harder. Even Jose, looking at the children, clenched his teeth.

Every man of them knew the Jiveros were inveterate polygamists; that their killings were actuated even more by greed for woman slaves than by cupidity for the grisly trophies of war; that it would be more merciful to shoot down these women and girls now than to let them fall into such hands.

They knew, too, that the Indian spoke truth when he cast on their shoulders the blame for the present defenselessness of his people, and that he voiced no idle threat when he predicted doom for all.

"I don't care what happens to the men – they would have killed us," Tim blurted. "But the women and kids – "

McKay's voice cut in. "Do as I say and you may live. Run on a little way. Turn to the water and run back through the trees as the edge. Do not step on the sand until you see us at our canoes. Come to us there. We will fight for you. Quick! Go!"

The other's mouth twisted in disbelief. These gun bearers, who had been their prisoners, would fight for them? No hope of that! But, as drowning men clutch at straws, he grasped at even that hopeless chance. As the imperative commands snapped in his ears and the guns sank he bounded forward. Automatically he obeyed McKay's pointing finger, indicating the rear of the hut. Around the shelter he plunged, pressed close by the fugitives blindly following his lead.

"Jose! Get back and watch for Jiveros!" barked McKay "When you see them don't shoot – run back here. Dave, hop to the canoes! Tim – Merry – bear a hand on these cases. Snap into it!"

Without a pause to watch the passing horde he leaped into the hut and clutched a couple of heavy containers, with which he plowed toward the canoes. Hard on his heels came his two able-bodied mates, each carrying all he could snatch and hold. Rand, lugging the rifles, limped rapidly in their wake.

Meanwhile Jose, slipping swiftly along the disordered column, found himself obliged to draw off to one side if he was to spy Jiveros instead of fighting his recent captors. The women and children, obsessed by fear, gave him hardly a passing glance. But the men, following behind in position to do their desperate best when the pursuers should overtake them, saw in him the living reason why they now were fleeing instead of battling their foes with gun and spear and bow. They did not know he was truly the man who had thought of destroying their fortress and had put that thought into execution; if they had, not all the head-hunters in the jungle would have kept them from hurling themselves on him with their only weapons – bare hands or crude clubs wrenched from prone trees. Even as it was, the bold stare and mocking grin of the outlaw enraged them to the point of striking at him if he came within reach. So, keeping in mind his duty, he gave them plenty of room and sped on to the rear.

84

There, last of all, he found the chief, loping onward with frequent backward looks and grimly clutching a formidable tree branch. Coward though he might have been that morning when confronted by dread specters of disease, he now was all man, guarding the exodus of his fallen tribe and holding himself ready to fight and fall first when the relentless death behind should strike. And the outlaw, reading his face, ceased grinning and gave the ruler a friendly nod. His answer was a hollow-eyed glare.

The retreating line faded away. The Peruvian posted himself behind a tree at the edge of the new trail and waited.

Back at the canoes, the Americans dropped their burdens and shoved the dugouts into water deep enough for floating. McKay glanced along the bank. A short distance farther on, a bush swayed sharply, struck by a speeding foot. The Indian had obeyed orders, turned, and started back just at the edge of the sand.

"Time for one more load," the captain judged. "Merry and Tim, back to the hut! Dave, hold her ready to go. I'll have to boss this gang."

The blond and the red man, with pistol holsters unbuttoned, raced back across the burning sands. They had hardly disappeared into the bush when the head of the Indian line broke out behind them. McKay beckoned imperatively. The leader made straight for him.

He was halfway across the hot grit before his face contracted with pain. But his stride never wavered; he only jumped ahead like a spurred horse. A couple of seconds later he was ankle-deep in the cooling water and barking at the women, who had begun to cry out and hesitate on the scorching surface. Between the goad of his voice and the momentum of the following mass, the waverers were propelled onward into the shallow water lane.

The whole column followed fast. Soon all the fugitives were packed together in the inlet, and the grim chief was forcing his way through to learn from the young guide why they were here in the open, easy prey for the impending attack.

The guide had halted beside McKay and demanded the same information. Was this a cruel trap, calculated to destroy their last chance of life? He snapped the question with savage brevity. With equal curtness McKay snapped back at him the answer to the riddle.

Sudden hope flared in the tawny eyes watching his. As the chief reached him and growled a wrathful query he translated the American's talk into the Indian tongue. The tribal ruler, his feet still hot, threw a quick look at the sand, another at the point in the bush where the tribe had doubled on its trail, and a third at the water line stretching away. Then his hard gaze bored into McKay's face.

"You are at our backs," he pointed out, his voice rough with hostile suspicion. "Your guns at our backs, Jiveros at our faces."

"I know it," shot the captain. "I will do what I say. Take it or leave it. We go."

At that moment Knowlton and Tim came careening out with more cans. They jostled past, thumped their burdens into the canoes, and hopped in after them.

"Better beat it, Rod!" called Knowlton.

"Jose coming?"

"Not yet, but time's short. Where do we go from here?"

"Hold up a minute." Then, to the chief: "Your life or death is in your own hands. Do as you wish."

With which he shouldered his way out of the press, ran to his canoe, jumped in, and commanded: "Paddle!"

The two dugouts slid outward, leaving the little canoe of Jose empty and waiting. A couple of young bucks grabbed it. McKay dropped his paddle inboard and swung on them with rifle aimed.

"Hands off!" he barked. "The man taking that canoe dies!"

The guide and the chief grunted together. The pair lifted their hands from the canoe and sullenly swung toward their commanders. At once the chief began loping outward, feet in the water, at the very edge of the sand. The rest followed.

At the mouth of the inlet the canoes swerved to the left and glided along the lake, near shore. At the same point the chief turned and ran on in the same direction. A short distance up-lake the boats slowed and stopped. The fugitives, following, splashed up to them, still only ankle-deep. The chief halted and gave gruff orders.

His people drew together, standing at the water line, facing the jungle, which seemed to quiver in the heat waves ascending from the intervening sand. Behind them the canoes crept up and grounded.

"Here's the dope," McKay explained. "Jiveros, following trail, turn at that place over yonder. Trail runs back along shore. But they see their victims out here, unarmed, helpless, making a last stand. Naturally they don't loop back along the shore line — they come straight out to get these fellows. They don't see us. Between them and us are forty yards of blistering sand. By the time they — "

"Here's Hozy!" Tim broke in.

Jose was dashing at top speed from the tree line. He tore across the sand, bounded through the water, leaped in air and alighted in his canoe with a fierce down-drive of the legs that shot the craft outward and sat him down in the same instant. His paddle darted out and lashed the water in tremendous strokes even before he got to his knees. Thereafter he fairly lifted the boat along toward the waiting group.

"Whew! Some getaway!" breathed Knowlton. "Our guests must be arriving."

"Get my idea?" demanded McKay.

"Sure," was the answering chorus.

Jose slowed to a stop beside the rest. "They come, amigos," he panted. "They are — "

"All right, listen a minute!"

Swiftly the plan of battle was outlined to him. His face cracked in a ferocious grin. Without another word he scooped up extra cartridges and stepped over the side, knee-deep. The others also slipped overboard and crouched.

To the Indian who spoke Spanish, McKay gave brief instructions. He grunted them rapidly to the savages standing before the knot of gunmen. Barely had he finished when a mutter of mingled rage and fear ran down the line.

It was swallowed up by an outbreak of exultant yells from the trees. Over there beyond the dancing heat waves a band of painted men, naked but for maroon loin clouts, broke cover. All were light-skinned, fierce-faced, equipped with jungle weapons and wooden shields. They pointed, gesticulated, howled in gloating flee at the sight of the almost unarmed men and the huddling women and girls waiting desperately at the water's edge. Their quarry was run down at last. Heads for the taking — women for the clutching — a revel of butchery and a Jivero holiday!

Out upon the sand they sprinted, vying with one another for first blood and first slave. The waiting victims cast anxious glances back at their new allies and took heart. The white men were tense, ready, peering through the fringe of naked legs concealing them, holding their fire.

Five — six — seven yards out — the first Jiveros began to bound higher and glance down at their feet. Ten yards — sharp grunts of startled pain broke from them. Twelve — fifteen — the grunts rose into yelps and yowls. The leaders tried to swerve aside.

They collided with one another, tripped, stumbled, and sprawled on the burning sand. Then they screeched.

**87**

An answering screech came from the water's edge – a shrill scream of laughter from Jose. Like a flash it ran along the line of fugitives standing cool-footed in the water. They howled and roared and twittered and squeaked, man and woman and child pointing derisive fingers at their foes. That ridicule stung more sorely even than the furnace below. The Jiveros, red mad with rage and pain, leaped forward again.

As they came they loosed a wild volley of arrows. The laughter ceased abruptly. In the waiting line men slumped down and lay still, long shafts protruding from their bodies.

"Now! Open!" roared McKay.

The Indian leader howled the command in his own tongue. Before the masked battery of white men a gap sprang open, Indians plunging to right and left. Through that gap darted flame spurts and crackling reports.

The foremost Jiveros, now only twenty yards away, sprawled again. This time they did not rise.

The clatter of four breech bolts and of one lever action rattled out. Then another swift rip of gunfire, terminating in the sulphurous bang of Jose's .44. Five more blood-mad slayers dropped on the sizzling sand.

The rest, shocked through with sudden fear at finding guns belching death into them, dug in their heels and stopped. But they could not stop long. The burning pain at their feet bit deeper. And in the instant of their pause the guns spat a third time.

The soft thumps of more bodies striking earth, the intolerable torment under foot, the swift realization that water and relief and their enemies all were nearer now than the trees, stabbed the killers into final fierce attack. Frothing, screeching, the survivors jumped ahead, throwing spears and whirling war clubs. In another crash of flame and smoke five more of them pitched headlong and died.

One more clatter – one more rip and bang – then the gunmen sprang up, reaching for their pistols. The last five Jiveros of the thirty-strong band were almost upon them.

But the hand-guns remained silent. In a sudden pounce the men of the white Indians hurled themselves on the remnant of their foes. Without a signal, without plan, without reason except the simultaneous primal impulse to avenge themselves on the merciless creatures who had harried them through the jungle and who now were within arm's length, the men who had just been the hunted became the killers. With tree-branch club, with fist and nail and tooth, they battered and tore those last Jiveros into mangled pulp.

The burning sands, only a moment ago alive with charging head-hunters, now were belted from bank to water with contorted bodies. Along that hot lane of death nothing moved. The Jivero band was wiped out.

## XIV. JOSE TAKES A CHANCE

The white men, watching the ferocious annihilation of the few remaining warriors, backed away and reloaded their rifles.

"A wolf pack," McKay warned. "Look out they don't turn on us. Get aboard."

A wolf pack it seemed, indeed, when it drew away from the corpses it had made from fighting men. Gashed, bruised, bloodied by the last desperate thrusts and blows of the head-hunters and by injuries inflicted on one another in the savage melee, it glared hotly around as if seeking fresh objects on which to vent its fury. But, now that it had made its kill, the pack speedily cooled. Perhaps the steady stare of the white men and the silent menace of ready rifle muzzles peering over the canoe gunwales aided the cooling.

For a long, quiet minute savage and civilized men looked one another in the eye. Then the chief stepped forward, harsh, grim, barbaric, streaked with red from a deep slash down one cheek, but holding up a friendly hand. In tones far more mellow than before, he spoke at some length. As he finished, he waved a hand toward the women.

McKay made a sign of incomprehension. The chief looked about, seeking his interpreter. With the same thought in mind, the Americans also searched faces. Then Tim pointed.

"Tough luck," he said. "We'll never know what he's trying to tell us. Look there."

Huddled in the shallow water lay the chief's right-hand man: the only one in his tribe who could speak Spanish. Through his throat, and out from the back of his neck, jutted a Jivero spear.

With a sudden unintelligible sound, the chief sprang toward that motionless figure. Dropping on one knee, he turned the face upward. Despite the unmistakable deadliness of the wound, he seemed loath to believe that the younger man was not still alive. Presently, however, he slowly arose and stood staring out across the water as if unseeing. When he turned back to his people his face was seamed with new lines.

José, watching, felt a sudden twinge of sympathy. Between those two must have existed a closer bond than that of chief and subject.

"Hijo?" he asked.

The somber Indian gave no sign that he heard. McKay, who had picked up a few words of the Quichua tongue in Andes, repeated the question in that language.

"Churi?" Son?"

The hollow eyes turned to his. "Zapai churi," he croaked. "My only son."

The captain nodded and strove to express condolence; but the effort was fruitless, for the requisite Quichua was not in his vocabulary. The chief, however, seemed to understand. He spoke again, a short sentence in which McKay recognized the words "iscun" and "ushushi," and motioned again toward the women, a number of whom now stood staring sorrowfully at the dead guide.

"Chief has nine daughters," he translated. "But his only son is dead. Too bad. I rather liked that young chap. Well, we may as well go back to camp and get the rest of our stuff. May be more Jiveros along later."

"Not unless another band is out," Jose disagreed. "None of these escaped."

"Sure?"

"Certain, capitan. I made it my task to watch those nearest the bush and to shoot some who tried to turn back. There is none to carry news of us."

"Good head!" Knowlton complimented. "You're a cool one, Jose. Well, Rod, I don't see any necessity for abandoning our camp. These chaps aren't likely to bother us after what we've done for them, even if we did burn their house a while ago. Tell them to beat it, and we'll resume housekeeping in our new jungle bungle-o."

McKay considered. The white Indians, who now owed their lives to them, were hardly to be regarded longer as enemies. Moreover, even if devoid of gratitude they would not be so senseless as to attempt an attack on the riflemen whose prowess now was ineradicably fixed in their memories. Rand's leg, too, must be worse than ever by this time. And they needed the jerked meat they had planned to get.

"All right. But we'll have to shift camp," he compromised. "Plain trail leads to it now, thanks to the feet of this gang. We'll go back there for the present. After we've shooed these people out we'll make another camp farther along."

The three canoes floated backward, turned, and journeyed to the inlet. More slowly, the Indians came swashing behind, a long stoical file, the women watching the gliding dugouts of the bearded outlanders, and the men carrying the bodies of their fellows who had gone down before Jivero arrow or spear.

**90**

The end of the homeless procession passed the spot where sprawled the disfigured bodies of the head-hunters last to die. It receded down the edge of the scorching sand which had slowed the enemy attack and aided the five to annihilate the assailants. Then through the heat quivering over the battlefield came a swift rush of wings. On the motionless Jiveros settled the black army of the upper air, which had been gathering from the four quarters since the first rifle volley, and which now fixed rending beak and talon in the fallen.

Again the canoes grounded at the shallow end of the water lane. Jose hopped out, thoughtfully watched the approaching horde, glanced at the stretch of sand, and spoke.

"Halt them here, capitan. They move slowly with their dead; and the feet of the young are tender."

While the others looked puzzled, he sprinted across the hot space and was gone among the trees. Then from the bush came sounds of a chopping machete.

"Funny sort, isn't he?" queried Tim. "He's going to bridge over this sand, I bet, to save the feet of the women and the kids. And yet he doesn't think any more of killing and mauling men than of smoking a cigarette."

With which he belied his own words by legging it across the furnace to aid Jose.

By the time the chief reached the halting place the pair were emerging with great armfuls of poles and long palm leaves, with which they rapidly threw a path of comparative comfort across to the head of the inlet.

"Women and children first!" commanded Tim. "This stuff will shrivel up in no time. Make it fast!"

So, after the chief caught the idea and gave his orders, the weaker ones of the tribe scampered along the green lane, which already was curling up in the heat. After them the body bearers strode heavily. The men behind got across as best they could, for no more leaves were put down for them. Last came the Americans, Rand trying not to limp, and the other two carrying ammunition cases.

Back to the camp trudged the five. And back to the camp the whole homeless tribe flocked with them. For a minute or two, before giving further attention to the Indians, the adventurers were busy glancing over the effects which they had been compelled to leave behind.

"Jiveros found this place, all right," commented Rand. "See how the stuff's been pawed over? But nothing's gone. They figured on looting the shack on their way back with the heads and slaves."

"Probably figured to find our trail, too, after they cleared up these folks, and get some more ornaments," agreed Tim. "But say, cap, why are these fellows hanging around? If they think we're going to feed them and build a new house for them they better think again."

It was quite evident that the white Indians wanted something; or, at least, that their chief did. He stood before the hut, grave eyes on the bearded men, obviously awaiting a chance to speak. McKay turned to him and pointed toward the river in a plain gesture of dismissal. But the chief made no move. He looked calmly into each alien face in turn. Then, in monotone, he talked.

What he said the five did not understand. The chief, seeing their blank expressions, seemed to repeat. He pointed solemnly down at his dead son. He pointed toward the women. He waved a hand along the line of white men. Several times he reiterated two words; "Churi chascai."

McKay, frowning, fingered his jaw in perplexity. "Don't get you," he confessed. "Only word I understand is 'churi' -- son. Anybody know what 'churi chascai' is?"

"Dave, try the old boy with some of your Javary cannibal talk. Maybe he'll understand that," said Tim.

But the tribal ruler, listening to a series of monotonous gutturals from the lips of the former Wild Dog, showed no comprehension.

"Wish we had a Quichua vocabulary along," Knowlton regretted. "The old fellow wants something and intends to get it, and he evidently can talk some Quichua, though I don't believe it's his usual language."

"Perhaps he knows the Tupi tongue spoken by the Amazonian Indians down below," suggested Jose. "I can speak it, though not well. And I know some Zaparo words also. Let us see." To the chief he spoke two words: "Herayi? Niato?"

This time the chief understood. "Niato," he repeated, nodding down at his son's body. "Noqui cunian."

"Ah," said Jose. "He speaks the Zaparao, but not the Tupi. He has just said in Zaparo what he said before in Quichua: 'Son. My only son.' Perhaps I can learn -- "

The chief interrupted. With another slow wave toward the white men and then toward the women, he said: "Acamia."

Jose started.

"Acamia?" he repeated incredulously, pointing to himself. "But no!"

The Indian nodded firmly. He pointed at the outlaw, then

**92**

at each of the Americans in turn. While Jose still stared, he spoke five words. Slowly, shyly, five maidens came forward and stood beside him; graceful, handsome girls, shapely, dark-eyed, smiling a little, coy but conscious of their charms.

Tim gave the little bevy a wide grin, and five perfect sets of teeth flashed a response. But as the maidens let their deep eyes stray along the other American faces, their smiles faded. Knowlton's blond-bearded face was unresponsive, Rand's dark-haired jaw was impassive, and McKay's black-whiskered countenance was cold.

"Acamia?" muttered the captain. "I don't know Zaparo, but I'll bet I know what 'acamia' means."

Jose, recovering himself, pointed to the ground and squatted. The chief sank down into position for lengthy conference. Whereafter, by words and signs frequently repeated, with pauses and puzzlings and new starts, a laborious process of exchanging ideas proceeded.

After a time the three able-bodied Americans stirred.

"Looks like a protracted powwow," said Knowlton. "We'd better be making ourselves useful as well as ornamental. Some of our cans are still broiling out yonder, and time's getting away."

"Right," the captain agreed. "Dave, keep on sitting in your hammock and twiddling your gun. We'll finish our moving."

Leaving their rifles with Rand, they returned to the canoes and loaded themselves with the hot tins. Neither going nor returning did one of them speak a word, though Tim broke into sudden chuckles at times. Though none was positive, each had a strong suspicion regarding the subject of the conference — a surmise amounting almost to knowledge.

Back at the camp they coolly busied themselves with preparations for moving farther along, as McKay had intended. The Indians, standing about in aboriginal patience, watched them and gave ear to the progress of the difficult conversation between chief and outlaw. The five girls smiled no more, but soberly contemplated the dead younger chief, lifting their gaze now and then to see what the bearded men were about.

At length Jose and the tribal ruler arose.

"Comrades," the outlaw announced with a grin, "the words 'churi chascai' and 'acamia' are not the same, but they mean the same thing to us now. The chief who yesterday wanted us for victims now wants us as — acamia. And the Zaparo word 'acamia' means 'son-by-marriage'!"

He paused dramatically. The Americans only nodded slightly, as if they had known it all the time.

"Behold, amigos, our brides!"

With a mock-courtly gesture he indicated the five jungle beauties. His partners complied, beheld, and looked back at him without facial change.

"Por Dios!" sputtered the exasperated Latin. "Are you sticks? Have you no eyes – no hearts – no bowels – no – "

"We've got plenty of guts and we're not blind," retorted Tim. "But tell us something new. We knew that an hour ago."

"Si? And you knew also that these are the highest and most beautiful maidens of the tribe – the handsomest daughters of the chief himself?"

Eyes opened at this. Jose, having scored a sensation at last, recovered his aplomb.

"Si, of the chief!" he repeated. "So you did not suspect you were so greatly honored. It is as I say. The chief – his name is Pachac – has never created a son, and says that Piatzo – the Great Father, or God – will give him only girls. So now that his only son is dead – "

"Hold on!" expostulated Knowlton. "You're stepping on your own foot. You say he can't have sons, yet his only son is – "

Jose guffawed, drowning the rest.

"Ah yes, amigo," he laughed. "Yet it is true. What Piatzo would not do for Chief Pachac, a Spaniard did. So says Pachac himself. Years ago a Spanish adventurer fell into the hands of Pachac – and when Pachac was not looking into the arms of one of the wives of Pachac. Where the Spaniard afterward went the chief does not tell me, but from that wife was born this man who now lies dead on the ground."

Looking down into the Spanish face of that dead man, the listeners nodded.

"That explains a lot," said McKay. "Go on."

"Si. That bold, lone devil of a Spaniard must have been a man after my own heart – ready for love even in the jaws of death – a true son of the Conquistadores! Hah! If we Spaniards were not so busy with blood and gold we could people the world with men – fighting men! And Chief Pachac knows it.

"He has seen what kind of son that man gave him. He has seen us kill six times our own number of Jiveros without winking an eye. He has seen us, prisoners in a mud cell, outwit his whole tribe and destroy his power. He is no fool, Pachac. Now he will make us all his sons, and behind the protection of our guns he will make his tribe strong again, and through us he will become the grandfather of many man-children who will

94

grow into great fighters against the accursed shrinkers of heads."

There was a pause. Pachac and his winsome daughters and his broken people watched the five. They stared coolly back at him — except Tim, who grinned and finally laughed outright.

McKay's mouth twitched.

"Jose, we're highly honored and so on, but we're here for gold, not girls. Tell the chief to trot along home."

"Madre de Dios! You refuse?"

"Speaking for Roderick McKay, I do. Every man can make his own choice."

"The gang sticks together," seconded Knowlton.

"But, capitan — amigos — comrades! These are not dirty, unkempt women — they are daughters of the chief! And if you have no fire in your veins, think of the gold! By joining the tribe we increase our own power. When they are strong again we lead them into the cordillera. We go with fighting men of the jungle behind us — "

"And then what?" demanded the captain.

"We find the gold, and then — "

"That's it. Then?"

Jose cogitated.

"I see. You senores are of North America. With gold, you return to your own land. You are not outlaws, like me, with no land to call home. To go, you must abandon your new wives. You would not. So you will have no wives. You will be free. I see."

His black eyes dwelt on his fighting mates, then on the handsome girls. His head tilted, and a reckless smile grew on his face.

"You all refuse these girls?" he demanded.

Four nods answered.

"But you stay here until Senor Dave is strong and you have shot and cured much meat?"

"Unless we have to move."

"If these people will be your friends you will not drive them from you?"

"Certainly not."

"Bueno!"

With that devil-may-care smile still stretching his mouth, he turned to Pachac. Another conference ensued. At length the chief, after a dubious pause, consented to something.

The girls looked startled. Then their teeth flashed again. But this time the smiles were not for Tim or his countrymen. They were for Jose.

And Jose, with swaggering stride, stepped among them. He slipped sinewy arms over the two nearest pairs of shapely shoulders, drew the giggling girls masterfully to him, and grinned diabolically at the four "sticks" from North America.

"Gracias!" he mocked. "As you have said, capitan, every man makes his own choice. Since you scorn these little tigresses of the Tigre Yacu, I take them all!"

## XV. THREE PASS OUT

"All right, old-timer," said Knowlton. "Sorry to lose you, but we wish you luck."

"I am not so easily lost, senor," Jose laughed. "Remember that I started up this Tigre Yacu before you did. And do not think that because I have paused I have stopped."

McKay's jaw set. "Meaning that you don't intend to stick by what you've done?" he snapped. "If you only expect to amuse yourself a few days and then desert these girls, you've stopped for good, as far as we're concerned."

The outlaw jerked his arms from their soft resting places and stepped forward.

"Capitan, have care!" he warned. "I am not without honor. I abide by what I have done. I do not desert my brides. But I do not desert my quest. Nor do I desert my friends — so long as they are my friends."

Eyes narrowed to slits, he watched McKay's grim face a moment. Then, getting no answer, he went on, his voice turning harsh.

"No man who calls me traitor — no man who even thinks me traitor — can be friend of mine. No man, friend or enemy, can tell me what I shall or shall not do. If you do not want me with you longer, go your way — and the devil go with you! But I have not stopped. Hah! No! And I have yet to see the man who can stop me!"

A flush shot across McKay's face. Perhaps he had wronged Jose; but the outlaw's volcanic retort was too hot to pass unchallenged. He stepped forward. Jose instantly stepped to meet him.

Rand's voice, cold as a knife-edge, came between them.

"Cut it out!" he drawled. "You're both wrong. Going to fight like a couple of fools?"

Both slowed. Another step, and they paused. Behind Jose the Indians stirred and looked at their chief. Behind McKay the Americans let their hands sink to their holsters.

"Yeah," rumbled Tim. "What's the matter with you? Hozy, stay off cap or you'll get all that's coming to you. Cap, jump

Hozy and you jump the whole tribe − he belongs to them now. They're scrappers. Remember what they did to the last Jiveros. Want to start another war before our guns get cooled off?"

Common sense gripped both belligerents. They fronted each other, eye to eye, but each saw in the other's face realization that he had spoken too hastily.

"My fault, Jose," McKay coldly apologized. "I misunderstood."

"Es culpa mia," was the chill reply. "The fault is mine."

"Good enough. Now you're both right," came Rand's caustic comment. "Let it go at that."

But, though the sudden gulf yawning between the two men had closed, a split still existed: not only between the captain and the outlaw but between Indians and Americans. Standing solidly behind their chief, ready to back him in anything he did, the men of the jungle now were also solidly behind the new son of Pachac. The Americans were as doggedly loyal to their own leader, right or wrong. What might have become a harmonious alliance, even despite the refusal of the northerners to accept membership in the tribe, now was merely tolerance. Saxon pride and Spanish pride left the gap unbridged − with Jose on the other side.

Now the Peruvian, ignoring McKay, somberly eyed the three men in the hut. With resolute tread he strode forward, picked up his gun leaning against a corner post, gathered his meager personal belongings under his left arm, and stalked out.

"Senores," he stated with formal politeness, "it is a matter of regret to me that our companionship ends. It is not by my choice that it does end. But for the slur of your capitan it would not now be ended. My intention was − but that does not matter. To you, Senor Knowlton − Senor Rand − my old friend Tim − I wish all success. If at any time Jose Martinez, the vile outlaw and deserter of women, can be of any aid to you three, do not hesitate to call. Adios!"

Turning his back squarely on McKay, he faced the men of Pachac and extended his gun arm toward the back trail. Pachac himself led off. The line began to move.

Silently the Americans watched them go: the barbaric chief, still gripping his crude blood-stained club, belted with his sinister black hair-girdle, followed by men bearing the corpse of his half son; the naked, muscular warriors, some carrying the other bodies of their slain; the fair-skinned daughters of the chief, looking wistfully back at the motionless Jose but asking no questions; the other women, some

**97**

young and robust, some carrying babes on their backs, some bent from age and work; the children, stoical as their elders. On into the dim shadows they filed, heading back toward the desolate clearing where the remnants of their plantation would yield them scant food. Then Jose moved.

Down the bank toward his little canoe he started without a backward look. McKay, cold and straight, still stood where he had stopped after the mutual apology which had not restored friendship. From the hut behind him came no sound. But he felt three pairs of eyes on his uncompromising back — eyes whose combined weight of disapproval hung heavy on him.

"Jose!" he called.

Jose went stonily on. He faded among the trees. He was gone.

"And there," said Tim, morosely, "goes the fellow that let us in on this trip. He tipped us off to the gold when we didn't know there was any up here, and would fight for us till the last dog died, as long as we didn't kick him in that sore pride of his."

McKay faced about. The three pair of eyes now were not on him. They rested on the spot where the son of the Conquistadores had disappeared; and they were grave.

"My fault," he conceded again. "But he's gone. There's nothing we can do now but move camp as we intended. I'll scout around."

Rifle in hand, he went out alone into the bush. Knowlton hesitated, frowning at the forest; then grabbed his own gun and followed him.

"Always together, those two," said Tim. "Merry wants to give cap a swift kick, but he trails along just the same. Dave, cap's too sudden sometimes. No need to jump in Hozy's face with both feet like that."

Rand smiled slightly.

"Why didn't you take a couple of them yourself, then? You had your chance."

"I can get me a wife at home if I want one, which I don't. But look at the thing from Hozy's side. He's a lone wolf, man without a country, too much of a he-man to set down in a town and get fat and bald-headed even if he could go back. He belongs in these wild woods. Now he gets a whole armful of girls handed to him, gets elected son of a chief and head of a hard bunch that he can train into a fierce fighting machine — why wouldn't he take it? Better to be a king among pigs than a pig among kings. And those Indians aren't pigs, either. He'd be an idiot to turn it down — with a price on his head and no place to go. Isn't it so?"

The green-eyed man slowly nodded.

"Sure. And what's more, all that long conflab between him and Pachac wasn't about girls," Tim continued. "Hozy's got his eyes skinned all the time, and while he had the chief going he was getting a lot of dope about something. About what? About what's ahead of us, most likely: the gold and that wheel thing the young fellow spoke about, and what makes men crazy up here. If he didn't get all of that he got something, and he'd have shot the works to us if cap hadn't gone off half-cocked. And now what do we know? And the only wise guy in the outfit's gone, sore clear through. And I don't blame him."

He spat disgustedly. Rand said nothing. He knew Tim. He knew the grumbling veteran would carry on as loyally as ever behind the captain whom he now scored. He knew, too, that there was much truth in what Tim said.

"And now here we are, without a guide in the middle of a howling wilderness. If we ever get to that gold we'll find Hozy and his crowd there ahead of us. And I bet you something else — if he doesn't get killed first, Hozy'll make himself a big noise around here. He's not just stopping to fool round a few girls like cap thought he was. He's looking ahead, figuring on things way beyond where he is now. You wait and see."

"Hope we live to see it."

"Yeah. Hope Hozy lives to see it, too. Well, he's got our whole case of forty-fours to start with, and if he gets a Jivero with every shot he'll make head-hunters hard to find around here. And there won't be any Moyobambinos in Hozy's country either. I bet the first thing he does is to start after that trader that was stealing our stuff. Hope he gets him."

Wherein Tim erred on both counts — as he was to learn before dark. Neither the case of ammunition nor the trader who had attempted to appropriate it had gone as far as the Americans supposed. Nor was Jose thinking of matters so trivial as a pursuit of the pair whom he had scared away that day.

Down at the river he had expertly concealed his canoe and joined the column fording the stream; and now, first in the line, heading even the chief, he was stealing along like the jungle creature he was, his gun ready to clear from the path any menace to the people who had taken him to themselves. In his dark eyes burned a flame lit by thoughts known only to himself: thoughts not of the Americans, not of the Moyobambino, not even of his present position, but of the mysterious

**99**

land to the north. Truly, he had not stopped. But even he did not realize that he had only just started.

Meanwhile, McKay and Knowlton were threading the tangle in their silent scout. No word had been spoken between them concerning Jose, nor would anything further on that subject be said for some time. In his heart the stiff-backed captain was rebuking himself for his abruptness and realizing to the full what a serious loss he had brought on the expedition; but even had it been possible, he would not have recalled the Peruvian now.

Neither would he give up his purpose to go on into the sinister cordillera toward which he had set his face. Not if all his comrades turned back — not if he lost food and gun and clothing and had to attack the jungle barehanded — not so long as one inch of progress and one ounce of will remained in him, would he quit forcing his way onward. When he could go no farther he would go down, face still to the front and dead fingers clutching the ground ahead. That was McKay.

At length, some distance farther along the lake and well back, he paused and scanned the ground around a small timbered knoll. Past the rise flowed a tiny but clear brooklet. Primeval solitude, unmarked by the feet of men, surrounded it. Game tracks were plentiful, and monkeys flitted along the high branches. Meat, water, secrecy, all were there for the taking. Glancing at his compass, he turned back into the labyrinth, working toward the lake bank. The present camp would be easier to find by following the top of that slope than by worming along the devious way he had come.

A little later he and Knowlton emerged into a fresh path, showing marks of many human feet. It was the trail left by the people of Pachac and the pursuing Jiveros; the point where the fugitives had doubled back, and where the head-hunters had later plunged straight out on the bare sand. The ex-officers paused, stepped nearer to the edge, and looked out.

The sand again was empty of life: the vultures had finished their work and risen. Out there now lay only stripped bones, fleshless skulls, scattered shields and spears and bows and clubs, surrounded by sinister red patches. The eyes of the men at the top of the bank ranged out to the water where they had crouched and shot. They returned, noting the positions of the bones along that red trail. They glanced carelessly at the path left on the slope itself. Then the pair turned away.

But they wheeled back. There, under a tree on that slope, they had seen something: something hastily set down beside the path by Jiveros just before charging out to kill and be

**100**

killed. Their eyes widened. Then they went down, picked up what they had found, and, walking with hands well away from their sides, resumed their way to camp.

As they stopped beside the hut, up from the direction of the canoes came Tim, puffing under the weight of a tin case.

"Say!" he panted. "Know what that proud fool Hozy did? Threw the can of forty-fours back into our canoe. Took a few boxes, that's all. Huh! What have you got there? Cr-r-ripes!"

The officers set down their finds. Tim's mouth worked. Then the case of cartridges slipped from his nerveless hands.

He was staring at the severed heads of the Moyobamba trader, Torribio Maldonado, and his Indian satellite.

## XVI. NORTH

A fire, carefully masked, glowed faintly at the top of the little knoll back in the jungle. Dimly outlined by its vague glimmer, the columns of nearby trees, large and small, rose into the upper dark and vanished amid grotesque lianas and great drooping leaves. Among them, a scant half-rod from the smoldering blaze, stood two straight young trunks between which stretched a horizontal pole. Under the pole squatted four men, smoking.

That pole was the front rafter of a carefully concealed hut: a hut against whose other three sides leaned newly cut bushes and ferns and whose roof-line was softened and distorted by cunningly spaced bumps and slants and juts of palm leaf: a covert which even a jungle Indian might have passed without seeing it, unless warned by the odor of smoke which permeated the air even when no fire burned. The smoke tang clung both to the soil and to close-hung strips of meat under the palm roof.

No Indian was near at present. But other jungle prowlers, as savage and nearly as deadly, were restlessly moving around the camp. At times their fierce eyes shone beyond the fire, and at other moments their snarls and growls told of their baffled hunger for the meat which they smelled beyond the men. Yet they held their distance, partly because of the dread fire demon glowering at them and partly because even their ferocious hearts had learned that here it was well to step warily.

They had learned, those tigres, that the man creatures now living here, though clawless and gifted with no such fangs as theirs, possessed a deadly power: that they could suddenly spit out a sharp crack which struck their brothers dead. They had met men before, and more than one of those men had fallen

**101**

before their rending attack and gone down their ravenous gullets. But those had not been such men as these; they had been bare of body, beardless of face, able only to stab with spear or arrow and then die. These new two-legged creatures not only would not be eaten — they killed and ate the tigres themselves!

Yes, they were tiger eaters. They preferred other meat, such as monkeys and birds and agoutis; but after they spat that flashing report at a jungle king they stripped his flesh from his bones, ate what they wanted, and salted and smoked the rest to add to the monkey haunches dangling from their roof. And so, though the big cats nightly slavered at the tantalizing tang which drew them there, they kept moving. And, come when they might, they never could find that meat unguarded or all the men asleep. Always one was there, alert and formidable.

For days now the camp had stood there. For days three of its men had hunted in the surrounding tangle, killing as quietly as possible and bringing back their prey to the hut where the fourth, who was lame, sat with a gun close at hand. When their butcher work was done they had gone with the fresh meat strips to the lake shore, where, on frames constructed at the edge of the bush, they salted and dried their provender and then brought it back to camp for a light smoking. And now, thanks to skillful hunting, good shooting, good luck and steady work, they had tough meat enough to carry them many a hard mile onward toward the cordillera.

Now, also, Rand's leg was again in condition for use. Careful dressing and faithful though tedious resting had healed the wounds to such an extent that now he not only could walk about but could even squat beside his comrades in the nightly smoke talk — though he squatted on only one heel instead of both. He was not yet in shape to buck a hard trail, but by favoring the injured leg a bit he could do his full share of paddle work. Moreover, he had no intention of lolling here longer. Already he had demanded that the dugouts, which now were sunk in shallow water for concealment, be raised and loaded and the journey resumed.

"Don't get hasty," complained Tim. "You've had it pretty soft lately, but we haven't. We've been plugging all day, every day. Me, I'm willing to loaf a couple of days myself. How about it cap?"

"Wouldn't hurt to lie up one day, anyhow," McKay agreed, mindful of the fact that the delay would heal Rand's injured leg just so much more. "All hands rest until day after tomorrow."

Rand frowned, but gave no further sign of impatience. He puffed again on his cigarette and glanced at the vanishing gleam of a tiger's eye in the black bush beyond. The others also had caught that gleam, but they made no move. So accustomed to the cordon of cats had they become that they paid little more attention to it than to the ever-present mosquitoes – unless the animals grew too aggressive. They smoked on in silence for a time.

"You know, I can't get that Moyobambino's head out of my mind," Tim declared presently. "Keeps coming back to me. I've seen all kinds of dead men in France, and plenty here in South America, too, and some of them were tough to look at, but they didn't spoil my sleep any. But in some way a head without a body on it gives me the jimmies. I didn't like the Jiveros much before, but I don't have any use at all for them now."

"So say we all," seconded Knowlton. "Still, there's no reason why Maldonado should haunt you. You gave him a good deep burial – what there was of him. Wonder where the rest of him is."

"Somewhere between the river bank and the white Indian clearing, most likely. If he'd kept on burning the water downstream the head-hunters wouldn't have got him. If he didn't try to do us dirt with the white Indians before they caught us he tried it afterwards, I bet."

The red man's random guess was right. His terror diminishing after he lost sight of the men whom he had sought to despoil, Maldonado had reflected that their fierceness and their jeering mirth were hardly in keeping with their apparently diseased condition. Tricky himself, he speedily suspected that he had been tricked. Whereupon, in a burst of vicious fury, he had plunged into the jungle to see if he could find the white Indian settlement and goad its warriors into pursuing the men who had mocked him. What might have happened to him if he had reached that clearing and its raging people may be surmised. But he never arrived there. The head-shrinkers spied him first.

"Funny how things happen," Tim went on. "Take those white Indians. With the whole jungle to run into, they couldn't hit any other place but our camp – the last place on earth they'd expect help, and the only place they could get it. Seems like a miracle."

"Odd, but not miraculous," disagreed Rand. "They dodged the Jiveros somehow and started running up the path. Then they quit the path – maybe waded the river a little way – to

**103**

lose their trail. They undoubtedly know of this sandy lake on account of its turtle eggs and good hunting. Young leader thought they'd have a chance to escape in here, so took the chance: intended to hide the women and children farther in and then tackle the head-hunters barehanded. They hit our camp because it was near shore and they were following the lake line. Simple enough."

"Yeah, to hear you tell it. Now tell me something else — where's that swaggering rascal Hozy, and what's he doing right now?"

Rand shook his head

"Don't ask me. I'm no oracle. But there's a simple way to find out."

"How?"

"Go find Jose and ask him."

"Getting brighter every day, aren't you? But say, I don't know at that."

He glanced sidewise at McKay, who stared expressionless into the fire. Then he turned to Knowlton.

"Might do that little thing, too. Maybe Hozy's been over here looking for us before now, but couldn't find this new camp — we covered up our trail carefully. Anyway, it wouldn't do any harm to walk over and see how he's making out. What do you think, looey?"

The lieutenant met the appeal in Tim's eye, looked at McKay's stiff neck, smiled slightly. "I'm game if the rest are. I'd like to know if the old fire-eater's still alive."

"Same here," Rand added his vote.

A long pause followed. McKay said never a word.

At length Rand arose, stepped to the fire; put on more wood, yawned at another eye-flash beyond, and suggested: "I'm on first-trick guard duty tonight. Better hit the hay, Merry."

The blond man, whose night it was to keep vigil from midnight to dawn, agreed and promptly turned in. McKay, still silent, followed. Tim grinned slyly at Rand, jerked his head toward the obdurate captain's back, and retired to his own hammock.

"Wants to go just as much as we do, but he's too set to own up," was his thought. "If I ever get rich and go back home I'm going to hire a sculptor to carve a little mule out of the hardest rock there is, and then I'll name it McKay."

Wherewith he curled up and slept.

Rand returned to his former place and disposed himself comfortably, facing the fire, cocked rifle now resting across his knees. Several times during his watch he lifted the gun part way, then let it sink as a menacing form swiftly dissolved in the darkness. After Knowlton relieved him he slept tranquilly, undisturbed by any shot.

The day of rest followed, and another night unbroken by gunfire. Then McKay, ending the second watch at dawn, roused his companions to a day of action.

In the cool daybreak hour, when the sandy stretch between water and shore was as devoid of heat as the forested soil behind, the four passed back and forth through the mist with meat and cans and guns and hammocks and paddles. They waded into the lake, scooped from the sunken canoes the sand ballast holding them down, rocked them in the water until clean, loaded them up, and got aboard. Before the sands beside them were even warm they were gliding away, leaving behind only a vacant hut where the tigres now might enter and sniff and snarl in chagrin.

Out to the river they swung. And there, though no word of Jose had been spoken for many hours, McKay turned his boat downstream.

Down to the rocks where they had been captured by the men of Pachac they paddled. There they slid the canoes under cover and worked through the bush fringe to the path leading toward the clearing where Jose might or might not be. But the visit to that clearing ended before it could begin.

The path was beaten smooth by the passage of many feet. The feet had passed within forty-eight hours at most. The Americans moved along it a little way, Rand studying the toe prints along the edges, the spots where some foot had swung a little wide. Then they stopped, looked at one another, and turned back toward the canoes.

They knew that a journey southward to the clearing of Pachac's people would be only a waste of time: that there they would find neither Jose nor his adopted brethren. They visioned the scene at that place as truly as if they now were standing at the end of the trail and gazing across the opening — an empty, desolate space of stumps where a few ancient mud huts gaped vacantly at a charred ruin which had been a tribal house, and where the plantation at the rear was only an uprooted waste, despoiled of everything edible. The nomads who had tarried there a few months were there no more, and unless other wanderers should come and settle on the abandoned site the ever-encroaching jungle would steadily creep inward upon it until it was engulfed in a tangle of upshooting green.

"Too late," Rand laconically summarized. "All gone — north."

## XVII. THE TOELESS MAN

At the top of a steep ravine a half squad of men paused, breathing hard, to mop their streaming faces and renew the oxygen in their laboring lungs.

Below them, clear and cold, a little stream trickled along the gully out of which they had just climbed. Behind, a stiff slope dropped from a ridge topped by tropical timber. Ahead, a short rise pitched upward at a grade betokening another ridge and ravine beyond. And off at the right, only a few rods away but concealed from the sight of the quartet by intervening trees, the Tigre Yacu squirmed its way along a deep boulder-choked bed.

The four men knew it was there, but its only use to them now was as a guiding line. So low was its water level, and so choked its course with rocks, that it was no longer a feasible roadway into the hinterland. After days of paddling, poling, wading, shoving and dragging their canoes through one bad pass after another, the indomitable adventurers had at last been compelled to abandon the sturdy craft and take to their legs.

Yet they had not left the dugouts lying carelessly among the boulders, nor even secreted them under the cover of low-drooping bush or up a cleft in the bank. The boats now were high and dry, yet ready for quick use. They lay at the top of a stiff incline, high above the present water level, higher even than the old stains marking the topmost reach of the rainy season floods. It had taken nearly a whole day of strenuous labor to get them there, for they were stout craft hollowed out from solid logs, and astoundingly heavy. But there they were, lying on crude trestles, with bows somewhat lower than the sterns and dipping downward. In them lay the paddles and a number of tin cases which once had held oil, later had served as sealed receptacles for food and ammunition, and now contained nothing at all. Only one of the containers still was heavy: the one in which remained the "trade" .44 bullets which the party could not use here but would not throw away.

The positions and equipment of those canoes were significant of three things: that their owners might be gone for some time, but intended to come back; that when they did come they might bring something with which to refill the tins; and that they might wish to depart in a hurry. With the banks only moderately full of water, it would require merely a quick shove of the boats down the natural chute to get under way with the utmost speed. And the season for the setting in of the heavy rains was not many weeks away. In fact, even now the daily showers seemed to last a trifle longer than had been the case a fortnight ago.

Now the contents of the vacant tins, together with smoked meat and hammocks and other wilderness necessities, were dragging at the shoulders of the four dogged marchers. The men stood leaning far forward, hands on braced knees, distributing the weight of their packs and easing their shoulders as they breathed. Hardened though they were by paddling, and iron-muscled from their strenuous toil among the rocks of the upper Tigre, they were not yet accustomed to the unceasing strain and the grueling down-pull of their back burdens. And all knew that stiffer work must await them.

Tim wheezed hard. "I know now what it is that drives men crazy up this river. It's climbing up these gullies and then tumbling down into another one a little further on. Up and down, up and down, and not getting anywhere. If I ever get out of here and back to New York I won't be able to travel naturally on the sidewalks – I'll have to climb up the sides of the buildings and then fall off the other side." He blew a sweat drop from the end of his nose and again breathed hoarsely.

His humorous arraignment of the country now surrounding them was well merited. It truly was an up-and-down region, gashed athwart by water clefts of varying degrees of steepness, and steadily growing higher.

Had he or any of his companions taken the time and trouble to pick out the tallest tree thereabouts and climb into its lofty crown, he would have seen, to east and north and west, a maze of jungled hilltops shouldering upward behind one another; and beyond, on all three sides, a mountain wall looming mistily against the sky some thirty miles away. That wall, curving around like the rim of a great lopsided bowl from which the southeastern quarter had been knocked away, was the mother of the hills, the mother of the Tigre boulders: the Cordillera del Pastassa, with its clawlike eastern spur: the golden mountains of their dreams.

But, though so near the unknown range toward which they had toiled and fought, not one of those pack-burdened men had yet seen it. Theirs was not the free outlook of the creatures of the tree-tops; they were earth-fettered, swallowed in the labyrinth, able to see only a few rods at most in any direction, and then seeing only the eternal tangle in which

**107**

they seemed doomed to labor for all time. They were here only because they were stubbornly following the course of the shrunken river, their compasses and a dim track pressed into the mold by bare human feet — the upstream trail which, starting somewhere below the abandoned white-Indian settlement, still ran on and on into the north and seemed, as Tim said, to get nowhere. Where they were now they could not tell; all sense of distance, even of time, was distorted by their surroundings. They only knew that if they fought onward long enough they must inevitably reach the mountains and there find — perhaps treasure, perhaps barrenness.

"If we could only pick up a little gold to kid ourselves along it wouldn't be quite so bad," Tim added. "But there isn't anything. Seems like Hozy's yarn about the crazy man without toes must be a dream. Even Hozy himself seems like a dream now, and his Indians too. Nothing but jungle and work and bugs and sweat — that's all the real things there are."

Again he spoke the gaunt truth. In all their tortuous way up the river they had found no gold worth keeping since that day when Tim had captured the forty-dollar chunk. Though their gold pans and other mining tools had all been lost in their capture and escape from the men of Pachac, they had made shift to wash a little dirt from time to time since then. They had found color, but in such infinitesimal quantities as to prove a discouragement instead of a lure. But for three things they might before now have decided their quest to be hopeless — though they still would have pushed onward.

Those three things were the nugget itself, still jealously prized by Tim; the tale of the mad Pardo, which they implicitly believed, though told by an outlaw who now was no longer a comrade of theirs; and the fact that the narrator of that tale was still pressing on toward the cordillera.

How far ahead of them Jose and his band now were they did not know, but they knew they were ahead, and that they had gained much distance over the far slower canoes of the following Americans. Traveling at the tireless pace of the jungle nomad, unburdened by packs, snatching their sustenance from the forest where civilized beings would have starved, they had pressed steadily onward while the Americans wrestled their canoes up through the boulders. Now their trail was old — washed dim by the daily rains, trampled under by the fresher tracks of animals. But it was there, and at long intervals the men following it found unmistakable signs that the new son of Pachac still led them.

Those signs were few, and so small that only the jungle-

**108**

trained eye of Rand spied them: a few threads caught on a thorn, which were recognized as torn from the Peruvian's raveled shirt-sleeve or ragged breeches; an exploded .44 cartridge shell glinting dully at one side of the path; the marks of a machete blade on some severed sapling or vine. The three former soldiers, though by no means blind to trail signs, would not have spotted these things as they labored on. But to Rand they spoke as plainly as if they had been printed placards announcing:

"I, Jose Martinez, have passed here."

And soon they were to find larger and grimmer signs of the progress of the deadly-handed outcast.

Having caught their wind, the four straightened up.

"Feel better, Tim, now that the hourly growl is out of your system?" Knowlton quizzed, in the low tone habitually used.

"Oh, yeah. Let's go, fellow idiots."

They fell into route step and plodded away.

Over the ridge they filed, Rand's eyes ceaselessly scouting ahead and aside. Down into another gully, up another slope. On again, down again, up again. And so on, as it seemed always to have been and destined always to be.

Then, on an upland somewhat longer and more level than usual, the scout slowed. His head slipped forward, and he sniffed the air like a hunting animal. But he did not stop. His nose told him that whatever was ahead was dead.

Just beyond the top of the hill he found it. It lay scattered along on both sides of the trail, which here led among sizable trees and comparatively thin undergrowth. It now was nothing but bones. But a few days ago it had been a body of perhaps twenty men, who had lurked behind the trees and attacked from ambush. Broken weapons, red-stained shields, splintered arrows jutting from tree-trunks, remnants of maroon loin clouts, and trampled ground bore mute testimony to the fierceness of the fight.

"Tidy little scrap here," said McKay, speaking for the first time in hours.

"Pachac's gang must be armed again — with clubs, anyway," added Knowlton, indicating a crushed skull.

"Yeah. And old Hozy was on the job as usual," Tim chimed in. "Look at this one. And there's another. And a whole handful of forty-four shells scattered around."

The two skulls to which he pointed bore the gaping holes of heavy bullets.

"Good swift action, all right," agreed the lieutenant. "Must have been a grand old free-for-all for a few minutes. Jiveros,

109

these fellows. Same equipment as the ones we sent west. Some must have gotten away. Remember the drums we've been hearing lately?"

The question was hardly necessary. The mutter of those drums off to the west had caused even sharper vigilance by day and more careful concealment of the nightly camps. Because of it, no fires had been built for days. Its menacing note had throbbed in the mind of every man long after it had died out of the air. Now each glanced searchingly about. But nothing showed itself.

"Uh-huh. Well, if more of them are out they're probably after Hozy's gang, not watching us," was Tim's comforting suggestion. "And they'll get plenty of trouble if they catch them. Look here, there isn't any hair anywhere around. Pachac must have enough scalps in his belt to make a whole shirt by now. If he cleans up another band of Jiveros he can start making a pair of pants."

Grim smiles answered him. But the same thought was in each man's mind — Pachac's band must be smaller now than before this ambush. Was Jose leading the tribe to victory over all raiders, or to ultimate destruction? Or was he still alive and leading? This might have been his last fight.

Rand hitched his pack and resumed his vigilant advance. The short column filed onward past the other relics of jungle warfare, dipped down into another valley, and left the battlefield behind. There was no further talk.

For some time they kept on before halting again. Then their pause was caused, not by men nor beasts, but by weather. The light faded, a murmur of approaching rain came to them, big drops spattered, and a spanking downpour set in — the daily shower. Picking a spreading tree, they squatted against the trunk, glad enough to slip their packs and rest.

Suddenly, some distance ahead, a faint yell broke through the slash of falling water. It came but once.

At its own good time the rain swept onward and the light brightened. The four arose and advanced, keenly alert. No sound but the steady drip of moisture came to their ears, and for a time no new sight met their eyes. Then Rand stopped short — looked — listened — and advanced on something at a bend in the trail.

There, face down, lay a man. He was naked, black-haired, but apparently not an Indian. His hands were dug into the dirt as if he had tried to raise himself after falling. His back was a welter of spear wounds.

Some one had run him down and stabbed him repeatedly in

**110**

savage ferocity; stabbed him again and again after the death-thrust. Then the killer had vanished into the rain-swept jungle, carrying with him the spear. Nowhere around the body now was sign of any man but the newcomers.

Rand stooped, looking closer. On the skin above and below the death-wounds were scars, not old, left by a whip.

Turning him over, the four looked down into a gaunt face overgrown by black beard: a face of Spanish cast, coupled with certain Indian features: the face of a mestizo, Peruvian or Ecuadorean. Their eyes ran down his frame. Then every one started.

Back into their minds flashed the words of Jose, describing the crazed Rafael Pardo who had reeled into Iquitos with his bag of gold:

"His skin was seamed with scars like those of a whip. His toes were gone − every one cut off!"

This murdered man on the ground, as they had just seen, also bore whip scars. And his feet were mutilated. Not one toe remained.

## XVIII. THE GOLDEN MOUNTAINS

Staring down at that maltreated man, the four muttered in growling undertones. When they lifted their gaze and peered again into the misty depths ahead their faces were hard set.

"We'll halt here," said McKay. "Unsling packs."

The burdens dropped. Tim, his blue eyes glittering, slipped the safety-catch off his breech bolt and lunged ahead, seeking the man who had speared the scarred victim.

"Dave! Stop him!" added McKay, without raising his voice.

Rand, also ready for action, loped away after the mad Irishman. Even when cool, there was nothing subtle or stealthy about Tim; and when enraged he charged like an infuriated bull, seeing red and oblivious of the disturbance he made. Now he was slapping down his feet and knocking aside drooping bush noisily enough to warn his quarry long before he could overtake it. Hearing the pursuit, the man − or men − ahead would undoubtedly slip into cover and spear him in the back after he passed.

But Rand did not attempt to fulfill the command literally and stop him short. He only sprinted up to him and hoarsely whispered: "Less noise! They'll dodge you!"

The fear of alarming and losing his prey slowed Tim down at once, whereas an appeal to "go easy" or to "watch youself" would have resulted only in a contemptuous snort and an increase of speed. Before long he stopped of his own accord, breathing hard and glaring around.

"We must have passed him," he panted. "He hasn't had time to get this far. Skulking in the bush back of us, most likely."

His companion thought otherwise, but he did not say so. The Indian probably had turned back immediately after killing his man and loped away on his back trail, moving without haste but eating up space at every stride. By this time he undoubtedly was well ahead, unconscious of the fact that white men were behind him. Further pursuit now would mean a long chase and probably ambush. Moreover, the rain had washed out any sign of fresh footmarks. Common sense demanded a return to their companions.

"Probably," Rand feigned to agree. "No sign up ahead, anyway. Let's look along back."

They looked, and found nothing. Returning to the body, they found Knowlton arranging a rough cairn of down-blown branches, while McKay watched in all directions.

"Best we can do," explained the blond man. "I'm going to give him what cover there is. Some thorn branches on top will keep off the animals."

"What do you make of it, Rod?" asked Rand. "Jiveros didn't do this. They'd have taken his head."

"Can't make it out," admitted the captain. "Looks to me like pure savagery. There may be some tribe in here that nobody's heard about. Certainly there's something around here that maims men. This fellow had no gold like that Pardo chap. Why he should be killed I can't figure."

"Personal enmity, perhaps," hazarded Knowlton. "Whoever downed him gave him enough stabbing to kill him a dozen times. A prisoner, possibly, who got gay with an Indian woman and then tried to escape."

"Prisoner of whom?"

"Don't ask me. I'm only guessing."

"Maybe if we keep on plugging we'll learn a lot," Tim morosely suggested. "And here's hoping I get the one that did this! Killing's bad enough, but this cutting off toes and stabbing in the back — grrumph!"

For a moment all stood squinting again along the empty track which led into the north. The same thought came to all at once.

"Jose's up ahead somewhere — or his gang is, or ought to be," Knowlton voiced it.

"Hozy wouldn't have a hand in anything like this," Tim remonstrated. "Maybe his gang would; but how would this fellow get past them all? Whoever got him was chasing him."

"And these feet have been toeless a long time," Rand added.

"Looks as if the Pachac crowd were side-tracked," said McKay. "Or else this chap came in from some other trail. Come. Let's move."

Tim and Knowlton bore the dead man to the cairn and covered him. Then they shouldered their packs. The file got under way.

Once more in the lead, Rand studied the damp trail more closely even than usual. It gave no sign for a time, the rain having blurred all marks except the fresh boot-heel tracks left by Tim's feet and his own. Not until they had labored up and down and onward for some distance did he find what he watched for. Then, reaching a spot where thick interlacing of branches overhead had formed a gigantic umbrella and thrown the downpour aside, he slowed, squinted, and nodded.

New footmarks receded ahead — the tracks of bare feet bound northward. And they had been made by more than one man.

He said nothing until an extra steep climb made all pause at the crest of another bank to recover their breath. When his lungs again were pumping normally he stated his deduction.

"Small gang of killers trailed that fellow purposely to get him. When they ran him down they finished him quick and started straight back. Looks as if they were working under orders and hurried back to report success. Otherwise they'd have hung around until the rain let up."

"Maybe they did."

"No. They went at once, regardless. Rain has been washing their trail. Good thing they did, too."

"Why?"

"Otherwise we'd be minus one crazy Irishman."

"Huh? Say, you think I can't handle myself — "

"With a bunch of spears in your back?"

Tim blinked. "Oh. I get you. Let me charge past and then heave their harpoons? Uh-huh. Well, that's the only way they could get away with it."

Nevertheless the belligerent ex-sergeant twitched his shoulders and sneaked a look at the forest behind him. He had been shot once in the back — in France, by a German infantryman who had pretended surrender and then used a short-barreled pistol — and now the old wound seemed to burn. Maybe he surmised why Rand had followed him in his recent reckless run and inveigled him back. At any rate, his next words

**113**

seemingly had little connection with his last utterance.

"You're all right, Davey."

Davey, the good skate, smiled and then plodded away.

As before, he kept watch of the retreating footprints before him, though not so carefully now, since he had learned that what he suspected was true. They were visible only at intervals, in spots where the ground was soft, wet, and protected from the bygone rain. At length the rainfall ceased to have any influence on the marks, and the scout knew that hereabouts the killers had emerged from the westward-speeding shower. The tracks faded out, reappeared farther on, vanished, showed again at another place; always spaced the same, showing a steady pace, and always following the mysterious trail toward the mountains.

He noticed, too, as automatically as he breathed, the creeping slant of the shadows cast by the westering sun. For many weeks – ever since descending from the Andes into the lowlands, in fact – this had been their only means of gauging the passage of the hours; for every watch in the party had stopped after a few days in the heavy moisture charging the air east of the colossal cordilleras, and thus they had been reduced to the most primitive means of time measurement. Now he knew that in little more than an hour the grueling advance must end for that day, if a safe and snug camp for the night was to be made.

The hour dragged past, filled with nothing but Tim's summary of their previous marching – "jungle and work and bugs and sweat." The feet of the men behind, and his own as well, were slipping now on roots and in wet spots which, earlier in the day, they would have cleared without effort; the legs now had lost resiliency, and the hungry, overworn bodies were becoming like engines whose fuel was burning out. But the present spot was unsuitable for camping – an upland, devoid of live water. So he tramped on, seeking a night haven.

The ground still rose. It held no more of those heart-breaking gullies, however, and progress was not too difficult, even for nearly exhausted men. Doggedly they kept putting one foot before the other until half an hour more had passed. Then the light ahead grew brighter. The trees seemed to thin out.

Studying the forest around him, the scout presently spied something and paused. The column stood hunched over, the three behind looking the questions they had not the breath to ask.

"Dry camp," puffed Rand. "Getting late. Got to stop.

**114**

Water trees here. We can make out."

He jerked his head aside. Scanning the timber, the others recognized a tree which they knew but had never yet had to rely on — the huadhuas, or water tree, a bamboo from whose joints could be obtained quarts of clear water. They nodded, dropped packs, staggered, adjusted their balances to the sudden loss of weight, and looked about for a good place to make camp away from the trail.

"Over there," directed McKay, picking a place well bushed but not too thick, and near a couple of widely spaced huadhuas. Heaving up their packs on one shoulder, they threaded their way into the covert, cast about for snakes, found none, and sank down for a brief rest.

Presently Rand arose and, with no explanation, returned to the trail. Along it he journeyed toward that thinning of the trees. He was gone for some little time. When he returned his eyes glowed.

"Didn't mean to slack on camp work," he said, glancing around at the results of the labors of his mates. "Been scouting. Come on. Want to show you something."

They followed him. Along the path they went, feeling almost fresh again without their back burdens. The forest grew thinner and thinner. All at once they stopped, subdued exclamations breaking from them.

They stood at the brink of a sharp declivity where, years ago, a land-slip had occurred. Under them yawned a sizable gulf, partly filled with water dammed by the fallen earth. But, after one glance, they gave no attention to it. Their gaze darted off to the northwest.

For the first time in many a weary day they saw mountains. For the first time they looked on the end of their long trail.

There in the north, blue-black at the base and gleaming golden at the summits, rose the tumbled upheavals of a bygone age: the looping range of the Pastassa, sprawling outrider of the tremendous column of the Andes. The misty atmosphere of the lower lands, which usually blurred the vista from this point, was swept clean for once by a stiff north wind now hurling itself at the faces of the four invaders; and in the fast-lifting light of the dropping sun the glowing peaks seemed looming over them, aglitter with unminted treasure — a promise, a lure, which might prove true or false.

Somewhere beyond that range, draining its northern slopes, the Curaray flowed down its golden bed to the Napo. Somewhere beyond its western segment stretched the river valley of the Patassa, home-land of the head-shrinkers whose

**115**

roving outposts twice had come into the trail of the four. Somewhere ahead in that great pocket of the mountains the trail must end at – what? The grim place where men went mad? The final port of all the missing men of the Tigre Yacu?

Whatever might wait in the few remaining traverses between here and the cordillera, it now was masked by the rolling jungle and the long shadows thrown from the western wall. Below the sunlit summits stretched a twilight land wherein showed no sign of man; an expanse which, for all the eye could discern, might have lain untrodden by human foot since first it rose out of the waters of the vast inland sea. Only the vague path still leading onward, only the bodies of the mutilated man and of the head-hunters who had come down it, proved that men moved somewhere under that baffling jungle cover girt by the mountain rim.

McKay, first to move, drew out his compass. The quivering needle verified the sun slant: they were gazing north-north-west. Returning it to his pocket, he remarked in a matter-of-fact tone: "Better move. It'll be getting dark soon."

Rand, who had looked out at the same scene once before, faced about promptly. Knowlton, his blue eyes shining with the light of the dreamer who sees his vision at last coming true, stood a moment longer before reluctantly turning away. Tim pivoted on one heel, yawned, and agreed: "Yeah. I'm hungry."

Through the thickening shadows they filed back to their covert. There Knowlton spoke.

"Well, by thunder, we've something to look forward to now. We're almost there. The golden mountains!"

"Maybe," said Tim.

"Maybe what?"

"Golden. If gold's there, it's setting tight and doesn't go down the river. Say, where is that river, anyway? We lost it."

"Over east somewhere," said Rand. "It's no good to us any more. The trail is the thing to follow."

"If there's no gold, Tim," challenged Knowlton, "where did Pardo get his? He came out of here – scarred and crippled like the fellow we met today."

"Uh-huh. Well, here's hoping. We've had a run for our money – now I want to see the money for the run."

"If it isn't there we'll keep on going until we find some," smiled McKay. "It's only two or three hundred miles farther to the Llanganati. There's gold there – if you can find it."

"Toting a pack all the way, of course?"

"Of course. But when you get there all you have to do is to find the Incas' lake and get out the gold."

**116**

"What's this yarn about the Incas' lake, Rod?" asked Rand. "Same old stuff you hear in Peru?"

"Same stuff. Incas threw billions of gold into an artificial lake on the side of the Llanganati during the Conquest. Good many men have lost their lives trying to find it. Still, it seems to ring truer than most of those Inca lake stories.

"They tell about one fellow named Valverde — a Spaniard — who was poor as dirt and went native. Awhile after he took his Indian wife he became enormously rich. Girl's father showed him how to get at the Inca gold and helped him raise a lot of it. He went back to Spain, and when he died he told the king of Spain how to get at the rest of the treasure. But it's still there."

Tim's eyes began to glisten. This was a new tale: a tale of lost treasure hundreds of miles away — far more alluring than the possiblity of equal treasure within a few leagues. Inca gold! The dream of every Andes adventurer for more than three centuries!

"And nobody's got it?" he demanded.

"No. Expeditions don't come back. Even one led by a priest — Padre Longo — didn't come back. After that, nobody else had the nerve to try for it."

"Say, if we don't find anything here, let's keep on going! We can get there some time — if our cartridges hold out — and it'll take something fierce to lick this gang after we land there. What do you say?"

The others laughed. Pessimistic a few minutes ago, croaking over the lack of gold in the Tigre — and now all afire to dare hundreds of miles of cordillera in chasing a new rainbow: that was Tim Ryan all over.

"We'll see what's here first," chuckled McKay. "Let's eat."

Silence fell on the darkening camp, broken only by masticatory noises and gulping of water previously drained from the huadhuas. Then across the jungle roof swept the sunset noise of birds and animals, announcing night. Gloom enveloped them. They ate on, wordless.

All at once they stopped chewing and leaned forward. On the wings of the wind still pouring out of the north came a new sound. It was not the roar of a tigre, the death scream of stricken animal or man, the snarl of jungle battle, the report of a gun. Any of these would have held them alert for a time; but the thing they did hear made them squat motionless as frozen men until it ceased. Even after it died they held that same rigid pose, staring dumbly into the dark.

Deep, slow, doleful as a requiem for the lost men who had

**117**

never returned from their quest into this fastness – a bell had tolled.

## XIX.  DEAD MAN'S LAND

Noonday sun stabbed down through the branches stretching over the curved crest of a long, rambling ridge. In scattered splotches it lit up sections of a faintly marked path leading along the upland. Filtering through tall ferns beside the path, it sprayed over bearded men in torn, jungle-stained clothing who sat on their packs and smoked.

Another fireless meal had just been finished, and the usual cigarettes were aglow. But the four were not lounging in the careless attitudes customary to men relaxing in the languor induced by food and tobacco. Each leaned a little forward, his feet under him, ready for a sudden upward jump. Each faced inward toward his companions, but his eyes kept swinging back and forth in vigilant watch of the forest beyond the man opposite. Between his knees, butt on the ground and left hand curled around the barrel, each held an upright rifle. And every man's pistol hung ready for a swift draw.

"If they'd only show themselves!" complained Tim. "If we could only get a look at them! They been trailing along with us the last two days, but never a hair will they show. Me, I'm ready for a scrap any time, and the sooner the quicker. But this thing of expecting a spear or a poison arrow in the ribs any minute and not seeing anyone – I don't like it."

The tense attitudes of the others showed that they felt exactly the same way. For two days, as Tim said, they had been under that strain – the knowledge that they were escorted by flitting Things which they could always feel, could sometimes hear, but could never see: an unceasing harassment which wore on their nerves more than half a dozen deadly fights. For two nights, standing guard in two-hour shifts, they had felt the invisible Something close by, ready to strike yet never striking. Even now they were positive that the stealthy movements which they heard from time to time were not those of animals; that the slight waving of a bush here and there was not caused by a breeze.

"Next time I see those ferns over there move, I'm going to shoot into them," breathed Knowlton, eyes fixed on something beyond Rand.

"Hold in, Merry!" warned McKay. "That's a rookie trick."

"I don't give a whoop! They're there, and if they won't start it I'm willing to."

"Take a brace, man! You'll hit nothing. You'll start more

**118**

than you can finish. Don't be an old woman!"

"I've got a theory about this thing," stated Rand, as calmly as if he did not feel Death lurking at his shoulder blades. "These fellows, whoever they are, are willing to keep us coming along. They have a use for us — up ahead somewhere; up where that bell rings. If you really want to start something, start back along the trail instead of ahead. I'll bet you wouldn't get ten feet away."

McKay nodded.

"Remember how that toeless chap's back looked," he added.

At the memory of that red welter the lieutenant twitched his shoulders.

"While you're springing theories, I've got one of my own," Tim hinted darkly.

"Well?"

"I'm not much of a hand to believe in things that aren't. Just the same, there's some missing men up here. They'll stay missing — they're dead! And they're what's around us now!"

"Ghosts? Nonsense!"

"Maybe. But why can't we see them? Why don't they cough or spit or breathe like live men? Who pulls that there funeral bell at night? How does a bell come up here, anyway? I tell you, it's not a real bell! These things aren't live men! And it's that bell, the dead men snooping around, that drives live men crazy up here! If I were alone here long I'd be raving."

There was no levity in his voice. And, though the others tried to laugh, their mirth was forced. Despite himself, every man had fallen under the uncanny spell of the deep jungle during the weeks on the weird Tigre Yacu. And it is a fact, as experienced jungle rovers know, that in the vast tropic wilderness are things which none can explain. Sounds like the clang of an iron bar, where there is no bar or iron; the ringing of a bell where no bell could possibly be; a penetrating, nerve-destroying hiss like that of a huge steam pipe, hundreds of miles from steam; these and other sounds, which the Indians ascribe to demons, coupled with the sudden and absolute disappearance of men who leave no trace of their fate — these are a few of the unearthly occurrences in the great green abyss below the Andes which confound reason and sense. And those four were overworn by hardship.

But none except straightforward Tim would admit, even to himself, that the weird espionage of those invisible Things was undermining his scorn of the supernatural.

"If there were such a thing as a Dead Man's Land, and if

**119**

this were it," the lieutenant doggedly combated, "you'd never catch Pachac and his people going up here. They're still ahead."

"How do you know they are? We haven't seen a sign of them lately. Ask old Eagle-Eye Rand. There's nothing to show that they ever got this far."

Rand shook his head half an inch. Tim spoke truth.

"Then where did they go, if not up here?" Knowlton persisted. "There's been no sign that they turned off."

"Where did the others go that came up here? How do we know what got them?"

There was a silence. Now and then a fern nodded, a slight creeping sound floated to them, but no life showed.

"Theories are no good," bluntly declared McKay. "But I've got one, too. That bell belongs to some old Spanish mission; those old Jesuits would go anywhere – the more God-forsaken the place, the better. The descendants of their converts are still here. Maybe they're virulent fanatics and practice a few fancy torments on fellows who don't come up to their requirements. Remember what was said about the wheel awaiting us."

Another silence. Then Knowlton said:

"Sounds more reasonable than Tim's nightmare. That might explain the whip scars and the toe-cutting, too."

"Wait a minute," exclaimed Tim suddenly. "Maybe I can get a rise out of these fellows."

He rose, facing a spot where he had detected several unexplainable dips of a bush. Slowly he made the sign of the cross.

After a minute he made it again. No sound or movement answered him.

"Nope. Your idea's no good, cap. The cross doesn't mean anything here. Now let's see if a little Irish nerve will get us anything."

With steady tramp he advanced at the spot he had watched. Ever so slightly, the bush dipped again. A faint rustle, hardly audible, came from beyond it. Eyes narrowed, jaw out, the ex-sergeant plowed into it and stopped. After peering around he backed out again. His broad face was not so florid as before.

"Not a sign here! No footmarks – no broken leaves – nothing! By cripes, it's like I tell you – they're not human!"

The others, who also had risen and stood ready for action, glanced around and at one another. Knowlton shrugged.

"You fellows have all sprung your theories. Now here's mine," he announced. "We'll get to the bottom of things if we

**120**

keep going. And we'll get nowhere stopping here. Let's go."

With this pronouncement everyone agreed.

One by one they slung their packs – one by one, so that three always could maintain their readiness for anything. The donning of their burdens was not so difficult now as it had been a few days ago, for the men were hardened to them and the packs were lighter: too light, in fact, so far as their food content was concerned. But Tim, though anxious to be moving away from the masking ferns, could not forbear his customary half-serious growl.

"Dead men don't get humpbacked lugging these blasted packs, anyway. If these fellows are going to knock me in the head I hope it'll come quick, so I can get a little rest out of it. I'd hate to get killed just when I got to a place where I could drop this thing for good."

With a final heave of the shoulders to swing the weight into the right place, he fell into position in file and took up the step. The column plodded away, heads moving from side to side in constant watch. Around a huge tree it wound, and into the northward trail it vanished.

As it disappeared, a louder rustle sounded among the ferns and bushes, which swayed more abruptly than before. Then they stood motionless again, and the sound died. The encompassing Things also had moved on.

Foot by foot, stride by stride, the four forged onward along the curving ridge top. Inch by inch the sun shadows crept eastward. Hour by hour the hot afternoon grew old. And as steadily as the little file swung ahead, as smoothly as the sun rolled in its course, the escort of silent Dead Men kept pace on either flank of the advancing force.

The ridge seemed to have no end. It rose in long grades, sloped away again, lifted and ran level, dipped at another easy slant, but still remained a ridge. At times, as the forest growth thinned, the marchers glimpsed the sky on either side. But they saw nothing of what lay out beyond those occasional side openings, nothing of what waited ahead at the end of the upland – and nothing of the Things trooping along in the cover at the sides of the path.

As the hours passed, no halt was made. None was needed on this ungullied upland, where no sharp declivities had to be scaled and the lungs functioned as rhythmically as the feet swung. Mile after mile crept away behind, until Tim's unspoken thought was reflected in the minds of his comrades:

"We're really traveling now! We ought to get somewhere by night!"

And get somewhere they did. At length, with an abruptness that halted them short, they emerged into open air. They dug in their heels and gave back, smitten with sudden qualms at the pit of the stomach. Almost under their feet yawned a gulf.

A sheer drop of hundreds of feet — a wooded country below — a tremendous mountain wall fronting them a half mile away; these were the things their startled minds registered in the first flashing instant of instinctive recoil. So long had their vision been confined by the dense tropic growth that the sudden burst into emptiness shocked their brains and sickened their bodies. Dizzily they wavered backward.

For many seconds they hung there in a close-drawn knot, while eyes and nerves and equilibrium readjusted themselves. At length they cautiously edged forward. A little back from the brink they peered downward, studying the green carpet far below.

It seemed a solid mass of jungle, unbroken by any clearing, unlined by river or road: a somber abyss wherein might live weird monsters spawned in the hideous Mesozoic age, but where the foot of man never had trodden. It curved away at both ends, its continuation cut off from the eye by jutting outcrops of the wall on which they stood. A yawning pit — nothing more.

Out of it, on the farther side, towered the mountain — a huge bulk, densely overgrown in its lower reaches, clad more thinly up above, nearly bald at the top. Along its side showed no indication of life except an occasional pair of parrots winging their way from point to point. Grim, forbidding, it brooded over its chasm as if guarding its fastness from invasion.

Up and down the four studied it, and back and forth along the gulf they swung their gaze. At the first appalled glance the drop had seemed to be at least a thousand feet, but now that they had steadied themselves they estimated it at not more than five hundred. The mountain shooting up beyond might be three thousand feet high; possibly several hundred more. How long the curving valley might be they could not tell. But there seemed to be no reason for exploring it, nor any way —

Tim drew in his breath sharply. The others glanced at him and found him looking over one shoulder, ashen-faced.

"Oh cripes, I knew it!" he breathed. "Here they are, and they're dead as hell!"

They whirled. At last they saw the Things.

A bare spear's-throw away, blocking the trail, stood men. But such men! Their ribs projected. Their arms seemed bones.

Their eyes gleamed hollowly under matted black hair. And their skins were green.

Green as the jungle around them, they were. Had they moved and slipped into the bush, they would have vanished like specters. But they did not move. At least a dozen strong, they stood there in a solid body, holding javelins poised at their shoulders. The points of those spears were long, saw-edged, and dark with the stain of poison. One cast, one scratch from those venomed edges, and the explorers would be doomed.

Fronted by death, backed by death, the four stood like statues. Then one of the ghastly creatures slowly lifted its left arm. Its green forefinger pointed beyond the trapped men. With dread significance, that finger turned down. In the soulless eyes of the creature was a command.

"Oh God!" groaned Tim. "We've got to jump off!"

## XX. INTO THE ABYSS

Motionless, wordless, breathless, the other three stood facing the gruesome things blocking the only avenue of retreat from the brink.

The green arm pointing to death hung rigid, the cavernous eyes remained fixed in a snaky stare. The poisoned points neither lifted nor lowered, poising as if truly held in dead hands. Only the regular rise and fall of the breathing lungs under the gaunt ribs proved that the Things were living men.

Rand, without moving his lips, spoke nasally from a corner of his mouth.

"Drop flat and shoot from the ground. Spears may go over us. Give the word, Rod."

But McKay did not speak that word. Instead, he took his eyes from the green menace and glanced behind. Then he coolly turned his back, stepped to the extreme edge, and moved along it, looking down.

"Not necessary," he said after a moment. "Trail goes down here. We'll follow it."

"Trail?" Knowlton echoed in amazement. "Where?"

"Rock stairs drop to a shelf. Pretty risky, but possible. Not much worse than some places we struck in the Andes. Come and look."

Gingerly the blond man backed. Tim and Rand maintained their wary watch of the Things.

McKay pointed a little to the left of a segment of the ragged edge. There, as he had said, a flight of crude steps jutted from the sheer face of the precipice – perhaps a dozen of them, widening as they descended to a narrow shelf leading away to the westward. The top stair was hardly two feet wide, the shelf not more than four: a precarious passage flanked on one side by the upstanding wall and on the other by nothing at all.

"Ugh!" muttered the lieutenant. "Dangerous even for an Indian. Impossible for us. The slightest bump of a pack against that rough rock throws you out and down. And our boots will slip on those slanting stones. Can't be done."

"Got to do it, or end our trail here."

It was stark truth. This was the trail. To quit it here meant, at best, only a long, sour retreat to the canoes and back down the Tigre. At worst, it meant death from the poisoned spears still closing their path. And there was little chance that all those spears would miss their marks.

"Once we're on that shelf, we can travel," Knowlton conceded. "But getting there is the job."

"Take off pack. Take off boots. Go down backward, easing the pack after you with your hands, step by step. If the pack slips let it go overboard. I'll try it out first."

Stepping back a little from the edge, he nodded to the green men. The spearheads wavered slightly, sinking a little lower. McKay unslung his pack, sat down, and began unlacing his boots.

"Tim – Dave – get ready," he urged. "Never mind those fellows. They won't do anything just now."

His calm voice expressed more confidence than he felt. Yet he was reasonably sure that no attack would be made unless precipitated by his own party. These green men, he reflected, could have attacked at any time during the past two days, and with greater safety to themselves. Their object, as Rand had said, seemed to be to herd the invaders onward, not to kill unless they attempted retreat. What fate waited beyond those stairs he could not even surmise. But they could hardly be trapped in a more hopeless position than the present one; and they still retained their weapons.

"Ouch!" blurted Tim, when he saw what must be done. "Go down that? I'll fight this gang bare-handed first!"

"Then you'll fight alone," retorted the captain, tugging at the first boot. "The rest of us are going down."

Rand said nothing. He studied the hazardous path, clamped his jaws tighter, and began preparations for descent. Tim looked at him, at the others, at the green men; opened and shut his mouth; mumbled dolefully, and took off his pack.

As McKay arose, with boots slung around his neck and rifle looped across his shoulders, a sound from the southwest throbbed across the silence. It was the far-off boom of drums.

"They're at it again," commented Tim. "Same old message we been hearing — Hello! What ails these dead men?"

At the rumble of the drums the green men had started. Now they had turned their heads and were looking back into the jungle. They stirred, lifted their spears higher in an involuntary gesture of defense, drew a little closer together as if threatened with attack. For the moment they seemed to have forgotten the Americans.

If the adventurers had snatched the opportunity quickly enough they might have poured a devastating fire into those momentarily unready foes; might even, by fast work, have wiped them out completely. But none moved. All watched the weird creatures in wonder. Soon some of the green faces turned back. They now bore a trace of human emotion: fear.

"Guess those drums don't belong to these greenies," said Knowlton. "They're Jivero drums, undoubtedly, and they seem to spell trouble for our genial hosts. We're not going into Jivero country down below, then. That's something."

"We're going into Dead Man's country, I'm thinking," croaked Tim. "This hole is where all the rest of them are waiting for us. I wonder if we'll look like these men in a little while."

"They're a good Irish color, Tim," the captain grimly joked. "Maybe old Saint Pat is waiting for you down below. Here goes to find out."

"Saint Pete, you mean. Waiting to hand me a harp the minute I fall off of those rock steps. But I don't want a harp yet — Hang tight, cap, and go slow, for the love of Mike!"

McKay was dragging his pack to the edge. Cautiously but coolly he laid it at the top step, turned backward, let himself down on hands and knees, straightened a leg and felt for the second stair. Finding it, he slid over and worked down until he had his knees firmly braced below. Then, very carefully, he drew the pack toward him and tested its balance on the rock above.

"Too heavy and too wide," he decided. "Haul it back, Dave."

Rand dragged it back, and the captain rose. Once more on the top, he began unstrapping his roll.

"You were right, Merry — we can't handle these things," he granted. "Every man take what he can carry in his clothes. Get all the cartridges and matches, and whatever else you can tote

**125**

without making yourself clumsy. Leave the rest."

"How about grub?" queried Tim.

"One meat strip apiece. Down below we'll have to shoot our grub or starve. Don't overload, or you'll be twanging that harp in a few minutes."

Faced by that alternative, the four picked from the opened packs what they could safely stow in pockets, shirts, and empty boots, plus their hammocks, the two short axes, and the light table gun, which could be stuffed under belts or taken down by hand. The remaining duffle was ruefully cast into the edge of the bush. The green men watched wolfishly, but made no move toward the abandoned equipment.

Again McKay essayed the perilous slant, going backward as before, keeping his eyes on the rock stairs as he passed downward, feeling his way with sockless feet. Once his rifle butt hit a projection on the wall, jolting him suddenly. His mouth twisted, and for a second his eyes swerved outward. But he gripped the stair above, raised himself a bit, swung his hips somewhat away from the wall, lowered himself again inch by inch — and the gun scraped past. A few more careful moves, and he stood on the shelf.

"One down," he announced, his voice a little husky. "Who comes next?"

"I," volunteered Rand. And, grimly steady, he made the descent without mishap.

"Let me go now," begged Tim. "My feet are getting colder all the time. If I wait any longer my legs will be stiff to the hips."

Knowlton, who stood ready to go, drew back and made room for the red man — who now was not red, but distinctly pale — to pass. Tim got on all fours, fumbled to a footing on the first step, and drew a long breath.

"Here goes nothing!" he quavered, trying to grin. "And may God have mercy on my soul!" His last utterance came from the bottom of his heart.

"Slowly and easy does it, old man," the lieutenant warned. "Take all the time in the world. Don't look down. Just ease yourself down slow — slow — that's the way! Get a good foothold every time. Slow — easy — it widens out at every step, you know."

Set-jawed, glass-eyed, Tim inched down. For him the passage really was harder than for any of the others: he was too broad and stocky. His left side hung out over the abyss, and his muscular but short legs lacked the reach of McKay's, or even of Rand's. The pair below watched every movement, coached him at every downward reach, warned him of every projection. And at last, shaky, gasping like a fish out of water, dripping with cold sweat, he found himself beside them.

"Well, I – huh – came through without a – huh – harp in my hand," he panted, grasping at the wall. "But I wouldn't do it again for a – million dollars. I'm sick to my stomach!"

"Stand still a minute," counseled Rand. "Watch Merry come down."

Knowlton already was backing over the edge. He threw a final glance at the green men, who showed no sign of intending to follow. "So long you fragrant hunks of green cheese!" he mocked.

The menacing figures spoke no word. Their lusterless eyes showed no glint of anger at his taunting grin. Only their spearheads, now almost resting on the ground, lifted a little and pointed at his face.

Knowlton dropped his eyes to the rocks and concentrated his attention on the deadly serious work of getting down. And now the hand of Death, hovering close over the head of each man traversing that treacherous spot, showed itself.

Perhaps it was because he was last in line and anxious to join his waiting comrades and move on; perhaps it was a touch of recklessness; or perhaps the sloping stones were slightly slippery from the passage of three perspiring men. At any rate, the lieutenant descended just a trifle too fast. Reaching for the fourth step, he slipped.

His unbooted feet caught the stair and clung. But the butt of the rifle on his back hit solidly against the same ugly projection which had caught McKay's. The barrel slapped sidewise and struck the blond head a vicious blow.

He lurched out toward the chasm, dazedly clutching at the step above. Then, balanced on the utter edge of the abyss, he lay limp.

Another movement, a slip of the gun, a shifting of something in pockets or belt, would turn him over and slide him into the green maw gaping below.

With a hoarse croak Tim jumped upward. Tim, who had confessed cold feet; Tim, still actually ill from dread; Tim, who would not touch those stairs again for a fortune, sprang up them like a mountain goat. His body slithered against the face of the precipice. His big hands clutched, one at the edge of a step, the other at his lieutenant's slack shirt. In one smooth, steady haul he slid the stunned man in toward the cliff.

And while the two below stood frozen, unable to help, he

worked his own way backward and slipped the reviving man down stair after stair. He did not look to see where he stepped. He planted his feet with unerring surety, grasped tiny projections without seeing them, balanced himself as lightly as a fly. In hoarse tones he muttered over and over:

"Just lay still. Lay limp and we'll make it. We're most down and going strong. Lay still, la-a-ay still!"

And he reached the shelf, laid his man out straight beside the wall, and grinned gray-faced at him. Then he wavered, clutched at the crag beside him, and sank down. And for the next few minutes he was absolutely and utterly sick.

"By God!" breathed McKay. "I've seen men awarded the D.S.C. for deeds not half as brave as that!"

But when Tim sat up again and weakly mopped his face he had a reward worth far more to him than government medals — a silent grip of the hand and a straight look from the "looey," alive and once more ready to go on. No words were spoken. No words could have said what eye spoke to eye in that long quiet minute there on the face of the wall.

"Let's go," said Rand.

Carefully they turned about, and slowly they filed along the trail, hugging the rock. Up at the top of the stair the green men stood watching them go. Presently they drew back, and for the first time sounds broke from them. With animal grunts, they fell on the stale food left behind by the Americans.

On along the narrow shelf the four adventurers trudged, looking down into the dizzy depths no more than they had to. It led on and on, widening at times, narrowing again, now roofed by overhangs of stone, again open to the high blue sky. Under a jutting outcrop it burrowed, and there it turned abruptly to the left. The marchers had rounded a shoulder of the hill which had cut off their view to the west and south.

There, on a natural platform beyond the corner, they halted with sudden murmurs. The jungle below was no longer without signs of man.

Perhaps a half mile farther on, in a wide waterless bay among steep green mountain slopes, the trees were thinned out at the top of a curving knoll. In that opening, dingy gray, showed the lines of stone walls and a house — masked by intervening tree-tops, but unmistakable. Whether men now dwelt there, what they did and why, were questions which only closer approach could answer; but men had been there — men who built with stone — and not so long ago. Otherwise the jungle would have swallowed up the place.

Down toward it the high trail now dipped at a stiff grade

**128**

for perhaps three hundred yards. Then it vanished into trees, and at that point the precipice also ended; the tree-clad slope was a slope only, not a drop. The path must wind on down that green slant and then swing out to the house-capped knoll. Was that knoll the end of the trail, the end of all adventure, the lair of the dread ogre who swallowed missing men?

Suddenly the watchers started. A sullen, low, awful murmur was shooting toward them from the farther mountains. Instantly the solid rock under them quivered and swayed.

"Quake! Down!" barked McKay, falling prone.

The others dropped flat, hugging the stone. It moved sickeningly, became still. A few seconds passed. It shuddered again, was motionless.

Up from the depths rolled several clangs of a deep-toned bell. From somewhere below, seeming very near, broke a grinding roar followed by a great thumping crash. The rock quivered once more, but this time as if from a blow.

After a few minutes of waiting for another tremor, the prostrate men sat up and looked around. Nothing seemed changed.

"Pretty easy," remarked Rand. "I'd hate to be caught up here in a hard one."

"Something dropped, and mighty close," said Knowlton. He crept to the edge and peered down. "Not along this side," he went on. "Maybe around the corner." Rising, he stepped to the other side.

"Did you hear the bell ring? It was down there by the house," said Tim. "That same deadman's bell we've been hearing – "

"Great guns!" Knowlton's voice broke in. "Look here!"

As they joined him, he pointed downward, then out along the shelf where they had just passed. Below, a great chunk of the wall grinned up from among crushed trees. Beyond, a long gap opened in the face of the cliff.

"This trail's closed forever," declared McKay. "Unless we can find some new way out, we're in for life."

## XXI. THE END OF THE TRAIL

Sunset, blood-red, burned behind the mountains.

Against its fiery flare the great misshapen bulks loomed dusky green above the sinister gulf in which stood the stone-crowned knoll. In that chasm the shadows were welling rapidly upward toward the top of the eastern heights. Moving along the bottom of the bowl, the four invaders found everything around them growing dim under the jungle canopy.

They had swung down the remainder of the steep trail without mishap, and without meeting any living thing. Soon after entering the trees the path had begun to zigzag back and forth along the steep, but no longer precipitous, side of the towering hill; and now it had become merely a succession of easy curves rambling on toward the walls guarding the house hidden beyond the trees. Along it the file was passing at good speed, each man still carrying his boots around his neck. As always, Rand led, scanning all ahead and aside.

Abruptly he halted, jumped back, collided hard with McKay, who now was second in line. Before him in the dimness a sinuous form moved slowly out of the trail.

"Snake," he said. "Nearly stepped on him. Guess I'll put my boots on."

With more alacrity than caution, the others followed his example. The odds and ends of equipment which had been carried in the battered footgear were shaken tumbling on the dirt, and every man hastily jammed his feet into the leather legs. By the time the lacing was completed and they were once more protected to the knee, the swiftly deepening shadows had grown so dense that it was difficult to find the articles they had dropped. And the path was swallowed in gloom.

"Better halt here and eat," said McKay. "There'll be a good big moon in a little while. Can't see our way now."

"We haven't got far to go," objected Tim. "And maybe there's some water ahead – I'm bone dry. And that snake's right around here somewhere. Let's go a little way."

His only answer was the sound of three pairs of jaws biting into the last of the smoked meat supply. The others had accepted McKay's dictum. With no further protest, he straightway clamped his jaws in a meat strip of his own.

The meal was brief, both because of the meagerness of the provender and the speed with which it was bolted. No man squatted or sat, for no man knew how many reptiles might be within striking distance. In lieu of water, each finished with a cigarette.

"No need of going without a smoke," said Knowlton. "We're in, we can't get out, and anybody who spies my cigarette is welcome to come running."

"Me, I'd like to see something coming – something alive, I mean," declared Tim. "This place is too spooky. Haven't seen anything here but one snake, haven't heard anything – "

Like a blow, the boom of a bell struck his words and knocked them into nothing. It came from the right. Solemnly

**130**

it tolled a dozen times. Then it was still.

No other sound followed, save the usual night noises from the gloomy depths around. No human voice spoke. No dog barked. No cat or cow or other domestic animal called. No squeak or rattle or bump or footfall betokened the presence of men in that house somewhere near by. Even the jungle noises here seemed weird, ghostly, echoing hollowly among the surrounding heights. Tim shivered.

After a prolonged silence Rand spoke.

"A queer hole. Good thing we stopped here. We were heading into the woods. Path curves back, probably, but we'd have blundered off it."

Nobody replied. All stood waiting for the moonlight.

At length it came. The obscurity grew less dense. Silvery patches of light appeared here and there on the earth. The eyes of the waiting men, already dilated wide by the darkness, made out clearly the shapes of the near-by trees, but not the path. Vague even in daylight, that trail now would not again be visible before sunrise.

But McKay moved over into a spot of light, studied his compass, and laid a course for Rand. "West-northwest. That'll fetch us out near that bell."

Rand, after contemplating his compass and the trees, nodded and dropped the instrument back into his pocket. Now that he had the direction firmly fixed in mind, his old jungle instinct would carry him straight, despite necessary windings, without another consultation of the magnetized needle. He turned and stepped away.

Slowly the party followed his lead, traveling in slants and detours, but ever swinging back to the prescribed course as surely as if Rand's eyes were glued to his compass instead of roving all about. They slumped into muddy spots, turned sharp to dodge boulders, straddled over down trees, and in places chopped their way with the machetes. Nowhere did they find flowing water. Their thirst, already keen, became acute discomfort as the meat they had swallowed demanded liquid. But none spoke of it, or of anything else.

All at once the trees opened. They halted at the edge of the forest, looking up at the cleared knoll.

They saw only stumps, low shrubs, scattered trees of great girth, and, at the top, a high stone wall, above which protruded the outline of a long, low roof. For a time they studied the wall, seeking some moving figure, but seeing none. Under the cold moon the hard gray pile fronted the wilderness like a forgotten sepulcher guarding its dead.

131

Toward it the hard-bitten little column advanced, instinctively changing formation to a line of skirmishers. Each man picked his own way around tree or bush clump, but none fell behind or went far ahead of his comrades. At times they paused to listen and watch; then went on.

Soon they stood under the old wall itself, looking along its length. Nowhere could they see an opening. For a hundred feet or more it ran straight north and south, then ended. Beyond rose the black mountains, looking down in insensate savagery at the line of stones taken from them by hands now mouldering and piled up to bar out whatever foes might come, and at the four lost men who, all chance of return destroyed, stood under them and looked about.

To the men themselves came a queer feeling that they were back in some former life, outside the walls of some medieval robber baron's castle, likely at any moment to be spied by mail-clad sentries above and riddled with long shafts or dragged in and thrown to rot in some noisome dungeon. Knowlton caught himself listening for the grind of steel-shod feet above, the clink of armor, the rattle of a sword. Then he smiled at his own folly. But the smile faded and his eyes widened. No martial sound came to him; but another sound did.

Somewhere farther down, beyond the wall, a vaguely confused murmur arose: a noise which might have been caused by shuffling feet combined with low voices; a sound as if men, or pigs, or both, were moving sluggishly about.

"Cripes! The dead men are getting up out of their graves!" breathed Tim.

In truth, it seemed so. If living men moved on the other side of those stones, they had little energy. There was no calling out, no song or laugh; only a dead, brutish sound which neither increased nor died out of the air.

McKay motioned along the wall and stole away. The others followed. Down almost to the end they passed, and there they paused again. From across the barrier that gruesome sound still came, more clearly now: grunting voices, bestial snores, the faint slither of feet passing about as if dragging in utter weariness. Something else came over, too — a rank odor as of an unclean pen.

The captain gauged the wall — a good twelve feet high — as if meditating an attempt to look over by climbing on the shoulders of some one of his companions. But he decided otherwise and once more moved on, stopping again at the end, or what seemed the end, of the rock line. It proved to be a corner.

Around that corner the wall receded for perhaps forty feet, then turned again and ran back to a sharp uplift of the ground. There it merged with the shadows and the rising earth. It looked like a passageway leading into some tunnel, which in turn might run back for many yards into the steep slopes beyond. The spies had little doubt that such was the case.

The captain shook his head, signifying that further progress in this direction now would lead them nowhere. They retraced their steps. To the other end of the wall they passed, and around the corner they turned without reconnoitering. Then they stopped in their tracks.

Drawn up in a close-ranked body, stolid and silent as if they had been patiently awaiting the Americans, stood ten men. Each held a rifle. Each rifle was aimed at a breast. And each eye behind the gunsights glinted as coldly as that of a snake.

They were Indians all. But they were not green men; not Jiveros; not men of the vanished Pachac. They were brutes; brutes in human form. Though the lower parts of their faces were half-hidden by the leveled rifles, their low foreheads, beady eyes, and bestial expressions were clear enough in the moonlight. They were more merciless than animals. And they held the lives of the intruders in the crooks of their trigger fingers.

Yet, after the first shock of surprise, the four looked them over coolly. One thing was very obvious – these were no dead men. They were alive, well fed, armed with repeating rifles of the universal .44 bore. The sight of those prosaic guns, threatening though they were, exerted a steadying rather than an alarming influence on the soldiers of fortune. Tim even grinned, though in a disgusted way.

"Faith, getting caught seems to be the best little thing we do," he remarked. "Outside of the Jiveros we caught on a frying pan, we haven't licked anybody since we came in here. If I ever get back home I'm not going to brag much about this trip. What's the word, cap? Drop and shoot, or stick up our hands?"

"Stand fast." Then, in Spanish, McKay addressed the Indians.

"Do not fear. We are not enemies. Put down your guns."

The guns remained leveled. One of the Indians replied in a harsh growl. "Go within."

"Within what? Where?"

"The gate."

The captain glanced along the wall.

"I see no gate."

"Go. You will find it."

He moved aside as he spoke, still covering McKay. The others likewise slipped aside.

"We go."

And, with unhurried tread, they went. Flanked on one side by the wall, on the other by the ready guns, they filed along toward the invisible gate. As they passed, the Indians swung in behind, muzzles point at the white men's spines.

Some distance beyond, a tree cast a deep, wide shadow on the wall. In that shadow the Americans found a stout gate of rough timbers, standing ajar. Three more of the brute-faced aborigines, also armed with guns, stood there. These stepped in, swinging the gate wide enough to admit two abreast. When all were inside, the big barrier was bumped shut. Heavy bars thumped into place.

The Americans, looking rapidly about them, saw the front wall of the big house; a bell suspended from a stout tripod near at hand; and a sort of scaffolding running along the inside of the stockade walls, about four feet below the top. The house front was pierced by a few high and extremely narrow windows — scarcely more than loop holes — and a wide doorway in which solid double doors stood slightly open. From the peak of the low-pitched roof jutted jagged stones which at one time probably had been a belfry, now ruined by some long-forgotten earth shock. The bell, hanging within the triangle formed by logs solidly braced in the hard-packed earth of the yard, was black with age. The scaffolding along the walls formed a narrow runway where men could pass in patrol or fight against enemies outside. If well manned, the place was virtually an impregnable fortress against any jungle foe.

This much the four absorbed in their first survey of their surroundings. Then their gaze riveted on the big door.

Slowly that door swung farther open. Beyond it a face showed dimly in the shadow cast by the big tree outside. The Indians looked toward that vague figure, and one of them spoke.

"They are here," he said.

The figure stood motionless a moment. The peering Americans saw that it was not tall, and that against the gloomy background its face seemed white. Then they nearly dropped. The figure replied; and its voice, though clear, was soft and low — the voice of a woman.

"It is well. They shall come in."

As if the words were a cue, light shone in the darkness. The

**134**

doors swung wide. Prodded by the Indian, the amazed soldiers of fortune moved forward, staring at a slender, graceful woman, bare-armed, black-haired and red-lipped, gowned in clinging purple, who stood with head saucily tilted and smiled at the shaggy men who had forced their way to the end of the long trail of the Tigre Yacu. Around her stood fair Indian damsels, nearly nude, holding bare-flamed lights.

Across the threshold passed the four, and down a bare corridor the bevy of girls and their mistress retreated before them. The Indian men remained outside, and one of them reached and swung the door shut. The lights passed into a side wall, and the Americans followed. They found themselves in a big room hung about with the same purplish cloth worn by the woman, in the middle of which stood a massive table from whose top flashed yellow gleams as the lights moved.

"Bienvenido! Welcome!" smiled the woman. "You have traveled far. Have you hunger and thirst?"

The eyes of the four searched the room. No men lurked there. They relaxed, smiled in reply, and doffed their battered hats.

"Thirst we have, senorita," answered Knowlton. "A thirst that gnaws. But not hunger."

"It shall be quenched."

She made a sign, and the girls, who now had set their yellow lamps on little wall brackets, went out by another doorway.

"Sit, senores," added the mistress of the house, nodding toward a long padded couch. "Water shall be brought for bathing, and I myself shall prepare that which will banish weariness."

With another smile she disappeared through the other doorway. Still almost dumb with amazement, the men sat down on the couch, unconsciously gripping their guns, and staring all about.

Tim breathed heavily. "What do you know about this? We came looking for dead men, and we tumble into a harem!"

## XXII. CIRCE

Four girls, bearing wide yellow basins, entered and crossed the room. Each stooped before one of the men, holding the bowl at the level of his knees. Restraining an impulse to snatch the vessels and drink the cool water in them, the travel-stained men laid their guns aside and immersed their hands. As they did so, each narrowly scanned the basins.

"Gold!" was their conviction.

The yellow metal could hardly be anything else. It certainly was not brass. The yellow lamps, too, and the gleaming things on the table – all must be gold.

"This place is a regular mint," whispered Tim.

"Looks like it," agreed Knowlton. "First time I ever washed my face in gold, anyhow."

Running a hand down his face to squeeze the water from his beard, he reached with the other for a small towel hanging over an arm of the girl serving him. As he did so, she bent nearer and whispered something.

The sibilant words meant nothing to him. Puzzled, he stared into her face. Then he blinked, rubbed his watery eyes, and stared again.

He was looking into the brown eyes of one of the wives of Jose.

A glance at the other girlish faces told him that they also were of the winsome daughters of Pachac. Not only that, but they were of the five whom the son of the Conquistadores had taken as his brides. Only one of the five was missing, and she must be among those now beyond the doorway.

In the wavering lights, which did not fully illumine the room, the Americans had not previously recognized the girls. For that matter, they had paid scant attention to them in their amazement at finding themselves amid such unexpected surroundings. But now a startled grunt from Tim showed that he, too, had realized who these girls were. McKay and Rand, after a glance at him, also looked more carefully at the faces so near theirs. Their lifted brows revealed their recognition.

Knowlton's girl whispered again. Again he could not understand. Her face fell, but she moved her head a little backward, toward the door where the purple woman had gone out. In her eyes was a plain warning against something.

The blond man nodded to show that he comprehended her effort to caution him, though unaware of just what the effort signified. Then he toweled his face and gave her the wet cloth. She turned away.

"Keep an eye peeled, fellows," he muttered. "Something slippery around here. Can't tell what's in that next room, for instance."

"Wear your poker face," advised McKay. "Don't show that we know the girls. Maybe we're not supposed to."

Then through that farther doorway came the fair-skinned woman in purple.

Behind her advanced girls bearing a large steaming pot and several cups of the same lustrous golden hue. Eying them

**136**

keenly, the men saw that among them was the fifth bride of Jose. And, remembering that the chief of the white Indians had had nine daughters, and noting features of resemblance among all these girls, they concluded that every one of them was of the blood of Pachac. But each man kept out of his face any sign of recognition, or even of interest.

They arose, as if in honor to their returning hostess. But in doing so they unobtrusively picked up their rifles and glanced beyond her to spy any furtive movement in the room beyond. No menace showed itself. The purple woman looked at their guns with an expression of amused contempt.

"Have no fear, my friends," she said. "Within these walls no guns are needed. Here are only rest and welcome after a long journey."

"Your men gave us a strange welcome," McKay asserted.

"Ah, but you then were outside the walls! In this wild land one must be on guard against all who come, until one knows them for friends. Of what country are you, Senor Gold Hair?"

Her long-lashed eyes had turned to Knowlton, whose tumbled hair shone under the light of a nearby lamp.

"Of the United States of North America, senorita. We all are of the same land."

"So? I have never seen one like you," she naively confessed. "Nor like this one whose hair is so red. These two," nodding at McKay and Rand, "might be men of Spain. But come, let us quench the thirst with guayusa."

She turned toward the stout table, on which the great golden pot now had been placed. With another quick look toward the door beyond her, the men laid their rifles back on the couch and moved toward the steaming bowl. Deftly she dipped up cupfuls of the hot liquid and set them along the edge. After a bit of maneuvering, the four took positions along a bench beside the table, where they could watch doors and their hostess, too. And, though consumed by thirst, none lifted his cup just yet.

They knew the guayusa tea well enough — an infusion from the leaves of a wild shrub found here and there in the upper Amazon country, which, like the yerba mate of Paraguay, exhilarates the drinker and banishes weariness. They were fatigued enough and thirsty enough to consume cup after cup of it. But they were also on their guard against anything and everything, and they waited for her to drink first.

"You do not like the guayusa, no?" she asked, dipping up a measure for herself.

"It is hot," Knowlton evaded. "And in my country it is the

**137**

custom to await the pleasure of the hostess."

Her dark eyes smiled wisely at him. She lifted her cup, sipped at it, drank in little mouthfuls, set it down empty.

"Of what are you afraid, Senor Gold Hair?" she mocked. "Should I let you pass my guards only to poison you?"

The lieutenant flushed and raised his drink.

"To you, senorita," he bowed. "The most beautiful woman I have seen in many a long day.

Which was not quite so florid a compliment as it sounded. But she took it at its face value, and as he smiled and quaffed the stimulating draft her eyes caressed him.

Tim gurgled into his cup. "Feed her a little more, looey, and she'll be in your lap."

McKay choked suddenly, spilling half his guayusa. Rand bit the edge of his cup to hold his face straight. Tim gurgled again and swallowed the tea in two gulps. Knowlton expressed a hope that he might speedily choke.

The dark eyes watching them narrowed, and a glint of anger showed in them. Though the alien words meant nothing to her, the suppressed mirth among the men hinted at something uncomplimentary — else why should it be suppressed? But she said nothing. She signed to one of the girls, who refilled her cup.

For a minute or two all sat frankly looking at her. They saw that she was indubitably Spanish; that she was not altogether beautiful — the features were a trifle coarse — but far from ill-favored: of Castilian countenance, shapely form, and mature years — mature, that is, for the tropics; perhaps twenty-five. Her red lips, thin, but pouting a little; her eyes, with a hint of passion in their depths; her languorous movements and her side-long glances — all were sensuous and sophisticated. Her dress, they now noticed, was only a sleeveless frock of llanchama bark cloth dyed with achote, ending at the knee, drawn tight at the waist by a broad girdle of the same material. And from that girdle, slanting a little forward, jutted the hilt of a poniard.

In his mind each man labeled her: "Dangerous."

Yet there was no hint of danger in her manner as she now studied each man's face in turn — and not only his face but the hardy frame beneath it. To three of those figures she gave fully as much attention as to eyes and jaws and expressions. Her gaze hovered a little curiously on Tim's red hair and beard, but she scanned his muscular body with more interest than his wide countenance. On McKay's stalwart frame and Rand's solid build she bestowed thoughtful looks. But on Knowlton's

**138**

thick, uncut yellow hair, golden beard, and twinkling blue eyes her gaze lingered; and under her lashes burned a soft glow of approval and allure.

"You've started something, looey," murmured Tim, sotto voce. "We three are just hunks of beef, but Angel-Face Knowlton is the candy kid."

"Shut up," requested the badgered man. Then he gulped his second cup of guayusa, noting, as he did so, that the woman now was eying the red-haired man in evident dislike. Tim was rapidly putting himself out of favor.

After another wordless minute or so of tea drinking, the woman turned her gaze again to Knowlton.

"What do you seek here?" she asked abruptly.

Involuntarily each man's glance darted to the great gold pot on the table. She threw back her head and laughed in a scornful way.

"You come for gold, yes? I knew it must be so. For that yellow trash men dare all. And when they have it, what then?

"Where gold is, there death is also. So my fathers have learned. Many years ago they found gold here. They fought the wild men, they made their captives build these walls, they mined the gold — and what then?"

"The earth shook and the mountains broke and slid. The way in and out of this gulf closed. There was no escape except the long way down the Tigre, through savages who let no man pass. So my fathers stayed here with their gold, which was worth nothing — what is gold in such a place as this?"

"Still they mined and got more gold, against the day when another temblor should open a new way out. It came, the terrible earth-shaking — and did it open a way? No! It crushed the mines, destroyed the men in them, buried even the gold which my fathers had taken out and stored in a walled-up cave. And so they died, and I alone am left — Flora Almagro, last of the fighting family that would tear wealth from the savage mountains of the Pastassa.

"I, and Indians, and tumbling walls, and a few paltry utensils which my fathers made from their gold — that is all. But the gold is in these mountains round about. Dig, senores, dig! Ha, ha, ha! In twenty years of digging you may reach that which my fathers reached — and then be crushed like them!"

Again she laughed — a mocking laugh with a wild note in it. "Four lifetimes of fighting man and beast and jungle and devil-rock — and this to show for it!" she shrilled, with a contemptuous wave toward golden cups and bowls and lamps. "If you would find gold and keep it, friends, bring in an army

**139**

— bring in cannon — blow off the tops of these mountains until they can no longer fall — then perhaps — if the jungle men will let you, you can pick up your treasure in safety."

None answered. All thought of the slight earth shock only a few hours past, of the fall of the cliff and the destruction of the trail. Her words rang true. And if they were true, Fate had tricked them into a barren trap indeed.

Thoughtfully they drained their cups a third time. The potent stimulant already had routed their fatigue, and now their minds were leaping nimbly from one thing to another — the quake, the mysterious green men above, the obvious servitude of the Pachac girls, the sinister absence of the rest of the tribe and of Jose — a dozen other things in incoherent sequence, all of which perplexed and disturbed them. At length McKay bluntly asked.

"How did you know we were coming?"

The suddenness of the query did not disturb her. Widening her eyes in mock innocence, she returned: "The approach of travelers always is known. The little parrots of the forest sent the word."

"Ah. Green parrots, no doubt."

"All parrots here are green, Senor Black Beard," was her laughing retort.

"So. And they drum with their wings to send their news."

At that her smile vanished. Involuntarily her hand darted to her dagger hilt, and she threw a look toward the outer door. The gesture, the look, were strikingly similar to the fearful attitudes of the green men on hearing the distant drums.

"Valgame Dios! Those drums!" she breathed. Then her head turned back and lifted again. "But now, you have it wrong. You have heard drums, yet? They are drums of the men who cut off the head and make it small — the hunters of the heads of men and the bodies of women — the old enemies of my fathers. Their land is beyond the mountains to the west, but they come at times — many of their bones lie in this gulf, where they died in fight. We have lived only because they came in scattered raiding bands. If ever they come in an army — "

Her hand tightened on the hilt. With another swift change she laughed out, the same wild laugh as before.

"They may capture the head of me, but that is all!" she vowed. "Flora Almagro never goes a captive to the hut of a Jivero — not while good steel can reach her heart! But — caramba! let us forget them. Tomorrow death may come, but tonight let us live! Now that the guayusa has rested you, there

**140**

is a stronger draft of friendship for strong men who have dared the Tigre and come to me here."

She signed again to the girls, who had been standing mute behind her. Three of them turned toward the rear room. Among those who stayed was the one who had attempted to convey a warning to Knowlton. Now she looked straight at him and again tried, by furtive nods at her mistress, to caution him. Puzzled, he stared back at her.

"Why do you look so at my maidens?" demanded Flora Almagro. Her eyes were narrowed again, and she watched Knowlton as if trying to read his thoughts.

"I was wondering, Senorita Flora," he coolly replied, "how, in this wild place, you obtained such handsome slaves."

His tone implied that they were not to be compared in beauty with their mistress. The subtle flattery was not lost. She smiled again. But her eyes still searched his.

"You look as if you thought you knew them, senor."

"One of them resembles a girl I saw months ago, far up the Maranon," he lied serenely. "But she cannot be the same. That one was taller."

For a moment longer she studied him. He carefully preserved his poker face. The suspicion faded from her eyes.

"But no, Senor Gold Hair. All of these have been with me for years. They are of the people who served my fathers. Now they shall serve — "

A stumble and a slight confusion at the door halted her. The three girls were returning, bearing another great golden bowl. One of them had tripped, and all three were struggling to keep the heavy vessel from falling. From it splashed a reddish liquor.

A flash of anger twisted the face of Flora. Her dagger leaped out, and with a feline spring she darted at the trio.

"Pigs! Lizards! She-dogs!" she screamed. "Have care! If you drop the wine, clumsy beasts, you shall feel the point of this!"

The three caught their balance, steadied the bowl, and bore it dripping to the table. The purple-clad woman, her breast still heaving with fury, looked down at what had been spilled, spun toward the table, her poniard half raised — and caught the cool stare of four pairs of eyes. After a silent minute she slipped the weapon back into her girdle and laughed in a forced way.

"I forget myself," she said. "But this wine, senores — it is old, precious. To see it cast on the floor by footless fools — it is too much. But now it is safe. Let us drink deep — of the wine of life — and love!"

With the last words her eyes burned deep into those of

**141**

Senor Gold Hair, whom she had plainly selected as recipient for other favors to come.

"Hm! This is getting a bit thick," thought the blond man. "But the evening's young yet, and if she drinks enough she may blab a lot of interesting things. On with the dance!"

Wherefore he smiled blandly at the senorita, accepted the cup tendered him, and gazed appreciatively at the fragrant contents. Red wine in a cup of gold, tendered by a seductive woman in a room hung with purple and lit by golden lamps, with nude maidens at hand to pour new drafts — here in a jungle chasm into which he and his comrades had been driven by green-skinned creatures at the points of poisoned spears! It seemed an impossible dream, from which he soon must awake to find himself again in a gloomy pole-and-palm camp surrounded by avid tigers. Glancing at McKay, he found the same feeling reflected in the gray eyes contemplating the scene.

"You have not yet told me your names, my friends," the last of the Almagros reminded them. "Now let us drink to each of my guests in turn, and then you shall tell me of your travels, yes? Tomorrow, if my poor hospitality has pleased you, we shall talk more seriously — of those things which are to come. But now — "

She nodded and lifted her cup to Senor Gold Hair, who promptly arose.

"My name, Senorita Flora, is Meredith Knowlton, an humble member of this party commanded by — "

He paused. Behind their mistress' back two of the Pachac girls were frantically signaling at him. This time there was no chance of misunderstanding. They were pointing at his cup and shaking their heads: warning him not to drink of it.

" — commanded by El Capitan Roderick McKay," the lieutenant went on, "the caballero seated at my right — "

There he let the cup slip from his fingers and drop.

"Don't drink, fellows!" he snapped in English. "It's doped!"

"By cripes, and there's a row outside!" helped Tim. "Hear it?"

A low muttering sound beyond the house walls flared into a snarling roar of hatred. Sharp yells — a bumping, splintering sound — a sudden roar of gunshots. With a bound the men threw themselves on their rifles.

Dios!" screamed Flora Almagro. "Las bestias — out!"

ghting creatures outside were animals, then they were s with the voices of men. They yelled, screeched, howled in a bedlam of blows and crashes punctuated by the recurrent rifle shots. Yet beneath the human voices sounded a ferocious undertone of bestial grunts and snarls: a fearsome, inarticulate growl more appalling than the death shrieks momentarily scaling high and breaking off short.

"Where away, cap?" called Tim, gun cocked and pistol loosened for a quick draw.

"Stay here!" snapped McKay. "Back behind the table! Heave it over!"

"That's right," approved Knowlton, glancing at the high wall slits. From the outside no man could shoot through those openings, nor could any creature larger than a house cat squeeze in at them. With the wall at their backs, the massive table as a bulwark, and only two entrances, they could hold this strong room against all comers until their ammunition ran out — and even longer, with their machetes.

They leaped around the table, tugged at one edge, swung it up and let its heavy top slam down with a crushing thump. The gold bowl and cups clanged on the stone floor, the liquor splashing on the purple dress of the woman and the bare legs of the girls.

"Here!" ordered the captain, pointing. Flora, her poniard gleaming, dashed around the table and sought to get behind them. The Indian girls followed with less speed — in fact, they seemed unafraid and kept looking at the doors.

"No, madam," McKay said darkly. "You do not stand at our backs with that knife. Over there, if you please — farther along."

"Cristo!" she spat. "You think me an assassin? You would let them kill me — "

"We let no man kill you. But we know what was in the wine!"

It was a snap shot, but it scored. Her face blanched, her eyes and mouth opened, and she slipped away from him, poniard up in a position of defense.

"Over there!" he repeated inexorably, pointing again. "And stay there!"

Several feet away, still staring at his bleak face, she stopped

**143**

where he had designated: protected by the upturned table, beyond reach of any of her defenders. Still farther on, the daughters of Pachac clustered well away from her, and in their faces now plainly showed sullen hatred of the woman they had served.

"Lights out along here!" commanded McKay, knocking a lamp from its bracket with his rifle muzzle. The others threw the lights nearest them to the floor and trampled on the oil which splashed out, killing the flame. That side of the room now was very dim, while the two entrances were well illumined.

Two nude figures came slipping in at the farther doorway. Four rifles darted to an aim. But they sank without a shot. The pair were women — daughters of Pachac.

At sight of them Flora Almagro hissed like a cat.

"You devils! she screamed. "You, you freed the beasts! You opened the gates! When they are driven back I kill you!"

Whether the girls understood the Spanish words or not, they evidently recognized the accusation and cared nothing for the threat. Their lips curled and their heads lifted in a defiant gesture worthy of their maddened mistress herself. Tauntingly one pointed toward the infernal tumult outside. The other flashed her teeth in a triumphant smile. Obviously they were not only guilty but proud of it.

Infuriated by their insolence, she sprang at them with dagger uplifted, forgetful of the shoulder-high table top intervening. She collided with the solid barrier so forcibly that the blow crumpled her gasping to the floor. The poniard fell from her hand. The Indian girls near her surged forward.

But, sensing the menace from those whom so recently she had threatened, she closed a hand over the weapon and lifted its point against them. They paused, hesitated, hung back. Holding them off with gleaming blade and blazing eyes, she hitched back to the wall and leaned against it, struggling to regain her breath.

Outside the conflict was advancing under the unglassed slits serving as windows, ventilators, and loop holes. The gunshots had dwindled to an occasional blunt roar, and those inside heard more clearly the impacts of blows, the gasping grunts of close-locked antagonists, the moans of wounded and dying. Thus far no man had entered the house. A stubborn hand-to-hand battle evidently was going on, with one side slowly gaining ground. Through the turmoil sounded a hoarse voice exhorting:

"At them, camaradas! Over them, esclavos! Kill! Kill!

144

Butcher the accursed torturers! Strike! Bite! Crush their skulls! Kill! Kill!"

Rand, after scanning the hollow embrasure of a slit above him, clambered up to its firing-step and leaned into the opening, peering down. Out there in the moonlight he saw wrenching, wrestling figures heaving about in mortal combat — naked arms and knotted fists clutching clubs, rising and battering down — shaggy heads and hulking shoulders hurling themselves past at some foe just beyond — distorted, red-smeared faces falling backward in death — the flare of an exploding rifle. Over the fighting forms hung a haze of dust and powder smoke, and from them rose the rank odor of bodies long unwashed.

This was no Jivero attack. It was an eruption within the walls of the fortress itself. In Rand's mind burned the word he had just heard from the throat of that unseen leader — "esclavos" — slaves.

It came again, from almost under him: that savage voice, that same word.

"Hah! El capataz de esclavos — the slave driver — the foreman! Welcome senor — welcome to death and hell!"

Back into Rand's range of vision reeled a stocky, brutal-visaged Indian, a rifle clutched aloft in his fists. He struck downward. The gun was torn from his grip. A long, lean white body, topped by a black-bearded face split in a grin of hate, leaped into view, swinging down the captured gun with terrific power. The crunching thud of the blow sounded above the rest of the tumult. The Indian capataz collapsed, his head a red ruin.

"Hay!" croaked the deadly voice again. "I have long owed you that blow, you fiend — how do you like it? On, camaradas! They break! On to the doors!"

In another bound he was gone. So swift had been his movement that the watcher's brain retained only a fleeting memory of black hair and grinning teeth. Before his eyes now passed a surging hurlyburly of other black heads, upshooting arms, lurching bodies —

"Dave!" crackled McKay's voice.

At the same instant came a struggling, thumping noise from the outer door. Rand jumped down and took his place in the line.

Bump — bump — bump — a grinding creak — another struggling sound. Then that hoarse voice again.

"So, you pig! You would block the door, hah? You hug the wood, hah? Then hang your brains on it to show your love for

**145**

it!"

Another bump, followed by the thud of a falling body. Hoarse breathing, the slap of bare feet in the corridor, and a triumphant yell.

"Now for that hell-cat who steals the brains of men! Let her drink her own devil-brew and — Por Dios, what is this?"

Into the room bounded the lean killer of the capataz de esclavos, followed close by his naked fighting mates. At sight of the upturned table, the four grim figures behind it, and the gun muzzles grinning at him, he halted in his tracks. Slit-eyed he peered into the dimness along that farther wall, and his jaw dropped. At the same instant four trigger fingers slacked their tension, and across the faces of the Americans darted the light of recognition.

"Begorry, it's Hozy!" rumbled Tim.

Jose it was. But not the same Jose whom they had last seen. He was naked as any wild man of the jungle: naked as the men pressing in at his back, none of whom had a rag of clothing save a narrow loin clout. His black hair and beard, which he had always kept scrupulously clean, now were dingy and matted with dirt, and half his face was smeared red from a gash on his forehead. But, despite his dirt and blood, notwithstanding his loss of clothing and kerchief and machete and knife, there was no mistaking his hawk face and his tigerish poise. And behind him showed the saturnine countenance of Pachac, his adopted father.

"Ho! It is the Senor Tim and — But quick, my friends, tell me! You have not eaten food given you by that woman Almagro — where is that foul corrupter? — you have not drunk of her cheer? Quick, senores, before it becomes too late!"

"Only some guayusa," answered Knowlton. "Make that gang of yours keep back!"

Without turning his head, Jose ripped out commands in Spanish and some Indian tongue. The men behind, who had been shoving to get past, stood still.

"And you feel alert, amigos? You feel no heaviness coming on you? No?"

"No."

"Bueno! Then you are safe. But lower the guns, friends — these are no enemies of yours. They are poor creatures much abused, who at last break free from the vilest slavery ever laid on men. All they now seek is the cruel cat who made them what they are. Si, and I, too, hunt her! Where is she?"

Knowlton, glancing sidelong toward Flora, found her still on the floor below the table top. But she was no longer leaning against the wall. Crouching, her poniard still lifted and menacing, she was creeping closer to the wooden bulwark between her and her foes, hiding from them and darting looks here and there like a cornered wild thing seeking a line of escape and finding none.

"Why?" curtly demanded McKay.

"Why?" echoed the naked outlaw, his voice strident. "Why? Use your eyes, Capitan McKay, and see! See what you, too, would have been in another day!"

He turned on his heel and grunted monosyllables at those behind. Then he walked before them to the middle of the room, eyed the still ready rifles and the hard faces above them, laughed harshly, and drew an imaginary deadline with one extended toe. Turning again, he extended his arms sidewise as a sign to his followers that none should advance beyond that line. Over one shoulder he jeered:

"Look at them, capitan – and see yourself in them! Are they not handsome?"

The captain and his companions looked. They saw men whom they recognized as members of the band of Pachac. They saw others, both white and brown, whose faces were new. And in those visages they found something that sent a chill crawling up their backs.

Many of those faces still were working with blood lust, many of the savage eyes were hot with unquenched thirst for revenge. But they were brutish, those countenances – the faces of men debased; and the eyes were those of animals – of dogs, of pigs, but not of men. Some of them were grimacing like caged lions; some grinned without mirth; more were sullen, sodden; and all, or nearly all, were well-nigh empty of human intelligence. Behind those leering masks dwelt darkened minds which responded to the commands of Jose only as the mentalities of broken beasts respond to the crack of a whip.

"Bestias," the woman had called them; and "bestias" they were. For that Spanish word means, not only "beast," but "idiot." These men were both.

Nor was that all. On the bare bodies shifting about were welts of slave whips – not only welts, but cruel scars years old. And among them moved some which stepped jerkily, as if partly crippled. As those short-stepping men came to the edge, where the lights struck them fair, the reason for their grotesque gait was revealed. Like Rafael Pardo, who had stumbled into Iquitos with madman's gold; like the unknown man speared in the back on the ridge trail, those men were

147

maimed — their toes amputated.

"Look at them!" Jose mocked again. "Look at the bodies that dared all hardships, to find such a fate! Look at the feet that carried them through savages and tigres and snakes — to this! Hah! And ask again why we must hunt the evil woman who did this thing!"

Once more he faced the four who had been his partners. His voice sank to a low, deadly level. His eyes roved from man to man, glittering with ruthless determination.

"Senores, you have been my friends. All — except perhaps you, McKay — still are my friends, if you wish. But we will have that woman, whether you protect her or not. If you try to block us we fight — and you die. In spite of your guns, your pistols, your many bullets, your steel — you die. We are too many and too near, and you cannot get us all before you go under. And if you die so, you die as fools.

"I cannot hold these tortured men from their vengeance on her if I would. And I will not try. We will avenge ourselves, and we will do it now. Decide quickly what you will do."

Every man of the four knew he spoke the cold truth. If his implacable tone had not driven home his inflexible decision, the sight of those lowering faces behind him would have confirmed it to the last degree. Yet the woman was a woman, and they would not hand over any woman, no matter what she might have done, to such a mob as that.

There was a tense pause. Then the outlaw's mouth twisted in a mirthless smile. He shifted his gaze toward his wives and their sisters, bunched behind the table and watching the parley without fear but with spellbound interest. He studied the gap between them and Knowlton, who was Number Four in the defensive line. He glanced at the girls. In answer to his unspoken question, one of them pointed downward at the hidden woman.

"So!" he said. "She is there, hiding her cowardly body, as I thought. Shoot if you will, you who were my friends. I go to whisper sweet words in her ear."

He dropped the rifle captured from the capataz, which he had been holding as a club. Empty-handed, he strode toward the spot where the woman crouched.

But he had no need to lean over the bulwark and look for her. As he lifted a foot for the last step she sprang up.

"Si! I am here, pig!" she screamed. "Take me — and take this with me!"

Like a striking snake she threw herself at him. Her poniard thrust for his throat.

**148**

Then it was that the outlaw's quickness, which more than once in the past had preserved his life, saved him once more. Swift as was her stab, his recoil was a shade swifter. In one backward leap he was four feet away, grinning like a snarling jungle cat. She fell forward on the upturned table edge, balked by the wood wall that had hidden her.

But hardly had she touched it when, with another lightning movement, she threw herself up and back on her feet. Her eyes blazed with insane fires.

"Live, then, animal!" she shrieked. "Here is one well-beloved, who goes to death with me!"

Like a flash she sprang at Knowlton, her Senor Gold Hair. Her upraised dagger darted for his heart.

"Come, my golden one — " she panted as she struck.

Instinctively the lieutenant sidestepped and snapped his rifle upward in a parry. The barrel caught her wrist and blocked its slanting swoop. In the next flashing instant she was seized from behind and hurled down.

The wives of Jose, daughters of a fighting chief who belted his waist with the hair of his foes, had leaped. Maddened by the stab at their man, they were jumping forward even as she turned to Knowlton. Now they were on her like tigresses, tearing at her face, twisting the poniard from her hand. Screams of hate echoed in the room.

As Jose and his band hurled themselves at the table, as the Americans surged forward, something bright and keen rose out of the knot of struggling women. Like a lightning flash it fell.

Slowly, still quivering with rage, the daughters of Pachac arose and stepped back.

Flora, the last of the Almagros, the jungle Circe who changed men to beasts with her terrible drink, the enslaver of the missing men of the Tigre Yacu, lay still, her own dagger buried to the hilt in her breast.

## XXIV. THE DEVIL'S BREW

For a long minute the big room of purple and gold was still. In the silence the only sounds were the breathing of men and the soft flutter of flames blown about in the gold lamps by a breeze stealing in at the loop holes.

Then three groups again became conscious of one another. The Americans looked up at the Indian girls whose explosion of fury had swept their tyrant into death. Then both men and women faced toward the staring creatures now hanging over the edge of the table.

Vague though the minds of those lost men might be, they

**149**

had no difficulty in grasping what they saw. Violent death being as old as life itself, perception and understanding of it is instinctive in all creatures. And these men still possessed eyes to see and instinct to interpret. Gazing down at the motionless figure, the blanched face, and the sinister handle jutting from the still bosom, they gradually drew back and let their clouded eyes rove among the gold vessels bestrewing the floor. The fight was done, the enemy dead, and their groping brains already were forgetful of it all.

One among them, besides Jose, seemed more alert — grim old Pachac, whose gaze rested watchfully on the Americans. Yet his face was hard set, as if it were an effort to concentrate his attention and hold it unwavering. The blight on the minds of the rest evidently had touched his also, but lightly. Among the whole crew the only one retaining full mental vigor was the indomitable son of the Conquistadores, Jose Martinez.

Now that outlaw did a strange thing. Over the body of the woman whom he had just sought in implacable vengefulness, over the poniard which had licked out at his throat a few minutes ago, he made the sign of the cross.

"Sea como Dios quiera," he said soberly. "As God wills, so let it be."

But there was no hint of regret or forgiveness in his tone, or in the face he turned first to his followers and then to his erstwhile partners of the Tigre Yacu.

The Americans had let their guns sink while they looked down on the woman. They did not lift them again. With the butts grounded, they looked pityingly at the hulking wrecks of manhood beyond the barrier.

Even McKay's iron face showed his feeling for those poor creatures, tortured, maimed, darkened in mind. For the moment he had forgotten Jose. And Jose, studying him, suddenly stepped toward him.

"Capitan," he said impulsively, "I have been a hot-headed fool."

McKay's gray eyes met his. McKay's set mouth softened.

"And I, Jose, have been a bull-headed jackass."

Their right hands shot across the barrier and gripped hard.

"That is a queer animal, capitan — a burro with a bull head," grinned the Peruvian. "And it has no right to live. So let it not come between us again."

"It won't."

The hands parted. Both men looked again at the human herd, and down at the quiet woman on the floor.

"Does this end it, Jose?" asked Rand, nodding down at her.

**150**

"This ends it, comrades. Unless some of those slave-driving Indios outside escaped — and I do not think it — this whole nest of devils is cleaned. Now we have more cleaning to do: to clean this room and the yard and ourselves. Whether we can clean the minds of these poor people I do not know, but we can clean our bodies, and it shall be done. Then there will be a tale to tell."

"Then let's be at it," said Knowlton, wrinkling his nose at the rank smell filling the room. "You clean up outside and we'll fix up here. And for humanity's sake give this crowd a bath."

"It is not their fault, Senor Knowlton. Wait until you see the sty they were forced to herd in, poor devils! Si, and I with them    I am one of them, except that my brain is clear. And that it is clear I owe not to myself but to Huarma, one of my brides — the tallest one, yonder. But of that you shall hear later."

He touched Pachac on the shoulder and muttered something. The chief's face relaxed, as if it were a relief to have no longer to try to think, and he turned docilely to follow the lead of his stalwart foster-son. Jose's voice began to snap in commands, and his hand pointed toward the corridor. At once the listless, aimless crowd became alive and began to press out of the room. The Peruvian followed them up, rounding up stragglers, knocking a gold cup out of one man's hand, shaking to his feet another who had lain down on the floor and closed his eyes. Last of all, he and Pachac passed out, side by side.

The Indian girls had drawn away from the table now and stood grouped at the rear doorway, seeming a little afraid of the bearded men but not in the least awed by the realization of what they had done to their mistress. The Americans gave them no further attention.

Leaning their guns against the wall, they moved out the table and swung it back on its legs. Rand and Tim stooped and lifted the quiet form from the floor. Up on the board they laid her, and just below the hilt of the poniard they crossed the hands which had sought to wield it in death strokes when, brought to bay by the beasts she had made, she thought to take with her the leader of the pack or the stranger on whom her sensuous fancy had settled.

Then, moving about the room, the four gathered up the scattered cups and ornaments and the big bowl which, with its venomed liquor, had been thrown over by the upturning of the table. These they placed around her, the bowl inverted at her head, the cups and heavy ornaments down the sides in

**151**

gleaming array. When this was done they puled from the wall a long section of the achote-dyed hangings, and this they stretched along over the table top. Then they picked up their rifles and moved over toward the door.

What they could do they had done. On the dim side of the room the last of the Almagros now rested under a purple shroud, surrounded by the gold with which she had sought to betray four more men into hopeless misery worse than death. And the men, keenly alert, were masters of her house and about to explore its secrets.

McKay paused and glanced around.

"Better leave one man here," he decided.

"What for?" wondered Knowlton. "Nothing to guard against in this room."

"Maybe. But a knife is a knife — gold is gold."

Rand nodded. The girls still stood as if waiting for them to withdraw. And the captain was determined that there should be no pilfering from that shrouded table.

"I'll stay," he volunteered. "Go ahead."

He stepped back to the couch and sat down. The others lifted lamps from the brackets and went out.

In the corridor they found the big double entrance door standing wide, gaping vacantly at the moonlit yard, whence sounded the shuffle of bare feet and occasional orders from Jose. Along the passage other doors, all closed, showed in the soft lamplight. Nowhere was any staircase. The living quarters in this broad, low house were all on one floor.

McKay flung open the nearest door, advanced his lamp, and looked around. Then he stepped back.

"This is her room," he said. "Bring her in here."

The other pair complied. Back to the table they went, and slowly they returned, bearing with them the shrouded figure. While the captain lighted the way they took her to a great canopied bed and laid her down. Then they drew the purple curtains and left her in her last sleep.

Though they glanced around the room, they did not linger. Their roving eyes took in the lines of the high bed, various massive articles of furniture evidently built from some cabinet wood cut in the surrounding jungle, a number of old tapestries about the walls, and numerous gold ornaments carelessly strewn about on stands and drawer chests. There was no sign of occupancy of the room by any person other than the woman who now lay there.

Passing out, they shut the door firmly behind them and looked steadily at the Indian girls, who had come into the
**152**

corridor. Then McKay addressed Rand, who had followed them.

"All right, Dave. Come along. This shut door is all the guard needed here."

He judged rightly. As he and his companions turned down the hall, the girls moved to the outer entrance. Covet the shining trinkets though they might, they would not venture to open that portal beyond which waited darkness and death.

From room to room the men worked their way, wrestling with doors which stubbornly resisted, though none had a lock to hold it barred against inspection. Each time, after shoving and prying the wooden barrier open, they found that the difficulty was due to the sagging or warping of the door, indicating long disuse. And each time when they penetrated beyond it they found the room musty and dingy, its furnishings mouldy, and its weapons – for there were old weapons in some of them – coated thick with rust and spider webs. Bats veered out into the corridor or swirled around the walls, and countless shells of long-dead beetles and other insects crackled under foot. Everything told the same tale: here once had lived a large family which now was gone.

Not all the rooms, however, were so hard of access or filled with decay. A few showed signs of fairly recent tenancy, and one wide chamber obviously formed the quarters of the daughters of Pachac. Except this one, however, none gave indications that it was still being used for sleeping purposes. The others seemed to be occasional guest rooms. The eyes of the explorers narrowed as they surmised where the "guests" had gone.

At length they found themselves in a lighted room undoubtedly used as the kitchen. There, among other things, they found the gold bowl which still held guayusa, now cooled, and a long shelf filled with tall square-sided clay bottles, tightly corked with wooden plugs. One of these had been taken from the shelf and stood beside the bowl. Lifting and shaking it, Rand heard the telltale gurgle showing that some of its contents had been poured out. Its plug came out easily – in fact, it was still damp. He poured some of the liquid into one hand.

"Looks like tea," he said.

"Sleep tea, undoubtedly," Knowlton suggested.

Tim agreed. "That's the stuff that destroys your brain. Look at the line-up of it on the shelf, will you? Looks like a jungle blind-tiger, with the square-face bottles and all. She kept enough on hand to make a hundred idiots a day, if it

**153**

works quick!"

"Must work quick," McKay declared. "Pachac's people haven't been here long. And look at them now."

"Wonder what became of the women and children," said Rand. "We 've only seen men."

"I'm wondering about quite a number of things," added Knowlton. "Jose will straighten things up, perhaps. Come on, let's find him."

Passing through a smaller room, which seemed to have been recently used for lounging and dining, they entered again the great main hall where they had been entertained. It was empty of life. As they stepped into the corridor, intending to leave the house and explore the yards, the lean figure of Jose stalked in at the moonlit doorway. Behind him came Pachac, and after them more of the brainless crew swung into sight.

"Ha, amigos! At last Jose is himself again — without a shirt or a knife, it is true, but clean from hair to heel. Por Dios, what a difference water makes in a man! And all this crowd behind have become men instead of pigs, though it took much scrubbing. Now the women have been set free and take their turn at the bath. What have you found here? You have searched, yes?"

"Nothing but rust and spider webs — and bottles of brain killer," Knowlton told him.

"That devil-broth — it shall be thrown over the walls! But come, let us sit — and, por amor de Dios, give me a cigarette! I have had no smoke for years."

They entered the big room, where, even as he snatched the proffered tobacco and papers, he glanced about in search for Flora Almagro. Rand pointed a thumb backward across the hall. Jose nodded.

"Years?" echoed McKay.

"Years, capitan. Time is measured by life, not by suns. A man may live years in a week, or only a week in years. Is it not true? And I have been in this place for years, though it is hardly two weeks since I came. Ah-h-h!"

He gulped smoke into his lungs and exhaled rapturously.

Behind him the men who had been slaves came slowly sifting into the room. As their leader said, they once more were men, clean from scalp to sole, their skins glowing from the strenuous ablutions that they had given themselves; and somehow they seemed to stand the straighter now, to look a little more alive, as if that bathing had refreshed brain as well as body.

**154**

Yet, though they no longer were driven beasts, one glance at them showed that their minds still were fettered in a black bondage.

As they pressed in and spread out like an aimlessly flowing stream, the five reunited partners watched them soberly. Jose sadly shook his head.

"My people," he said. "The people who followed me into this, as well as those who came before me. And you too, senores, would have been spared much if you had never joined Jose Martinez at the mouth of the Tigre Yacu. I have a heavy task before me, friends – to clean the minds of these men as I have cleaned their bodies. I hope it can be done, but only my wife Huarma can do it."

"How?" puzzled Knowlton.

"She is wise in the ways of herbs and drugs. Though very young, she is the medicine woman of her people. And what one evil leaf has done, another good leaf may undo. We shall see."

"You mean to say that all these men were robbed of their brains by a jungle herb?" demanded Rand.

"I do, Senor Dave. You have heard of the floripondio?"

Blank faces answered him.

"You have not. Be thankful that you have none of it within you now. If you had, you soon would know more of it than words can tell.

"I am not a medico or a droguero – one skilled in drugs – but I know of that devil-weed, for I have heard of it from men of the Napo country. Up that Rio Napo – and in other places, too, no doubt – it is sometimes given a man by his woman when she tires of him and wants another; and he becomes an imbecile who will be the slave of that woman and of her new love, not knowing what he does.

"It is steeped like a tea, that is all; made like the guayusa. But where the guayusa drives weariness from the most tired man and makes him keen, the floripondio deadens the brain of the strongest. Put into food or drink, it soon does its deadly work without the man knowing what is paralyzing his mind. Then he is lost.

"So, friends, that is the reason why the missing men of the Tigre have not come back. That is the reason why you now see those who are before you turned to animals. Only a little leaf of the jungle, plucked and put into water – cooked by the same fire that warms innocent food – and then used by human fiends to wreck the reason of Memen!"

155

## XXV. PHANTOM TREASURE

The missing men of the Tigre and their new comrades in misfortune, the men of Pachac, stood for a time looking dully about them. Then, as if by simultaneous tacit consent, they lay down on the floor and disposed themselves for rest. Uncovered, unbedded, they relaxed and closed their eyes like men long inured to nothing better. Only Pachac himself still stood, pathetically dependent on the brain of his new son.

"Tired, yes," nodded Jose. "They have worked under the lash since sunrise, they have fought hard tonight. So have I. But my mind is not burdened like theirs, and it will not yet allow me to rest. Let us sit, comrades, and – "

A fresh padding of feet in the corridor interrupted him. In at the door flocked women and children, led by the daughters of the chief; the weaker portion of the white Indian tribe. Scanning them, the five partners saw at once that the curse of the floripondio had not been put on their minds. Their eyes darted eagerly about in search for husbands, brothers, fathers. Having found their men, they ran to them; then sank silently down at their sides without disturbing their rest.

The outlaw's sober face lightened.

"That will help much," he declared. "With the women to follow the orders of Huarma and care for their men, much may be done. I have not seen them since the accursed drug was put on us, and I feared that they, too, were darkened in mind."

He spoke to the tallest of his brides – the one who, he had said, was Huarma, the medicine woman. With dignity worthy of her father, yet with due deference to her hawk-faced lord, she responded. He nodded again.

"The women and children," he explained, "have been used as slaves on the plantation, which lies back among the trees to the west. The woman Almagro thought it not worth her trouble to drug them – she knew they dared not try to escape without their men. Is it not true, senores, that human fiends always are tripped at last by something they have left undone? If that woman had not held in contempt the women of Pachac, and in particular the daughters of Pachac, we should not now be here, nor would she by lying dead across the corridor. But now that we are all together once more, let us speak of what has been and what may be."

He dropped his cigarette stub, eyed the table, and, with a grin, strode to it. Shoving the big upturned bowl to the middle

156

of the board, he swung himself up and squatted on its broad yellow base. Then he beckoned with both hands to his wives and their sisters and father. Laughingly they approached and ranged themselves along the table edge, placing their parent in the middle. The Americans smiled as they contemplated the scene.

"Hozy, old-timer," grinned Tim, "you look like a — like a — "

"Barbarian," chuckled Rand.

The metaphor was not bad. Seated on a golden throne, with his foster father at his feet staring owlishly outward; with his comely women lined at his sides and his people prostrate before him; with the royal purple lining the walls of the spacious hall, the barc-flamed gold lamps glowing, and the jungle moon slanting its white beams in at the narrow openings behind — Jose Martinez, man without a country, naked and fiercely bearded, looked to be the truculent ruler of some forgotten kingdom resurrected from prehistoric time. And here in this untamed land, where the rise and fall of nations and the passage of centuries meant nothing at all, he truly was a king; for in his sinewy hand rested whatever power existed.

Now his gaunt face cracked wide, and he seized an empty gold cup and held it aloft in a grotesquely dramatic gesture.

"Dios guarde al rey!" he cackled. "God save the king! But of what good is it to be king when one cannot drink his own health? Tomorrow, my ambassadors from North America, we must search our royal cellar for wine not doctored. Then our treasure shall be doubled, for if we drink enough we can see two bars of gold where only one was. Hah!"

"What's that? Bars of gold? Where?" demanded McKay.

"Where? Where but here, capitan? Why do you think all these men have been held slaves, robbed of brains, driven with whips? For what, but to work in the mine?"

"Great guns! You mean that? What mine?"

"The mine of gold in the mountain to the rear. Si! Gold! The gold of mad Rafael Pardo! Hah! You are astonished, yes? You believed, as I did, the wail of the woman that the mine was destroyed? She sang you that same song, and you have not had time to think why these men were — "

He stopped short and sprang up, suddenly pale. The others, too, except the sleeping men, lost color and staggered. The solid floor had quivered under them.

From the cordon of mountains outside sounded a low rumbling growl. Again the floor shuddered slightly. Then all was still.

157

"Once more the temblor!" breathed Jose, his eyes darting about the walls. "Once more the ground shivers. But it is past — until it comes again. And these solid old walls have stood worse shocks, no doubt. Let us forget it."

Yet the gleam was gone from his eyes and the ring from his voice as he went on, and the sudden fire that had swept the veins of the Americans at the magic words "gold mine" had as swiftly cooled. Each felt the hand of an awful power hovering over the house, able, at its brute whim, to crush it and its occupants into jumbled stones and mangled corpses.

"Gold is here, amigos," said Jose. "And it is ours. But let us start at the beginning. First tell me how you came here, and what happened before and after."

He sat again on his yellow throne, and the four disposed themselves as comfortably as might be on the long couch. To stand would not help them if another quake came.

Briefly Knowlton detailed the happenings since Jose had turned his back on them at the lake of the burning sands. As the minutes passed and no further sound came from the mountains, all forgot the recent ground tremble. And when the tale was done the Peruvian's face again was alight with interest.

"So that was the heavy blow we earth rats felt this afternoon — the falling of the trail along the cliff. We felt the temblor, too, down there in our hole — si, it sickened us! — but what the blow meant we did not know. Nor did I know, until this moment, of that shelf along the rock. We came in by another way."

"Then there's a way out?"

"There is one — there may be others. We shall see. But when the rains fall hard, as they soon will, that way will be closed by water. We came in here, senores, through the ground!

"Si, es verdad; it is true. My father Pachac knew that way, and told me of no other. We came as he directed. We left the path at a watery ravine, going up in the water and killing our trail. And after wading far we followed Pachac, who went over the hills to more water, and so to here.

"If you looked about you today, you must have seen that this place is a gulf among mountains. And if it had no outlet, when the rains came they would fill it up, and it would be a lake. Yet it is dry and firm — why? Because at one place near its middle there is a hole, and that hole runs away under the earth to the other side of a mountain to the south, and through it all the rain streams run out. It has not much water now, and we came in along its bed without much trouble — though it was a long, black journey, and I had to club snakes to death as I advanced."

Thus the mystery of the vanishing trail of Pachac and his people was explained. The Americans made no comment. Jose went on.

"Now this is the tale of this place, and of the family of Almagro, as my Padre Pachac knows it:

"Long ago, before Pachac was born, and while his father's father was a very young warrior, there came from somewhere to the north a band of hard-fighting men who seemed all of the same family. They came as if seeking a place where they would not be found by some one or something they had left behind them — not fleeing, but always watching toward the rear. And they brought, besides themselves, their women and slaves, the women dressed and armed like men, and the slaves carrying burdens.

"They found this gulf among the mountains, which then was much easier to enter than now, for into it led a narrow twisting canyon. And they had no more than come into it when they spied gold — a yellow splash of it on bare rock, plain to any eye. So here they stayed.

"Not long after they came, another band, much bigger, without women, also came from the north as if hunting them. But the heavy rains were now beginning, and the waters rushing from every side not only swept away all trace of the Almagro trail but discouraged and drove away the pursuers. They never returned.

"The Almagro family made their Indians work on the walls and on the gold. They were hard masters, and the Indians died out. Then the Almagros went out into the jungle round about, and with their guns they killed chiefs and made slaves of their people. These, too, they worked to death in their mine — men and women and children, all were driven like cattle until they died.

"This went on for years, and much gold was taken out, but the family stayed on. The older Almagros died, and the younger ones also grew old and died; but the gold still was there. Earthquakes came and closed up the entrance canyon and wrecked the mine; but they opened up their gold hole again and kept burrowing. Yet, the more gold they got, the slower the work went and the weaker they grew.

"Two things made this so: they could not get enough Indians now, because the Indians either moved too far away or were too strong for them; and they would not mate with

**159**

Indians and keep their family big. They mated among themselves, brother with sister, and most of the children died young or were dull of brain. Some were killed by Indians, some by earthquakes, some by snakes or other jungle things. The family grew very small: too small to be able to leave the place. They knew the Jiveros would get them.

"Then, from trying to enslave Indians by force, they began buying prisoners from those Indians. With the Jiveros they could do nothing, but with other Indians they arranged trades. Whatever prisoners they could buy they took, paying with gold, which the Indians could trade out by crossing to the Curaray and then journeying down to the Napo.

"Pachac, and his father before him, knew of this trade in prisoners, but had nothing to do with it. They were wanderers, lived too far down the Tigre to make the trade profitable, did not want the white men's goods, and would rather kill their enemies than sell them. But when Pachac's half-Spanish son grew up he had different ideas. He wanted guns and cartridges, and Pachac let him keep prisoners and send them here. So that, amigos, was what was meant when we were told we should go to the wheel."

"What is the wheel?" queried Rand.

"It is a thing made to crush ore, and a man killer. In some ways it is like the trapiche sugar mill used in the Andes, which is worked by cattle going around and around. Here, men are the cattle. Many a poor slave must have worn out his life on the infernal thing."

"What's that big bell outside for?" Knowlton asked.

"What it was used for at first, or where it came from, I cannot tell you. I know only the tale as it is told me by Pachac. But now it has been used to call in the men from the mine. I suppose that if an Indian attack should come it would be rung at any time, but since I have been here it has rung only at night, after a day without end — a day of horrible toil.

"We were herded in a foul pen behind here, with stout gates which no man could pass. The pen opens into a walled passage leading into the mine. A rotten breakfast at daybreak — a day of torture under the whips of those unfeeling Zaparo brutes we killed tonight — another rotten meal after dark — a night sleeping on the filthy stones of our pen — then back to more labor. That is the life here.

"Men who have tried to escape were maimed so that they were not likely to travel far again — their toes cut off. Some of them now lie here in this room. One — Rafael Pardo — reached Iquitos as you know. And you say another was killed by green

160

men above? So some did try again — perhaps the floripondio was weak at times and men grew cunning and desperate for a while.

"But I think that accursed drug was put into the food at certain times to keep the men always dull of brain. I think, too, that the use of it was an idea of the woman Flora and not of her fathers — though I do not know that to be so. But Huarma, my wife, saw that woman of evil putting it into food after we men had been sent to the pen, so I know it was given us at times."

"How did you dodge it?" Tim wondered.

"I did not dodge it, Senor Tim. The woman betrayed us all. We knew nothing of her devil brew, and when she received us in friendly manner and gave us food and drink we took it gladly — and awoke in the morning unable to think and covered by the guns of those slave drivers — guns taken from men who had won through to this place before us and then had been made idiots.

"But Huarma, chosen as one of the house slaves, spied and learned what the thing was that had made us beasts. Then she told women sent to the plantation to find for her a certain herb — I do not know what — it is one of the medicine secrets of her people. This she brought to me at night, with clean food and drink, though she would have died if the guards had caught her. Night after night she came, and my mind grew keen, and our father's dullness, too, was partly cleared away — she had not enough medicine for us both, and she gave me the best of it. But she warned me to keep playing fool until her chance should come to open our gate and let me lead an attack. Tonight that chance came."

"A real woman, I'll tell the world!" admired Tim. "But where's all this gold you brag about?"

Jose arose, stretching his long arms wide, a triumphant grin lighting his face.

"Come and see, comrades — partners! It is put every noon into a vault — the pure gold which has been melted into bars. The guards alone handle it, but I know where it goes: in at a door in the wall near the mine entrance. There must be a huge room there in the side of the mountain, piled with the gold of four lifetimes. Come!"

They came. Out into the moonlight, down a yard where the stones still glistened redly and bodies lay piled beside the wall, they followed him. On into a patio where shone a deep pool of water — evidently the bathing place of the Almagros — and through a ruined gate like that of a prison yard; across a walled

**161**

space whose fetid odor told that it was the slave pen, they strode. There, after hauling open another solid gate, they entered a long runway terminating in a black tunnel. At the tunnel mouth their guide paused.

At his right showed a stout door, set in the wall and heavily barred.

"Hah!" he exulted. "Here lies the treasure of the Almagros! After all their crime and cruelty it goes to a slave, and to his comrades who tomorrow might also have been slaves. If you would use your gold, you Almagros, reach out now from the fires where you roast, and snatch it to buy a drop of water from your master, the devil! We come to take it from you. Ho, ho, ho!"

He tugged at a bar, which slid with an ease telling of constant use. Eager hands forced the other bars away. The door swung open.

Holding aloft the lamps they had brought, the four stepped in and stared about. For a moment they stood speechless.

"Cristo!" Jose spat then. "What demon's work is this?"

They saw a stone-walled, stone-roofed, stone-floored cell not more than twenty feet square. They saw nothing else.

The vault was empty.

## XXVI. THE HEAD-HUNTERS

Days passed.

Days of work, they were; days of striving to restore the drug-deadened minds of the former slaves to their one-time vigor; days of search for the vanished treasure of the Almagros, of exploration and critical examination of the mine. And each was followed by an evening of discouraged discussion.

Far more success was achieved with minds than with mines. Under the skillful treatment of Huarma the men of Pachac steadily shed the incubus of brain blight, awaking each morning with clearer eyes and quicker wits. Pachac himself, whose curative treatment at the hands of his daughter had begun while he still was a fellow-slave of Jose, now was wholly himself again, though gloomy in spirit because he had lost his most cherished possession – the gruesome girdle woven from the hair of his slain enemies. At some time during his term of bondage it had been cut off him by a guard who found that it served as a protection against whip blows, and now it could not be found despite the most persistent search.

But the survivors of the Tigre's missing men, who had been here long before the coming of Jose and his tribe, showed little response to the ministrations of the youthful medicine

162

woman. Their brains had been permeated for months, or years, by the terrible floripondio; and it was useless to expect a speedy revival of their mental faculties. True, they seemed a trifle less brutish, and in time they might regain full control of themselves. But for the present they gave little indication that they would ever again be the men they had been.

They were kept at work, those witless creatures, both for their own good and for the benefit of the community; but not at their former tasks in the mine. First they and the reviving warriors of Pachac were divided into squads which dug graves on the hillsides beyond the walls; and there Flora Almagro and the men of both sides who had fallen on that red night of revolt were buried deep. Then they were turned to cleaning up the house and its yard, making the mouldy old rooms again habitable and the former slave pen fit to traverse. After that the Pachac men were set by their chief at making new weapons, while the others were drawn off to work with the women on the plantation — light labor which gave them the fresh air and clean sunlight of which they had been so long robbed in the gloomy mine holes.

For the present, the mine was deserted by all except the restless five adventurers, who, after a thorough inspection, also left it and returned to their first search — for the Almagro wealth. Their examination showed that the mine was practically worked out. Some gold yet remained, but what was in sight made the inspectors shake their heads; and the place was so honeycombed with shafts and tunnels as to show that the mountain not only was virtually looted of its treasure but absolutely unsafe to work in. An unusually sharp earth shock would probably cause it to crumple on itself, crushing the mine into nothing. And in the past few days several more slight quakes already had occurred.

Yet the pinching vein of yellow in the mine was all the gold they found. Hunt high, hunt low, not one bar out of the tons which must have come from it could be discovered.

They ransacked house, yards, and even the mine itself for some trace. They pounded walls and floors, listening for hollow sounds. They swam about in the bathing pool, hunting under water. In only one place did they find sign that gold had ever lain. That was on the stone floor of the vault where, Jose swore, he had seen bars taken in at noon.

That floor bore out his assertion. Between its stones were many grains of the metal, evidently chipped from the bars by rough edges and corners of the rock. But where it had gone, and how, no man could tell, though all sorts of wild guesses were made.

"I wish we had saved one of those slave drivers as a prisoner that night," Jose regretted. "He could be made to tell things, perhaps. But then there was neither time nor reason to think of anything but killing. And now — dead men tell no tales."

They were standing at the tunnel mouth as they talked, the hot afternoon sun glaring down on one side, the dark empty mine yawning at them on the other. Along the walled passage leading from mine to pen no other figure moved. Somewhere up in the yards Pachac and his men were lazily working away at the manufacture of their new weapons. Out on the plantation, well away from the walls, the women and their male assistants were toiling as they pleased. Within the house the chief's daughters were busy at various occupations. For several days even the distant menace of Jivero signal drums had been stilled. All was peace. Yet, from force of habit, each of the partners was carrying his gun.

"Well," said Knowlton, as they turned toward the house, "it doesn't get us anything to keep coming back and mooning around this vault like a bunch of kids who have lost their baseball. The stuff's gone somewhere, and we've looked everywhere. The only thing left is to take this whole place apart stone by stone, and that would use up a few years of time. Guess we'd do better to scout around these hills and locate a new mine."

"The pot of gold was at the end of the rainbow, but somebody's moved the pot," nodded Rand. "Or maybe the rainbow's moved. Either way, it's up to us to move also, unless something develops soon."

He glanced around at the mountain tops looming beyond the wall. Jose followed his look.

"I doubt, Senor Dave, if you will find gold anywhere else in this valley," he said. "Remember, the Almagros were here many years. If more gold were here they would have smelled it out long ago."

"Sure. But there's a whole cordillera along here for us to browse in. Say, do you keep feeling as if these mountains were watching you — hostile — ready to jump on your back?"

"Always," the outlaw admitted. "Perhaps those Almagros felt it, too, and built these walls more to make them feel safe than to shut out the savages."

"Made them thick enough, anyway," said Tim. "You could run a tunnel right through them from end to end, and nobody'd know it was there."

McKay stopped short. His eyes ranged along one of the

**164**

walls – the one in which the door of that empty vault was set.

"By George!" he exclaimed. "Tim, I'll bet you've hit it. Secret passage in the wall from that vault to – some place under ground, maybe. We'll rip a hole in this wall and find out. What say, Jose?"

"Por Dios! Capitan, it may be – But no. We have tested the stones in that vault and found no entrance. Of what use would be a tunnel ending in a solid wall?"

"True. But there's something, somewhere, that we haven't found. I want a breach made in this wall, just to – "

"Hark!" Rand cut in.

Across the gulf, thin and high, echoed a scream.

It was the cry of a fear-stricken woman. It came from the direction of the plantation. It swelled from one isolated note of fright to the voices of other women breaking out in mortal terror.

"Demonio!" Jose cried sharply. "The women of Pachac do not scream unless the devil himself is after them!"

He darted away toward the yards. The others dashed after him.

As they ran, they heard the outcries coming nearer. Then the screams died down, the women needing all their breath for running. But from the yards where Pachac and his men lounged now rose a new uproar – a harsh outbreak of surprise and rage. Then, high over all, sounded another appalling note from the plantation.

It was the awful death yell of a man.

Through the old slave pen, through the patio with its quiet pool, and into the long yard beside the house ran Jose and his comrades. That yard now was empty; for Pachac and his warriors had plunged through the big open gateway, and their yells of wrathful defiance roared outside the walls. Jose tore on around the corner to join them, his swarthy face contracted into a fighting mask. But the Americans, with McKay in the lead, lunged straight at the wall.

There rose a crude ladder, lashed to the rough scaffolding which they had noticed on their first arrival: one of several short stair flights by which defenders could man the walls in haste. Up this swarmed the captain and the following three. Hardly had McKay jumped into position against the upper stones when his rifle began to crack. In rapid succession the other guns added their wicked voices in a chorus of death.

Streaming toward them, close at hand now, they saw the panting women, throwing themselves up the hill toward safety. Close behind, their paint-streaked faces grinning in mingled

**165**

ferocity and triumph, bounded warriors of the Jiveros.

The dreaded drums at the west, which a few days ago had muttered back and forth, had not been merely grumbling among themselves over the killing of an ambushed band by the men of Pachac back on the Tigre. The ensuing silence had not meant peace. Now the vengeful killers from the Pastassa were here to gain heads and women, and to destroy this stronghold which for generations had repulsed their fathers.

And the big gate was open, nearly all the defenders outside, and their women prizes almost within reach of their clutching hands.

But the hands of those foremost pursuers closed, not on the flying hair or bare shoulders of their prey, but in death-clawings at the ground. From their elevated platform the four gunmen stabbed flame and death downward. From the gate the roar of Jose's repeater broke out. From the disordered ranks of the men of Pachac a ragged flight of arrows whirred.

The sudden storm of lead and of five-foot shafts struck the nearest Jiveros to earth. Warriors collapsed, pitched headlong, kicked, rolled, were still. Others, disconcerted by the abrupt belch of death from walls which a moment ago had been empty, slowed to fit arrows to their bows. But behind them a thick stream of other savages came pouring across the bowl and up the slope. The rush was checked for only an instant.

Between shots Tim gasped, "There's a regular army of the hellions!"

The women reached the gate and reeled within, eyes glazed with terror and lungs gasping for breath. The Americans clattered their breech bolts without raising fresh cartridges. Their magazines were shot out — and the extra ammunition was inside the house.

"Jose!" roared McKay. "Inside, quick! Inside!"

Another defiant blast from the outlaw's gun drowned the command. An ululation of rage from the men of Pachac followed. Outnumbered though they were, they were seeing red and thirsting to close with their hereditary foes.

"God!" gritted McKay. "It'll be a massacre! Hold them, men! Hold them with your sidearms!"

He dropped his rifle, leaped down into the yard, sprinted for the gate. The three remaining on the wall unholstered their forty-fives and again opened on the enemy. The ripping roar of the big pistols, the impact of the heavy bullets among them, again slowed the Jiveros in the van, but did not stop them — except those hit, who were stopped forever. The others, though they flinched and batted their eyes at each recurrent

**166**

crash, loosed a retaliating storm of arrows. And they came on.

The deadly shafts splintered against the walls, hurtled overhead, hissed between the pistol fighters. Too, they plunged into the unbulwarked white Indians. Several of Pachac's men dropped, writhing.

Out on their rear now raced McKay with pistol drawn. In three bounds he was beside Jose and Pachac. His gun and his voice broke out together — the weapon hurling lead at the oncoming savages, the commands striking Jose like blows.

"Inside! Jump — you — damned idiot! Inside!"

Jose jumped. For once he had forgotten that, as fight commander of this gang, he must govern them — he had reverted to the lone fierce jungle rover fighting against odds, thinking only of killing as long as he could. McKay's voice brought him to his senses. He lunged at his men, cursing, shoving, hitting, propelling them in through the wall.

The Indians themselves were sobered a little by the fall of their kinsmen under the Jivero arrows. Under the crackling orders of Jose and the weight of his fist and foot they gave way, turned, and sprang for cover. But they took all their dead with them, and their wounded, too, though the stricken men still living would not live long with the poison of those arrows in their veins. No Jivero should take a head from them until the whole tribe of Pachac was down.

Last of all, McKay and Jose backed in, dodging javelins thrown by Jiveros leaping toward them. As the massive gate was heaved shut the firing ended. The pistols of the three above were empty.

An instant later the Jiveros struck the gate and the walls.

## XXVII. THE MOUNTAINS SPEAK

Later on, the survivors of this battle were to learn that only a wandering woman, seeking herbs in the forest beyond the plantation, had prevented a complete surprise of the Almagro ortress and a wholesale massacre of its men.

She had spied the first of the Jiveros slipping along through he jungle, creeping toward the house. Screaming, she had fled with the speed of mortal fear, first to the plantation and then toward the protecting walls, her sisters dashing after her. Thanks to their frenzied swiftness and the devastating gunfire, they all reached cover.

But the dull-brained men working with them on the plantation died. Whether they failed to grasp their peril and tood blankly gaping until the Jiveros were upon them, whether a sudden flare of manhood prompted them to leap at

**167**

the savages and attempt to protect the retreat of the women, will never be known. But none of them lived to move far from the spot where he was standing when the alarm broke out.

Now Knowlton and Rand and Tim, standing a few seconds longer at the wall after emptying their pistols, glanced around at a horde of rushing savages grimacing at them in fury howling a jungle hymn of hate, brandishing aloft the ghastly trophies chopped from those missing men of the Tigre who would never go out again. The sight of those severed heads and of the vindictive triumph in the faces of the wild men exhibiting them both sickened and infuriated the Americans. They threw their pistols into aim once more, then remembered their uselessness.

"Got to get more shells!" rasped Tim. "And then, you bloody butchers – then!"

He stooped and seized McKay's abandoned rifle prepara· tory to sliding down the ladder. As he did so an arrow impaled his hat and knocked it into the yards, the shaft hurtling on and slithering up and over the house roof. Others whizzed around Rand and Knowlton, who ducked and dropped to the yard below. A gloating yell swelled from outside, the bowmen believing the quick disappearance due to hits.

The three sprinted for the door, Tim passing McKay's gun to him on the run as they plunged inside. The captain clutched it automatically, his whole mind busy with the urgent problem of bringing order out of chaos, whipping the disordered rabble into an efficient fighting force. And a problem it was; for these men, little less wild than the ravening Jiveros outside, knew only one style of fighting – the slipping, dodging combat of the thick bush, the jungle animal method of grappling with a foe and dispatching him – and now that they found themselves cooped within white men's walls they hardly knew how to make use of themselves.

Those few who had been trained in rifle work by the dead Spanish-Indian son of Pachac were useless now as gunmen, for though the guns of the conquered slave drivers were at hand there were hardly any cartridges of that caliber – Jose himself had only a handful left for his own rifle. The others, though equipped with their new arrows and spears and clubs, had no poison with which to smear the points of the missiles and no chance to use the bludgeons. All were in a fever to meet their foes instanter, but none acted in cohesion with the rest.

Some shot arrows or hurled spears upward at random hoping to hit enemies outside by pure luck. Others scrambled to the fighting runway overhead, stood still while they loosed

**168**

at the Jiveros, and were swept down to death by counterflights of venomed shafts. A few even sought to reopen the big gate and jump out with spear or club. The whole yard was a furore of blundering action.

Jose himself, though struggling furiously to get his men in hand, hardly knew what he wanted to do with them. He, too, was a jungle fighter, not a soldier. And McKay, who saw that these raging warriors would never consent to herd themselves inside the house and do their battling through narrow slits, could not impress on their hot minds the only other expedient — to carry on a running skirmish along the walls. Nor could he get Jose, assailing his own men with fist and foot and lurid language, to listen to his roaring counsel. And Pachac, his teeth gritting in impotent craving to bludgeon some Jivero with a huge club gripped in his knotty fists, was neither able nor willing to understand the trained soldier.

The reappearance of his own comrades, their pockets and shirt fronts crammed with the reserve ammunition, was a godsend to the captain. Mechanically accepting a hatful of mingled rifle and pistol cartridges shoved at him by Knowlton, he yelled:

"Up on the walls! Merry, left wall — Dave right — Tim front! Shoot, duck, run, shoot! Up and at 'em!"

The three jumped for their respective walls. But each halted and threw up his reloaded rifle. Atop the stonework, hands and heads were appearing — heads of warriors who had scaled up on the shoulders of others and now were heaving themselves inward like old-time pirates clambering over the bulwarks of a fighting prize.

For a few seconds the yard roared with the rattle of gunfire. The heads flopped backward and were gone. The Americans reloaded and again ran for their stations.

By the time they had scaled the ladders more heads were rising across the stones. Each swiftly shot his own sector clear, then ducked to evade a hail of missiles hurled by Jiveros farther out. They crawled a yard or two, then popped up and slammed a few bullets into the enemy before sinking and moving on a little farther.

The renewed rip of the guns and the up-and-down-and-over tactics of the gunmen had drawn the eyes of every white Indian. Now, with their example plain before all, McKay hammered home his plan of battle.

"Jose!" he bellowed, his voice booming through the ferine chorus from outside. "Divide forces! Man the walls! Make your men keep moving! Like that!"

169

His rifle swept around, indicating the dodging three who were shooting down the enemy while keeping themselves protected.

"Keep them moving!" he repeated. "Or they'll be killed like those!" And he pointed to the corpses of Indians who had stood still long enough to become targets.

This time Jose listened, saw, understood. At once he began driving the idea into the head of Pachac. That veteran, after viewing again the way the three riflemen were working, put the plan into effect at once.

The warriors, whom neither Jose nor McKay had been able to handle, caught the idea quickly when their chief howled it at them, and sprang with alacrity to the sides pointed out. This moving, sliding method of warfare was not, after all, much different from bush fighting, except that it was carried on along a narrow wall path, above ground and behind a stone barrier. From every angle it was the best mode of defense under the conditions: it not only gave the men on the wall the maximum protection coupled with ability to see their enemies and shoot straight, but it kept them ranging all along instead of holding only small sections. True, their bows were clumsy weapons to handle in such narrow quarters, and the rear of the place was virtually unprotected, due to lack of men. But such strength as the defenders had was not put where it could be used with most deadly effect.

Scrambling along the runway, rising to heave spears and dart arrows out and down, dropping and moving on, civilized and savage allies carried on their jack-in-the-box warfare. Few heads now rose on the other side, for most of the Jiveros had drawn back to get a straighter aim at their quarry; and those who did attempt scaling were quickly shot down by the ready guns. Some of the assailants took cover around the big butts of nearby trees, but the main body scorned defense, moving about in the open and snapping spear or arrow at the appearing and disappearing heads within the walls. And into their mass poured a galling fire which carpeted the hillside with dead.

Yet McKay, though he now had marshaled his forces into the only feasible formation, felt in his bones that this was a losing fight. Rapidly he ran along all three walls, ascending ladders, glancing about, crashing a bullet or two into savages, then descending and dashing to another section; and he saw that, as Tim had said, there was a "regular army of the hellions," far outnumbering his own weirdly assorted garrison in both men and missiles.

170

It could not be long before the cartridges and arrows and javelins of his men would run out. Then only five machetes, a few empty rifles, and a meager supply of clubs would remain with which to assail the savages who would come crawling over the walls on all sides. To fight hand-to-hand in the yard against an overpowering force meant inevitable death. To withdraw into the house meant slower death; for the vengeful Jiveros, if unable eventually to batter a way in, would camp outside and besiege them until starvation claimed all immured within.

Jose, too, saw this. He, like McKay, was running from place to place, keeping his men moving up and down, preventing a bunching of forces at any one spot, scaling the ladders now and then to look out and spit bullets and curses at the beleaguering headhunters. The two met before the big house door, in which the women and children were packed, watching.

"Por Dios, capitan!" grinned the outlaw. "For once I think Jose is caught in a trap which he cannot break free from! But the Jivero who cuts my throat shall cross a heap of his comrades to get me!"

"Looks bad," admitted McKay, mopping his dripping face. As he spoke, two of the white Indians toppled from the runway, quivered on the stones, and lay still. "Too many for us. We'll have to get inside before long."

"Si. Our arrows fail, and — Hah! Down, you fiend!" His rifle jumped, and a head rising beyond the right front wall was gone.

" — and we go in and starve," he went on, pumping his lever. "I would rather stay out and fight to the end, but the women — Ho! Santa Maria! We have no women — we are all fighting men! Look!"

For the first time both noticed that those waiting women and children were armed, and that the faces which recently had been distorted with terror now were set in desperate resolution. The ancient weapons of the Almagros, the useless guns of the dead guards, the knives of the kitchen, all had been gathered up and were clutched in the hands of the women and boys of the Pachac tribe.

"That is the answer — death now in the open, not death like starving rats!" vowed Jose, his eyes snapping. "To the walls, all of us! Let us — "

He staggered. So did McKay. The ground was quivering again.

For a moment the fighting died. Defenders and assailants alike felt that tremor, heard a muffled growl in the mountains

**171**

looming around. Savage and civilized men felt an unnerving sinking at the stomach, a chill along the spine. And the women and children, though stoically resolved to meet death fighting to the end against their encompassing human foes, cried out and sprang from the doorway as the floor crept beneath their feet.

The ground became motionless and the growling ceased. For a few seconds the tense silence held. Then a rifle shot cracked, and Tim's gruff voice exulted.

A new yell of fury outside answered. Again arrows thudded against the house roof. A howl of defiance broke from the men of Pachac. The hopeless battle was on again.

"That settles it!" granted McKay. "If we get a bad shock the house may go. Get them out in the open!"

They were all outside already, and they stayed out. McKay and Jose parted. The captain loped to a section at the left front where several of the white Indians had been shot down, and where the other defenders were out of arrows. He clambered up just in time to blow away two fierce faces which topped the wall. To his dismay, he found no Jiveros now in sight. They had rushed in and were close to the stones, working upward in force. He grimly held his fire, awaiting the rising of the next heads.

Jose, working along the left wall, found the same condition. Knowlton, whose hot gun was the only firearm on that section, was doggedly firing as his chance came; but the Indians on his runway now were looking desperately around for clubs, loose stones, anything with which to continue their fight. Their bows were becoming useless, both because they had nothing to shoot and little to shoot at — for here, too, the Jiveros had closed in. Even as Jose looked along the weakening line he saw Knowlton hand his rifle to the nearest Indian for use as a club, draw his pistol, and loosen his machete. He clamped his jaws and jammed his four remaining cartridges into his own gun. Close work was at hand.

Tim and Rand, with their Indian fighting mates, were in similar straits. Tim had already shot his rifle out and now was working along with his pistol, drilling the upshooting heads. Rand was even worse off — his automatic had jammed, and pounding on the wall failed to loosen its action. And here, as on the other sides, the head-shrinkers were climbing in ever-increasing numbers.

Yet no man of the garrison left his wall. No man even thought of it. McKay, with his rifle, and Tim and Knowlton with their hand guns, were shooting faster and faster. Jose

**172**

sprang on the top of the stones and chopped with red machete. Indians who had clubs followed his example, crushing skulls with hoarse grunts of satisfaction. Indians who had none yelled to the women below to pass up their weapons.

Instead of complying, the women themselves climbed the adders and, with knife and ax and ancient muzzle loader, attacked the slayers and slavers crawling up and over them.

Huarma and her sisters, the daughters of Pachac, rose beside Jose and, screaming hate into the ears of the encroaching Jiveros, swung the clubbed guns of the late guards down on head after head. The other women of Pachac, with whatever weapons they had gleaned from the house, hacked and clubbed and stabbed. The men of Pachac grappled barehanded with antagonists who snaked themselves up to a footing. From somewhere roared the voice of Pachac himself, howling in ferocious joy as he smashed the skulls of his enemies. And the Americans, though a few cartridges still were left, sheathed their pistols and joined the hand-to-hand conflict with slashing steel. All along the top of the wall the last furious death grapple was in full swing.

"Hah!" shrilled the voice of Jose. "A fight of fights! Kill! Men of Pachac – women of Pachac – kill! Fight to the end! Kill!"

Suddenly a flare of orange flame shot high in the northwestern sky. A roaring inferno of noise burst among the mountains. The ground heaved like a rolling sea.

A grinding, cracking crash of collapsing stones and timbers echoed from the house of the Almagros. A deep stroke boomed from the big bell in the yard, terminating in a thumping jangle as it fell.

The walls, with their battling antagonists still heaving and clubbing and grappling, pitched outward in a harsh rumble of sliding stone. A long scream rang across the gulf. Then fell an awful silence.

## XXVIII. OUT OF THE WALL

Rain hissed down.

Cold, heavy, thick and fast it deluged a jumble of stones and timbers which had been a house; sluiced along between lines of other stones which had been walls; washed red stains from contorted men sprawling motionless on the sides of a knoll; beat back the senses of other men who groaned, stirred, sat up, stared dizzily around. Then it slid away down the hillsides, collected in new-born streams, snaked along depressions, and, at the bottom of the gulf, crept upward again in a

**173**

shallow but steadily rising pool.

In the memories of the first men to regain consciousness echoed receding yells of fear and the slap of bare feet fleeing into the jungle. Now from the wrecked walls a new sound crept into the swish and splash of the rain — moans of crushed and mangled fighters not yet dead but dying. Into the horrid chorus broke other noises — cries of men, women, children, revived by the wet chill and staggering up from the ground to learn the fate of those whom they held most dear.

Through the blurring sheets of falling water lurched indistinct figures holding arms before their faces to fend the drowning deluge from mouths and nostrils, peering about for relatives or friends, calling with voices growing sharper as those whom they sought remained silent. Then over all bellowed a fog-horn voice erupting from a tattered figure in dripping khaki; from whose red beard drizzled a stream of rain turned pink by a bleeding nose.

"Cap! Looey! Dave! Hozy! Where are you?"

For a time none of the voices for which he listened made any response. Other voices in plenty arose; some in joy of reunion, some in repeated shouts of certain names, some in dull groans of pain. Other forms came blundering into his path, but all were those of Indians who peered at him and then stepped away on their own quests. Again and again he roared through the unceasing tumult of the downpour. Then he jumped ahead, drawing his machete.

A tumbling thing on the ground a little farther on became two things. One of them pitched to its feet and glowered down from its six-foot height at a naked huddle of flesh which twitched a few times and became quiet. As Tim pounded up it turned sharply, and the bloody-nosed veteran looked into the swollen face and blazing eyes of McKay. Under him lay a powerful Jivero with head twisted aside.

"Huh! Don't you know this war's gone bust, cap?" demanded the red man, slapping his commander joyously on one shoulder. "Enemy's run for the woods, screeching their heads off — those that aren't jellied under the stones. What've you got to pick on this one for?"

McKay essayed a grin, tried to answer, made a wheezing sound, and rubbed his throat, in which showed the prints of big Jivero fingers.

"Alright, never mind apologizing. You sure broke this fellow's neck right. Come on, let's get the rest together."

They forged on along the tumbled mass of stone, squinting sharply at every prostrate form they found, the captain

**174**

turning his aching neck at times from side to side.

"I figure they got slung out, same as I did," Tim roared conversationally. "I was thrown clear and lit on my nose; went to sleep awhile. Nearly busted my neck, I guess – it feels sort of crackly now. How did you come to keep that Jivero? Fall on him?"

"Yes. Got thrown end over end. Struck on my stomach – also on his head. Knocked us both out."

"Uh-huh. And then you both came alive and did a dog-eat-dog stunt, hey? Oh, looey! Dave! Hoz – "

"Here!" came Knowlton's voice. Around a corner of the leveled walls a vague shape came stumbling as if hurt. In a few more steps it became the lieutenant, shielding his face with one arm. The other hung at his side.

"Good!" he exclaimed. "You two are still on your legs. Where's Dave?"

"Dunno yet. What ails you? Break something?"

"Shoulder's out of joint. Wrenched this leg somehow, too, but it's whole. Handsome nose you've got, Tim."

"Yeah? She feels like a dill pickle. Seen Hozy? Any Jiveros around that side?"

"Jose's all right. He's hunting around now for Pachac. No Jiveros, except dead ones. Must be a frightful mess under the walls – they were packed three deep when the rocks went over them."

"So much the better for us," was McKay's comment. "You sit down under this tree and let us snap that shoulder back. Then wait while we find Dave. He was on the other wall. Got any cartridges?"

"Nope. Shot out."

McKay dived a hand at the lieutenant's holster, drew out the empty pistol, replaced it with his own. The three moved to the shelter of the big tree nearby, where Tim braced his feet and held the blond man tight. McKay, with an outward pull, drew the dislocated shoulder back into place. Knowlton went white and leaned against the trunk.

"You won't need a gun, probably," added the captain, "but you'd better have one on. That one's loaded. Stick here until we come back."

He and Tim turned and squelched away through the streaming grass in search of Rand. Now that all others of their five-cornered partnership were accounted for, they gave no attention to the shifting figures or the medley of noises around them, except to watch for any belated Jivero creeping out of the debris and seeking escape. They saw none such, for every

**175**

headhunter able to get away had gone long ago, shocked witless by the cataclysm.

After passing the next corner, however, they slowed and began careful inspection along the line marking the right wall, where Rand had last been seen. Here the ruins seemed to have fallen both ways, as if the convulsed earth had twisted like a wounded snake, heaving some parts of the roughly cemented barrier outward while others toppled in toward the house. As they advanced, the rain began to decrease and the wreckage became more plain.

Along it was proceeding work of mingled succor and slaughter. Men of Pachac, armed with spears and clubs picked up from the sodden ground, were using them as levers to pry loose members of their own tribe or as weapons to exterminate Jiveros trapped among the stones. No quarter was given or asked. Head-hunters died with fierce defiance on their faces, savage to the last. The Americans saw, scowled, but said nothing. It was the primal law of the jungle – kill or be killed.

Some distance down the wet stones, they paused. There a little knot of white Indians, themselves smeared red from hurts received in the collapse, were working carefully to extricate a half-crushed man of their tribe. One of them, spying the American pair, pointed downward and grunted rapidly. Though the words meant little to the listeners, they saw in the Indian face something that brought them up on the rocks. There the aborigine pointed at McKay's boots, then down under the trapped man.

"Cripes! Must be Dave!" guessed Tim. "Pair of boots in there under this fellow!"

Their eyes met. Then each looked quickly away. If Rand was caught under those stones –

Restraining their impulse to jump in and help – for more men would only hinder the work – they stood tensely waiting while the hole was enlarged and the Indian drawn out, his face gray with suffering but his jaws clamped tight. Then they got a look into the ruin.

"Poor Davey!" McKay muttered.

They saw a dead Jivero. From below him, between his right arm and his side, projected a booted leg.

For a moment they stood motionless, dreading the sight of the mangled form which must lie beneath that of the enemy. Then they started. The leg had moved!

It strained weakly as if trying to draw itself back. The foot quivered, jerked from side to side, grew still.

McKay scanned the rocks rimming the opening. They were

**176**

loosely balanced, likely at any moment to slip and drop. He indicated a couple which must be held or braced. The Indians remaining — two had carried away their injured comrade — stepped to the menacing blocks and strained back against them. McKay and Tim stooped, braced themselves, and, with a slow, careful pull, drew the Jivero up and away from his death trap. Pitching him outward, they reached again and grasped the boots, both now exposed. With another steady draw they lifted Rand.

He was lying aslant, head much lower than his feet, curved in a strained position in a crooked cavern of jagged stones. If he had been conscious when that foot moved, he now had lost his senses again. His face, appearing from a dim crevice as he was raised by the legs, was dark and bloated from suffocation. Under him the rescuers glimpsed a welter of smashed things which had been men.

They drew him up and bore him away down the slippery rocks. The Indians loosed their holds on the stones and skipped aside. The blocks grated, slid, and fell with a sullen crunch into the place where Rand had lain.

Out on good ground they laid him down and tore off his shirt, which hung in ripped rags. McKay felt for his heart. It was beating.

Tim let out a breath, interpreting the slight relaxation of the captain's face. "He's hardly scratched! Head's all right — legs look straight — arms all sound — how's the ribs? Caved? No. Say, those dead men sort of cushioned him. Squeezed him black in the face, but that's all. Talk about luck!"

And a few minutes later, sitting groggily up and blinking at the figures which seemed whirling around him, Rand proved Tim's words true. His frame was whole, though wrenched and strained. His constricted lungs were functioning normally again, the congestion of blood had left his head, and the few cuts and bruises he had received were of no consequence. Yet, but for the fact that a living man of Pachac happened to be caught above him and attracted the attention of other Indians, he would have been squeezed to death down in the chaotic rubble long before he could have been found. He owed his life to pure luck.

" 'Lo, Rod," he mumbled. "Where's — Merry? What happened?"

"Merry's holding up a tree and waiting. Nothing much happened. Volcanic explosion somewhere up north — earthquake — everything tumbled down, including us. Jiveros are mostly buried. Now we're all taking a shower bath. That's all.

Feel like walking?"

Rand dizzily shook his head. But after a minute the surroundings stopped whizzing around him, and he began struggling up. His mates promptly aided him to his feet. Arm in arm, the three passed back down the line to rejoin Knowlton. And as they went, the rain ceased.

In the clearing air they saw Knowlton's blond head bobbing along beyond the rock jumble which had been the front wall, and before they reached the corner he came limping around it, his face beaming at sight of the rescued man. He halted and waited, gave Rand a slap on the back as they passed, and fell in behind. Reunited once more, the four went on to find Jose.

As they passed on, their minds now at ease regarding one another, they saw in stark detail the work of the sudden spasm of nature. The house and the walls were stone heaps. From them now sounded no more of the half-conscious moans; for the injured men of Pachac had died in their traps or were being taken out, while all the Jiveros caught alive had been executed. Here and there protruded a hand or a foot of some warrior who never again would fight. At intervals lay broken white Indians attended by little groups of their own people. And at one spot was a number of bodies lying side by side on the soaked earth. Among them were a few women — the fighting women who had gone to death like men.

In the hillside itself gaped narrow fissures. Beyond, the faces of the mountains were altered. Bare slides grinned out where had been unbroken green. In the precipice along which the four had toiled not many days ago yawned new crevasses. Many other changes, of which the Americans never learned, had been wrought around them. One, of which they were not to remain long in ignorance, was that the mine of the Almagros was no more. Another was that the underground passage through which Jose and his people had entered this placed was blocked forever.

As they rounded the corner beyond which Jose had last been seen, they found no sign of him. In the thin mist now rising from the drying ground moved only the forms of the Indian garrison and their women. They were alternately giving attention to their less fortunate fellows and scanning the jungle.

"If those Jiveros come back now — " muttered Rand.

"Come back from where?" demanded Tim. "Under the rocks? That's where nearly all of them are. Those that got clear are running yet."

A sudden yell cut him short. It came from the rear end of

**178**

the mass which had been the house. Up there the startled four saw the missing Jose. He had been clambering around to get a comprehensive view of the devastation. Now he was prancing and waving his arms as if demented.

"Senores!" came his shout. "Come here! El oro!"

"What! The gold?" burst in one amazed chorus from the battered soldiers of fortune.

"Si! We have it at last! Valgame Dios, it is a treasure like that of the Incas! It is — See! With your own eyes come and look! Santa Maria! What a yellow gleam!"

Still throwing his arms about, he disappeared down the rubble of stone and timber. Afire with excitement, the Americans leaped away along the line, even Knowlton forgetting his painful leg. Climbing over the ruins of the wall between, they joined Jose, and stood petrified at what they saw.

From the space where the rear wall had stood now slanted a pile of yellow bars. That wall, buckling outward, had spewed out with its stones what had been piled just behind those stones. There, in one gleaming heap, lay tons of the precious mineral. How many more tons were concealed within the ruin no man dared guess.

"See, it is as you said, Tim and capitan! Behold that wall — it ran from the vault to the end of the house. It was hollow — it has not so much stone as the other wall. There was a passage in it — some way of swinging aside blocks in the vault — another entrance here at the house. The house had a double rear wall with much space between the two — I have thought before now that somehow the house seemed longer outside than inside, but I never thought to measure. And the gold was piled to the roof! Por Dios! There may be an underground space, too — there may be — "

His voice cracked. Dazedly the others followed his gestures as he talked and danced about. They saw that he had hit the truth. Their eyes came back and clung to the golden glory rising from their feet to the wrecked treasure room of the Almagros. Then they sank down on the nearest stones and dumbly fumbled in their soggy clothing for something with which to make cigarettes.

So, at last, fickle Fate had thrown at the fighting five the golden lure which she had dangled so long before their eyes. And the grim mountains of the Pastassa spurs which had held the merciless Almagros in their unyielding grip until no Almagro was left, now had smashed all their handiwork into chaos. A little while, and the gulf where they had lived and died would be a noisome pest hole. And the booty wrung from the bowels of the stone by four generations of torture and treachery would go out on the backs of men who fought hard – but fought clean.

## XXIX. THE KING OF NO MAN'S LAND

The banks of the Tigre Yacu were full.

Between the shores where, a few weeks ago, clear water had crept languidly along at the bottom of a rock-strewn natural ditch, now rolled a turbid flood; and from both sides sounded the plash and gurgle of smaller streams hurrying in with the burden of water dumped on the hillsides by the latest rain. Now the sun had broken out again, and from every dripping leaf sparkled gems of moisture.

In a little cove, where the downward-sweeping waters slowed and swung about in a wheeling eddy, a grotesque object floated and tugged at its moorings of stout bush-rope; a nondescript creation such as the mysterious Tigre Yacu, which before now had washed many a weird thing southward on its eternal journey from the cordillera to the Maranon, never had upheld on its restless bosom. Two stout canoes, covered over, formed its nucleus; reinforced with logs, they upheld a platform with built-up sides and curving roof. A combination of balsa, pontoon, raft, and box, it was, and as ugly a vessel as ever traveled jungle waters. Yet, for all its homeliness, it was a treasure ship. The boxlike platform held a fortune in pure gold. Now the men who had created it stood lined along the bank: four Americans, one hawk-faced Spaniard, and some forty Indians whose skins were only a shade darker than those revealed by rips in the clothing of the khaki-clad men. Near the lean South American loitered a number of lithe young women whose dark eyes turned to him at his every word or movement. Farther back were a sprinkling of other women and children.

These were the survivors of the no-quarter battle with the Jiveros and the earth convulsion which had crushed that fight into nothingness at its desperate height; the five partners and the death-thinned people of Pachac. Among them Pachac himself no longer stood.

Caught and killed in the collapse of the wall he was holding, he had passed out as he would have wished – in the flaming fury of hand-to-hand battle with his foes. Now the commander of the tribe was the man whom he had taken as foster-son – Jose Martinez, outlaw, killer, and son of the Conquistadores.

For days after the wrecking of the house of the Almagros,

180

every able-bodied man, woman, and child had toiled feverishly at the great gold pile, the white men driven by their own treasure hunger and the Indians by the crackling voice of their Spanish chief. From dawn to dark, with hardly a pause to snatch food from the plantation, they had transported the yellow bars in a steady stream to a spot well up the nearest mountain, where the air was fresh and clean. Fortunately, the sky had remained overcast much of the time, and, as often happens in the Andes region after an earthquake, the air had been decidedly cold. Thus favored, the toilers had been able to labor long in the midst of the ruins before the sun turned hot and the air became pestilential. By the time they were compelled to flee, the place had been quite thoroughly looted.

Even had it been possible and desirable to extract and bury or burn the dead and reconstruct the demolished house, the grim decree of the mountains forbade it. Not only had they plugged the natural drain of the gulf in their spasm, but at every fresh rainfall they sluiced more water into the pool which had formed and was stealthily creeping farther and higher along the bottom and sides of the misshapen bowl. Henceforth no man should live in the chasm where so much of human maltreatment and misery had resulted from their first admittance of men. When the deluges of the forthcoming wet season should end, the sinister knoll and its stones and bones would be sunk under a stagnant lagoon wherein only reptilian creatures could spawn; and the Almagros, after all their ruthlessness and strife, should lie forgotten forever in a bed of slime. So the stern giants towering around had determined, and so it should be.

But none of those who toiled to salvage the treasure trove had any desire to remain. As soon as their prize was safe they sought a way out, eager to be gone for all time from that hole. And, thanks to the jungle craft of the nomads of Pachac, they found at length an exit whereby they could reach again the vague path by which they had journeyed up the Tigre. Thanks also to the Indians, they lived off the forest and the bush while the gold was brought out and packed down the trail and while the clumsy river craft was built and loaded.

Nowhere had they met Jiveros. But, a few days after the earthquake, they had heard the drums off to the west begin to grumble again, and guessed that the survivors of the savage expedition had returned to their own land with their tale of doom. Nor had they seen again any sign of the gaunt green servitors of Flora Almagro who had speared the escaping toeless man and forced the adventurers over the edge of the abyss. What had become of them only the inscrutable jungle could tell; and, as always, the jungle remained dumb.

Now the time for parting was at hand. And for a time no word was said. Wistfully, yet proudly, Jose stood among his people and looked at his four comrades who were leaving him. Like his men, he wore on his body only the loin mat of the white Indians; but, unlike them, he retained around his shaggy head a faded red kerchief, and in one hand he held his battered old rifle: his crown and his scepter as king of the little tribe. Down one bare leg, too, dangled his machete.

None of his hard-won gold was on the bank. In fact, it was miles away, secreted in a cave which he had discovered just outside the mountains ringing the gulf. His only visible possessions now were his gun, his bush-knife, and the partly filled tin of .44 cartridges which the Americans previously had left with the updrawn canoes.

"No, senores, I will not have my share of the treasure carried farther," he said when making his cache. "Of what good is it to me? Now that I have it, I can think of only one use for it; and the time to use it so has not yet come. You are eager to go out, while I — where should I go? Let us move on with your gold. Mine will keep here."

The Americans, though asking no questions, had guessed at what he intended eventually to do with his prize — and had guessed wrong. Now, standing beside their laden craft, they thought of it again. McKay bluntly spoke out.

"Where do you expect to hang out after you leave here, Jose? We'd like to keep in touch with you. Going back over the Andes to gild the palms of the authorities and enjoy life? Or down the Amazon? Or over to Europe?"

A slow smile passed over the outlaw's face and died. He answered with the cool dignity of a caballero.

"Once, capitan, a misbegotten creature arose between us — a burro with a bull head. It came up because you had a thought like the one you have now. But it shall not lift its head again.

"You think the natural thing, capitan, but you have it wrong. I, Jose Martinez, return across the Andes and buy the favor of officials? Bah! Who throws meat to yelping dogs which are too far off to bite him? Not I. Still less do I journey to those dogs and drop the meat into their greedy jaws.

"And down the Amazon, or across the sea, should I be content? No. I have been too long a wild rover of the jungle. In the jungle I stay."

His eyes went to the girls near him, and again his lips

**182**

widened — this time in the sardonic grin of Jose the bushman.

"And if I would desert my brides, amigos — for they never could come with me into the cities, and I must abandon them if I go — if I thought of forsaking my little tigresses of the Tigre Yacu, there is another reason why I should stand by them."

The four looked into his twinkling eyes, then at his girl wives.

"What! Already?" blurted Knowlton.

"Why not, senor?" laughed the other. "Did I not once say to you that if we Spaniards would pause at times between our fighting and our gold hunting we could people the world with fighting men? And every man should prove his words by deeds, is it not true? Unless Huarma and her sisters and I are much mistaken, soon there will be five little Joses asking me for little guns to play with.

"And that is not all. The four sisters of my wives have decided that they also should become brides of their chief. And who am I that I should deny them? So all the nine daughters of Pachac become the wives of the son of Pachac."

McKay threw up his hands.

"Come on, fellows," he said. "He's raving. Let's go."

"One moment, capitan," laughed the white chief. "Help me with a problem. With sons each year for twenty years, how many shall I have?"

The captain shook his head and glanced at the boat. Rand answered.

"Barring twins, one hundred and eighty."

"Oof!" grunted Tim. "Cap, you're right. He's crazy as a bedbug. Hozy, just wait until the first nine get squalling together, and you'll never wait for the other hundred and seventy-odd. You'll come running and jump into this river, squeaking: 'Here goes nothing'!"

"You do not know me, comrade," chuckled Jose. "If they vex me I shall go out and kill a few Jiveros. That is one reason why I stay — to kill Jiveros."

"A laudable ambition," conceded Knowlton. "But where does your gold fit into your plans? None of my business, maybe, but — "

"But why is it not your business, friend? I will tell you what is in my mind."

He looked along the line of his adopted people, and his face sobered.

"There was a time, before I had fought against those Jiveros, when I had for them some respect. I said to you that,

183

if my head must be taken by any man, I would wish it to go to those fighting wild men. But since I have fought them, since I saw the headless bodies of those poor fellow slaves of mine who were cut to pieces on the plantation, since I have heard the true tales of them told by Pachac and his people — No, I have no respect for those accursed ones! They are beasts!

"Now, as you say, I have gold. Now that I have gold, it means little to me — the gold itself. It was a bait, a lure, a thing that kept me striving on in spite of death and the devil. And that struggle to get it, senores, the fighting and adventure and hope and despair — that was the real prize — that was living! And far above all those things, amigos, I treasure the memories of the days and nights I have spent with my North American comrades: men I could trust, men I could like, men in whose company I could sleep without awaking to find a knife near my throat.

"But that time is past, and you go. Now I look to what is ahead of Jose — and of the people of Jose. I have looked on the mountains to the north and found them good. Not that hole of the Almagros, but the great wild cordillera which no man owns; where the shrinkers of heads travel, where more gold lies waiting, where the law of the yellow-dog men of the western cities does not reach. I will make those mountains mine!"

The old flush of enthusiasm was rising in his cheeks, the old ring creeping into his voice.

"Si! Mine! I will not be a petty chief of a vagabond tribe — I will be a king of the wild lands! A barbarian king, perhaps, as you said not long ago — but a ruler of hard fighting men, a maker of war on the demons who shrink the heads of men and make beasts of women. Si! I, Jose!

"Behold these people of Pachac. They have no tribe name that I can recognize. They call themselves only The White Ones. No, not Yameos. The White Ones. And in other parts of this thick country between the spurs, and north toward the Curaray, are more of The White Ones. So these tell me. They tell me, too, that they can lead me to some of those other White Ones, and from them we shall learn of still more. All are bitter haters of the Jiveros.

"Now for my gold. Already that young half-Spanish son of Pachac had trained a few of these men to use rifles. I shall carry on what he began. With my gold I trade for more guns — and I get the best! I buy many cartridges. I bring together the other White Ones. And there in the mountains we make a stronghold that shall make that one of the Almagros seem a house of clay. We drive the Jiveros howling west to the Morona – to the Santiago! Por Dios, we sweep them back against the Great Cordillera itself!"

The four stood fascinated as the magnitude of his ambition fired them. Then Rand spoke.

"And then, the first thing you know, you'll be at war with two governments."

"Si? The government of Peru, which has cast me out? The government of Ecuador, which cannot rule what it claims? They cannot even agree on their own boundaries, as you senores must know. Ecuador calls this its Provincia del Oriente, but what does it mean? Nothing. And to me the paper laws and decrees of both of them are nothing. This is No Man's Land, and I will be its king!"

"Just like I said!" exulted Tim. "Didn't I tell you, Dave, down by that red-hot lake? The King of No Man's Land. And I'll tell the world you'll make a rip-roaring king, too. I wish I could stick around awhile. If I only had a new outfit – But shucks, I've got to get my money home. So long, old-timer, and more power to you!"

He reached a red-haired fist and gave the chief of The White Ones a mighty grip. In turn the others followed his example. Then they clambered aboard their treasure ship, set themselves at the powerful steering oar they had built, and nodded to Jose.

Slowly, regretfully, the outlaw lifted his machete to sever the bush-ropes mooring the straining craft.

"Adios, camaradas!" he called.

"Hasta luego," countered McKay.

"What! You will come back some day?"

"Never can tell. We might get bored and come looking for some excitement."

"Hah! Come to me in the mountains and I will feed you excitement until you choke! Until then – Vaya con Dios! Go with God!"

The blade chopped down. The craft swung outward and checked. Again the steel fell, shearing another rope, and it floated free.

In a final chorus of yells it gathered headway and surged downstream, its crew swinging at the long rudder. Then it settled itself for its long voyage to the mighty Maranon. Hands shot up in the last gesture of farewell. Around a slight bend it drifted, and the jungle of the Tigre Yacu blotted it from sight.

For a time the red-crowned man at the water's edge stood motionless, his face somber, his dark eyes dwelling wistfully

**185**

on the spot where his partners had vanished. Then, with a sigh, he stooped and lifted the case of cartridges to his shoulder.

Upstream he turned, warily scanning the bush. Upstream the armed warriors and the rest of the little tribe silently followed him. And into the green shadows the coming King of No Man's Land and the nucleus of his army of The White Ones passed and were gone.

www.ingramcontent.com/pod-product-compliance
Lightning Source LLC
Chambersburg PA
CBHW020638180626
46816CB00003B/1031